UNLEASHED

AMY McCULLOCH

SIMON & SCHUSTER

First published in Great Britain in 2019 by Simon & Schuster UK Ltd
A CBS COMPANY

1 3 5 7 9 10 8 6 4 2

Simon & Schuster UK Ltd
1st Floor, 222 Gray's Inn Road
London WC1X 8HB

www.simonandschuster.co.uk
www.simonandschuster.com.au
www.simonandschuster.co.in

Simon & Schuster Australia, Sydney
Simon & Schuster India, New Delhi

A CIP catalogue record for this book
is available from the British Library.

PB ISBN 978-1-4711-6998-4
eBook ISBN 978-1-4711-6999-1

Typeset in Goudy by M Rules
Printed and bound by CPI Group (UK) Ltd, Croydon, CR0 4YY

For Kim,
most brilliant of friends

GLOSSARY

Baku: a robot-animal companion

Moncha Corp: the company that manufactures bakus

Monica Chan: the founder of Moncha Corp and inventor of the baku

Eric Smith: Monica's business partner and co-founder of Moncha Corp

Companioneers: employees of Moncha Corp responsible for the design and creation of bakus

Monchaville: a district of Toronto funded and maintained by Moncha Corp

Profectus Academy: the elite science, technology, engineering and mathematics school funded by Moncha Corp

BRIGHTSPRK: a rival technology company to Moncha Corp

Halo: the BRIGHTSPRK personal assistant device

Derek Baird: former professor at Profectus Academy and secret corporate spy for BRIGHTSPRK

PART ONE

THE UPDATE

CHAPTER ONE

M Y FIRST THOUGHT WHEN I WAKE UP
is that I am not in my own bed.

Bright lights shine above me, and I lift my
hand to shield my eyes. At my movement, a little robotic
creature springs to life.

>>Good morning, Lacey. How are you feeling today?
asks his soothing electronic voice.

I struggle to sit up, but my head is spinning.

>>Your vital signs are strong, but you might want
to take it easy.

The baku hops down the bed, curling its soft body around
my wrist. My vision swirls, nausea rising in the back of my
throat, so I close my eyes and tilt my head back against the
cool metal headboard. Slowly, I come back to myself. When
I open my eyes again, my vision is much clearer.

Wrapped around my wrist is a little chinchilla baku, its
shiny robotic eyes blinking up at me. 'Where . . . where am I?'
I try to say, but my throat is bone dry and the sound comes
out with a horrendous rattle.

>>I'll order you some water.

'Thank you,' I croak. Then he crawls back up my arm, projecting a keyboard on to my lap. I type out the rest of my questions.

Where am I? I ask.

>>You're in Toronto Main Hospital. My name is Picchu and I'm your designated hospital-baku.

Suddenly, the nausea is back with a vengeance. *I'm in hospital?*

My mind feels so muddled.

I check my body, but apart from the IV stuck in my arm, there doesn't appear to be any serious injury – no casts for broken bones, no mysterious bandages.

I cast my mind back, struggling to find a memory that might explain what's going on.

There's nothing.

Fear and shock make my hands shake. It takes me a moment before I can type again.

What happened?

The chinchilla burrows up against me, trying to calm me down.

>>I will call for a nurse.

I shake my head. I don't want a nurse. I want my mom.

'Jinx, call Mom,' I croak. I look around the room, searching for my black cat baku. Bakus are robotic companions, designed to keep us connected to our friends and family, to our social networks and to the outside world. But Jinx is even more than my companion – he's my friend.

4

There's no answer from him.

>>I'm sorry, but all personal bakus are confiscated in this ward, says Picchu.

I frown. I want to argue but I hardly have the energy.

'Can you open your messaging app?'

>>I'm sorry. We don't allow access to external messaging or social media apps for hospital patients.

He sounds way too chipper to deliver such a disappointing message.

Picchu might be cute, but he can't connect me to the outside world. I guess it's supposed to be for my own benefit – to keep me relaxed and ensure that my stress is low – but I just feel isolated and alone. And scared.

Really, really scared.

I focus on Picchu as he moves around my body, doing his routine checks. I've seen one of these chinchilla bakus before, at school.

Bits and pieces of information from my lessons come to me. His super-soft, synthetic fur is totally sterile, and while he is designed to be very affectionate and cuddly, he also takes care of monitoring my vital signs. His soothing vibrations are able to guide me to sleep and help with pain management too.

I frown. How come I can remember class lectures, but I can't remember what happened to me? Where is Jinx? Did I have an accident?

'Oh good, you're awake,' says a nurse, who bustles in with a poodle baku conveniently trotting at her heels.

Picchu immediately heads towards the poodle, his little tail connecting with the poodle's shiny black nose.

'What's he doing?' I ask, frowning as the chinchilla flashes a blue light.

'He's updating me with your vitals.'

'Oh ... and there I thought he was just being friendly.'

The nurse laughs. 'He is. But he's useful too. And so is Catcher here. He's able to monitor all the patients on my ward at the same time and – if there's a crisis – he can move a lot faster than I can. Very helpful, these bakus.' She hands me a juice box, which I gratefully take a sip of. The liquid soothes my scratchy throat.

'Oh right, we learned about that at the Academy,' I say, followed by an embarrassingly loud slurp.

'A Profectus student, are you?' She raises an eyebrow.

'Yeah,' I reply, feeling a blush rise in my cheeks. Profectus is the top high school in the country, a science and technology-focused academy whose graduates often end up with jobs at Moncha Corp, the company who manufacture the bakus. It's always been my dream to be a student there.

'Well, great news, Lacey – Picchu's data shows a marked improvement. In fact, your vital signs are normal and healthy.' The nurse pats Catcher on the head. 'I think we'll be able to get you out of here in time for the Christmas break.'

I sit bolt upright, a searing pain streaking its way across my forehead.

'No, no, still not time for any sudden movements,' she says, gently placing her hands on my shoulders and guiding me back down into a resting position.

'But ... but Christmas break? That means I've been out for ...'

'Almost a whole month. It's the strangest thing. You've been in and out of a coma that we can't explain. No obvious head injury or other wounds, except a little bruise on your arm.'

My head spins with that information. A whole month out for the count? A coma? *What happened to me?*

The last thing I remember is ...

Is ...

Just a blur.

I squirm in the hospital bed. 'Where's Jinx?' I ask the nurse. 'Where is my baku?'

Before I know it, Picchu is back, curled up around my throat. I can feel my muscles – which are so tense I feel like an elastic band stretched and about to ping – relax.

'I know you have a lot of questions, my dear. Visiting hours are coming up and your mom will be here. She'll be so pleased that you're awake and healthy. If things continue like this, you'll be home before you know it – and your baku will be returned to you.'

I calm my breathing. Jinx is okay.

My desire to see Mom is suddenly overwhelming. I want her arms around me.

'There's also someone else who's been visiting almost every day. He's very devoted to you.'

I frown. 'He?'

For some reason, that makes the nurse guffaw with laughter. 'I'll leave you to figure that one out on your own. For now, I have another dose of medication for you, and then you should get some rest.'

Rest sounds like the absolute last thing that I need. I want to move, to get up and figure out what's been happening in the month that I've been in hospital. My muscles feel thin and wasted, and I want to walk, to run, to do *something*.

Then the drugs kick in and I end up back in a deep and dreamless sleep.

CHAPTER TWO

'I THOUGHT YOU SAID SHE WAS AWAKE!' Mom sounds frustrated; frazzled. 'This is beyond ridiculous. I want to take my daughter home now!'

I can hear her, but she feels just out of reach. My eyes are glued shut with gritty sleep. I tilt to the side, reaching my hand out in the direction of her voice.

'Mom?' I manage to whisper.

'Lacey!' She's by my side in an instant, her warm hands clasping my outstretched one. I instinctively grip back. I'm coming back to myself. I can feel it.

I force my eyes open and wriggle until I'm sitting up. Mom wraps her arms around me, her embrace warm and comforting. 'Can we go home now?' I ask, speaking directly into her neck.

'Yes, honey,' she says, stroking my hair. She's holding me so tightly; I don't think she wants to let me go.

Her tone changes as she addresses the nurse. It's much sterner. 'Have you finally figured out what happened to her?'

The nurse makes a show of scrolling through the data

on Catcher's back. 'We've been treating her for mild hypothermia which she has now completely recovered from, which is why she is feeling stronger. And she hasn't lost consciousness in the past forty-eight hours so we're hoping this is the end of it, now.'

'So does that mean I can take her home?'

The nurse nods, and her expression softens into a smile. 'I think the doctor wants to do one more examination to give her the all-clear, then we can formally discharge her. In the meantime, I should mention that there's another visitor . . .'

Mom smiles too. 'Yes, you can let him in.'

The nurse pats my leg and leaves the room, Catcher trotting at her heels.

'Have I really been in this hospital for almost a month?' I ask Mom.

'Twenty-seven days, and I've counted every minute of every one of them,' she replies.

'Wow,' I reply. Then my voice drops. 'I don't remember anything about why I'm here . . .'

'That's okay, sweetie. You've been through a lot.' Petal, Mom's level 1 butterfly baku, flutters around her head, then connects to the small leash that is looped around her ear to charge. Instinctively, I reach up and touch my leash.

'Your baku is at home,' Mom says. 'I wasn't allowed to bring him to you while you're in hospital. I tried to get you transferred to the Moncha hospital, but an old teacher of yours, Mr Baird? He thought it would be a better idea if you stayed here. And then you were so unwell that it seemed silly to move you. No one could explain what was happening . . . you kept slipping in and out of consciousness.' Tears well up in her eyes, her voice breaking with emotion. A flash of memory comes back to me – of running through twisting hallways away from . . . away from what?

My mind draws a blank. I open my mouth to ask Mom about Mr Baird, when there's a knock on the hospital room door.

A familiar face pops around the frame and my heart skips several beats. It's Tobias, his dark brown eyes filled with concern. He's still wearing his Profectus uniform and in his hands is a tiny box covered in black cat wrapping paper. 'Can I come in?' he asks.

'Please do,' says my mom.

He grins widely when he sees that I'm awake, and rushes to my bedside. But then he hesitates as he approaches, glancing between my mom and me. A blush rises in my cheeks, and all of a sudden I can't figure out what to do with my hands. It's like neither of us knows how to act around each other.

Luckily, his baku breaks the tension. Aero, a beautiful level 5 eagle, follows him into the room, lands on the railing of my bed and squawks loudly. I reach out and brush his smooth golden feathers, and a series of lights ripple down his wing, where I'm touching it. I smile, wider than I have in a long time.

Tobias sits down on the other side of the bed to my mom, and squeezes my hand. I squeeze back. 'I'm glad you're awake,' he says.

'Me too,' I whisper back.

'I'll give you two a moment,' Mom says. 'I'm in dire need of some coffee. Can I get you anything, Tobias?'

Hearing Mom sound so familiar with Tobias threatens to deepen my blush. But he shakes his head and so do I. 'Thanks, Mom.'

'See you later.'

There's an awkward moment of silence as she leaves the room, and then Tobias and I are alone. My eyes dart around, unsure where to look – and I catch sight of my reflection in the window. I bite my lip – my hair is a rat's nest, and a month of lying down on the bed has done nothing for my complexion.

He grips my fingers again, and I look back at him. He's smiling. Maybe he doesn't care what I look like. 'I brought you something,' he says. He hands over the wrapped box.

'Thanks, you didn't have to do that.' I gently tear open the paper, revealing an old-fashioned wooden toy maze, with a marble running through it. I immediately begin turning it in my hands, directing the marble down to a small hole in one of the corners.

'I thought you weren't the flower-receiving type,' he says. Then he chuckles. 'Seeing that look of concentration on your face is exactly what I wanted! And look, you can adjust the maze at the back, so you can build your own by lowering and raising walls. Thought it was the perfect present for my bedbound engineer.'

The marble drops into the hole with a satisfying clink.

I look up at him, unable to help the grin on my face. 'I love it!'

He smiles, then turns more serious and leans forward, his elbows on his knees. 'So, do you remember anything about what happened?'

I shake my head. 'I wish that I could ... can you help me fill in any gaps?'

Tobias nods. 'The doctors said you had some memory loss that they can't explain ...' He lowers his voice. 'We were at Moncha headquarters that night. Carter had stolen Jinx from you to give to his dad.'

My breath hitches. Carter Smith. My academic rival. Well, our rivalry is more than just academic – it seems his hatred of me runs so deep, he's willing to steal from me. 'So we went to Moncha HQ to get him back,' I whisper.

'Yup.'

'And we got him!' I remember that. I remember holding Jinx in my arms. Running through hallways away from vicious security panthers.

Then there's another flash of memory. This time, it's of Jinx running away. 'Oh,' I say, my voice sounding small. 'He bolted.'

Tobias nods. 'That's where we lost you. You ran off after Jinx and got trapped behind some locked doors. I couldn't follow you.' His voice sounds strained.

'It wasn't your fault, Tobias,' I say.

His hand leaves mine and his fingers tighten into a fist. 'Do you remember what happened after you chased Jinx?'

I shake my head.

Tobias studies me, his eyes searching my face. Whatever he was looking for, he doesn't find any answers, and his shoulders slump. 'I still have nightmares about that night,' he continues. 'When I realized I couldn't follow you and Jinx, I freaked out. I waited for you in Mr Baird's car, just around the corner from Moncha HQ. I sent Aero out to scan the streets to try and find you. That's when we spotted you passed out in the cold, so I ran to get you. I was so scared . . .'

'You're the one who found me?' I ask.

Tobias nods. 'I brought you to the car, and Mr Baird drove us to the hospital.'

I close my eyes, willing more memories to come. But none do. I feel disappointment settling in my bones. I haven't been very helpful. I know that Tobias, Mom and the doctors had been waiting for me to wake up so that I could provide some sort of explanation. But I can't.

When I open my eyes again, I change the subject, unable to bear the disappointment reflected back in Tobias's eyes. 'The nurses say that I've been in here for almost a month. What . . . what have I missed?'

'Well, with you in hospital, Mr Baird said we didn't have enough evidence to go to the authorities about Carter or his dad. I mean, all we know is that his dad was trying to take back your baku and since it was Moncha property to begin with . . .' Tobias shrugs.

I nod. 'And what about at school? How's Ashley? And Kai? And River! Are they okay?' They had been with us, fighting

14

off Carter's security bakus inside the headquarters. I hope none of them were hurt.

'They're fine,' he assures me. 'They're worried about you. Ashley has been taking notes in all your classes; she said she'd drop them round as soon as you're back home. You'll catch up quickly though, I'm sure of it.'

'And the Baku Battles?'

His smile slips a little. 'Gemma and her team . . . they won the final round.'

'Oh, Tobes, I'm really sorry.' I know how much Tobias had wanted to win. The Baku Battles were a fiercely competitive Profectus tradition, and an opportunity for students to show off the skills they learned in class. As the captain of the winning team, Tobias would have earned a summer internship at Moncha with Monica Chan herself – the founder of the company. It would have placed him on a par with his older brother. His parents, who also worked for Moncha Corp in high level positions, would have been so proud of him. It was everything he had worked for all through high school. Not only that, but Gemma's team victory meant Carter Smith had won too.

Tobias is lost in thought. Then he shrugs and smiles again, although this time it feels forced for my benefit. 'Don't worry; I have loads of options. I'm not worried.'

'I know how much you wanted it. I'm so—'

'Don't apologize. Nobody's even seen Monica Chan for weeks.'

Pain spikes in my head at the mention of Monica's name,

and I wince. Tobias's eyes widen with concern, but I shake my head. 'I'm okay. I just want to get out of this hospital bed.'

'It will be good to have you back. Things can go back to normal now, can't they?'

Images of security panther bakus with snarling, snapping jaws; of Carter Smith with an axe to grind; of Jinx running away from me through the hallways of Moncha HQ, flash in my mind. If that's what normality is, then maybe I don't want it. Despite everything, I smile weakly at Tobias. 'Let's hope so.'

At a noise by the door, we both look up. Mom arrives back in the room, a backpack slung over her shoulders. 'I spoke to the doctor outside, Lacey. They still don't know the exact cause of your black-outs and memory loss, but as long as we keep an eye on you and take it easy, I can bring you home.'

'Thank goodness! I can't wait to get back and see Jinx,' I say, my smile broadening.

Mom and Tobias exchange a look.

'What is it?' I ask, crossing my arms over my stomach. I have a bad feeling about this.

'Honey? I don't know how to tell you . . .'

As she's talking, it hits me in a rush.

Jinx is gone.

CHAPTER THREE

THE ELEVATOR RIDE UP TO OUR apartment seems interminable, stopping at almost every floor. Petal flutters around Mom's head.

'Petal, did you put the heating on?' she asks.

>>The apartment is set to 21 degrees Celsius.

'Lights on as well; I want it to be as welcoming as possible for when we get back.'

I know Mom is saying this for my benefit, reminding me that I'm home. But even the thought of being in my own bed, with all my things around me, doesn't feel quite right. Because Jinx won't be there. My companion. My best friend.

I miss having his cheeky voice in my head. Our telepathic conversations had become normal to me but were so *not* how other people communicated with their bakus. Jinx was special. He didn't obey my commands, but he was always there when I needed him.

But now he's gone.

On the ride home, Mom had filled me in a bit more about my hospital stay. The doctors weren't able to find any sort of adequate explanation for my coma. All they knew was that whenever I woke up, *something* would pull me back into a deep sleep and affected my short-term memory.

In the meantime, they treated me for hypothermia, and the *something* seemed to pass on its own, with time. They said I'd powered my way through it.

It wasn't a good enough explanation for Mom or for me. But what could we do?

Our apartment is small – two bedrooms, a bathroom and a cramped open-plan living room and kitchen – but it's home. Even the view out over the city is comforting, grey as it is outside. I see that our little plastic Christmas tree has come out of the cupboard – although it's not decorated yet. I bet Mom has been waiting for me.

It's another stark reminder of how long I've been in hospital for. It's almost Christmas.

We walk into the kitchen and Mom fills the kettle and puts it on the stove to boil. We don't speak until there are two mugs of steaming hot English Breakfast tea in front of us, and we're both perched on our preferred stools by the counter.

'How are you feeling?' Mom asks.

'Better,' I say, with a shrug. 'A bit weak.'

She nods, then lets out a long sigh. 'The doctor said you might – but that you'll feel stronger soon. He reminded me that you weren't in a normal coma – there was no permanent brain damage or lasting side effects, other than the memory loss. And hopefully that will come back too. I'm just glad to have you home.'

'Me too,' I say.

'Are you feeling up for talking?' she asks. Mom has her serious face on, the one I don't see very often because, since it's only the two of us, she is nicer to me than I deserve. She lets me spend all night in my basement locker, tinkering away. She indulges my hobbies. She lets me attend the school of my dreams even though it must bring up terrible memories for her about my dad, who left us when I was five.

And how do I repay her?

By being dishonest and not turning to her for help when I needed it, at the first sign of trouble. Then I get into so much trouble, I end up in hospital for a month.

How can I explain all this to her?

Still, I answer her question with a small nod.

'Honey, you have to tell me everything that has happened,' she says, her tone soft but firm, brokering no debate.

I open my mouth, but I have no idea how to begin. Plus, there's something giant hanging over my head. I don't know how much I *can* tell her.

I pick at a loose string on the edge of my sleeve. 'When I started at Profectus, they made us sign an agreement that said we couldn't discuss what happens at school with anyone outside it.'

Mom tuts at me, but follows it with a wry smile. 'So, did you actually *read* that document before you signed it?'

That's not what I expected her to say. The only sound coming out of my mouth is an unintelligible 'Uhhh . . .'

'I'll take that as a no, then. Because if you had, you would have seen the clause that states how parents are exempt from that particular rule.'

My jaw drops. 'What?'

Mom sighs, and Petal brings up the agreement with my signature on the bottom. Or rather, my fingerprint, processed through my baku.

'See?' she says, pointing at the line. Sure enough, the sentence reads that I could have told Mom what was going on at school all along. My guilt seems several magnitudes bigger. 'Now, my little tinkerer. Tell me everything.'

I don't need any more encouragement than that. The words come spilling out of me like water from a burst dam. I start with the fact that Profectus hadn't given me money for a level 3 baku at all. I'd found Jinx – or the broken and mangled wreck of him – by the side of the railroad tracks. I'd spent all summer repairing him to full functionality. And then . . .

I remember what Jinx told me in the basement of Moncha HQ. *He* was the one who'd hacked into the system and orchestrated my acceptance into Profectus.

He really was no ordinary baku.

I tell Mom all of what I know.

She listens patiently, gasping and groaning at key points in the story, her eyebrows rising alarmingly high up her forehead when I tell her who was after Jinx: Eric Smith. The second most powerful person in the entire Moncha Corporation after Monica herself.

When I get to the part about Jinx running away from me

yet again, I finally break down, my words merging together, almost indistinguishable. I still can't remember much other than running through the hallways, and the frustration of losing my memory *and* Jinx is almost too much to bear. Before I know it, Mom wraps her arms around me and pulls me close.

'You should have come to me,' she whispers into my hair.

'I know,' I stutter back, my voice choked with tears.

'You don't have to tackle this on your own. Tomorrow, you and I will march into Moncha headquarters, demand an audience with Eric Smith, and ask him where Jinx is. Even if Moncha do own all the bakus, and even if Jinx is ... different ... they can't just steal him away from you with no explanation. And with Jinx still missing, that's the most obvious place to start looking.'

This time when I sob it's out of relief – not sadness. Mom looks fierce, her blue eyes, so different to my dark ones, shining bright. I haven't seen her this animated in years, and it ignites a spark deep inside my belly. Maybe things will be okay after all.

'But will Eric Smith see you?' I say through my sniffles.

Mom stiffens her shoulders. 'He had better. He owes me.'

I raise an eyebrow, despite myself. 'Owes you?'

'You might be surprised to hear this, but once upon a time, your dad and I knew Eric Smith quite well.'

I gasp. Mom never talks about my dad. Not since he disappeared when I was five. I've never had a proper explanation – maybe it was a mental health breakdown, or stress, or he simply abandoned us. Talking about him hurt her so much, so I learned never to ask questions.

'After your father ... left, Eric was the one who got us this apartment and my job. Because the one thing he could never give me was an answer. I think he will take my call about Jinx.'

'I ... I hope so.' I lower my head and my voice drops to a whisper. 'I really miss that little baku, Mom.'

She touches her index finger to my chin. 'You are so your father's daughter.' She pauses. 'I know he's no match for Jinx, but do you want your beetle baku back in the meantime?' asks Mom. She disentangles herself from me, then walks over to a small box next to our television, where Slick is lying – inert.

She picks him up and brings him over to me, ready to be leashed and recharged. I take him, seeing no other option. Sitting in my palm, I take a second to admire the engineering needed to create even a level 1 model scarab beetle baku. So much technology is hidden within his elegant greenish-purple carapace, a whole host of functions perfectly balanced within such a small package.

I plug him in to the leash at my ear, and he starts up with a tiny *whirr-click*.

>>Hello, Lacey.

I immediately detach him and throw him down on to the couch, my heart beating wildly.

'Lacey, what's wrong?' Mom asks.

Bile rises in the back of my throat. Something happened,

something that ended up with me lying in a puddle, getting soaked through with freezing water, leaving me with hypothermia and in hospital for a month with unexplained memory loss – and I have a feeling that Slick was involved.

But that's impossible. Bakus can't harm their owners.

'I . . . I don't know,' I say, still staring wild-eyed at Slick. I force myself to pick him up. I turn him over, staring at the rubbery pads of his feet, not quite sure what I'm looking for. Mom is looking at me as if I've lost the plot.

'I think Slick's not the only one in need of a recharge,' says Mom.

I yawn in reply. My head feels as if it's loaded down with bricks. Maybe she's right.

Mom leans down to kiss my forehead. 'Maybe it was too soon to give you your baku. You don't want to be bombarded with messages and social media right now. Let's get you to bed. And tomorrow, we will tackle everything else, okay?'

'Okay. Night, Mom,' I say, heading towards my bedroom.

But a loud knock at the door stops me in my tracks.

CHAPTER FOUR

I HANG BACK AS MOM OPENS THE DOOR. Wariness sets my teeth on edge. Who could it be? We haven't buzzed anyone in, and we don't get many random visits from our neighbours.

'Can I help you?' Mom asks, her voice tight. Instinctively I bury my hands deep in the pouch of my hoodie.

I poke my head around the corner into the hallway, so I have a view of the entrance. I gasp. It's a team of Moncha guard, dressed head-to-toe in black, complete with slick black panther bakus at their heels. They have a distinctive insignia on the shoulders of their uniform: the Moncha logo, a stylized letter M, with a cluster of stars in the corner. They're not part of the ordinary Moncha guard. They're part of Eric's team.

'Mrs Chu?'

'It's Ms,' Mom answers, jutting her chin out in front of her as she opens the door. She's trying to stand solidly, to show them that they can't intimidate her – but I can tell that they do. Of *course* they do. They're designed to intimidate – everything from their all-black outfits down to their terrifying, robotic-looking panthers. There's nothing cute and fluffy about these bakus.

'Do you live here with your daughter, Lacey Chu?'

'I do.'

'We have orders to search your residence for stolen Moncha intellectual property.'

'Whose orders?' Mom stands with her hand on the doorframe, her knuckles turning white as she grips it in fear. Petal is fluttering around her ear nervously, bleeping at her. 'Yes, I know who they are,' she snaps at her baku. She must be reminding her these are members of Eric Smith's personal security team. 'I can't just let you in because you say you have some "orders" from somewhere. We've just come back from the hospital – where my daughter has been for the past month. Can't you come back tomorrow?'

'No, ma'am. We were directed to search your property as soon as your daughter returned.'

She straightens her spine. 'This is an invasion of our privacy! Unless you have some sort of warrant ...'

'Actually, ma'am, we can search whatever we like, whenever we like. It's in the terms of your lease for the apartment.'

Her face drains of colour. 'No, it isn't. I would never have signed something like that.'

'Everyone who lives in this building has signed it. Moncha Corp owns this building, and as such we have a right to enter at any time. This request is a mere courtesy. Now if you and your daughter could step outside with your bakus, we will only need a few minutes.'

I've been cowering in the kitchen doorway, listening to their conversation. But if they're still looking for Jinx, that means they don't have him. I don't know where he is either – so I have no reason to hide. I step out into the hallway and take Mom's hand. She needs me to be strong with her. Slick is inert in my other hand. One of the security guards narrows his eyes as I pass, eyeing my unleashed baku, so I connect Slick as we step out into the hallway, swallowing down the bad feelings I had a moment ago.

Even though I know they won't find anything, it makes me sick to see them enter our little apartment. A few doors open down the hall and then quickly shut again – neighbours wondering what an earth is going on, but also not wanting to get involved. Word spreads in a building like this.

I'm sure they'll have plenty to gossip about with Mom and I backed up against the striped wallpaper in the hallway, guarded by panthers and looking like criminals. Mom has never been so close to a security baku, but it's not that long since I ran away from one. Not that long since I saw one attempt to sink its teeth into my friend's arm. So much for bakus not being able to harm people.

Mom's grip tightens around mine as we hear them move from room to room. Every so often we hear a man shout 'clear', and the security team captain sounds more and more frustrated when they don't find anything. There's no evidence of Jinx in the condo.

26

'You two.' The captain steps outside again and crooks his finger at Mom and me. 'Come with us.' Reluctantly we follow him back into our living room. Mom tenses as she sees what a mess they've created.

I'm stunned at how fast things can change. How a home can turn from a safe haven into a prison – how a company can go from beloved to feared. All those things we thought would never happen to us are happening.

We're told to sit down on the sofa. All four security guards are in front of us. 'We have it on good authority that you have been seen with this stolen property.' His security baku projects a 3D hologram of Jinx on to the table in front of me.

The hologram is so realistic; tears prick my eyes. My fingers itch to reach out and stroke him. But I try to remain calm. 'That *was* my baku – and I didn't steal him from Moncha Corp. I don't know where he is. This is my baku now. Meet Slick.' I hold the little scarab beetle robot out in my hand to show him, but the guard doesn't acknowledge it.

'We'll see about that. As you know, Moncha retains the right to record any and all conversations overheard by the bakus.'

Now it's my turn to lose the colour in my face.

'I'm going to ask your bakus to play back the conversations you've had since Miss Chu was discharged from hospital.'

Oh no. I told Mom everything about Jinx – which means that Petal heard everything too.

And then I realize something else. Slick was there when I was chasing Jinx – he likely has information about where

Jinx went that I don't remember. I wish I'd been clearheaded enough to think about that before the guards showed up.

It's all going to be over before it's even begun.

But then the strangest thing happens. They rewind back the recordings on the cloud for both Petal and Slick, but throughout our conversation about Jinx, there is fuzz and distortion. It's not obvious, because there are enough audible words to make it sound natural; it's as if the bakus had been recording during a loud traffic jam. The conversation has been rendered meaningless. I glance over at Mom, but her face is neutral. I wonder what she makes of it all. Even stranger, Slick's memories of running after Jinx are the same as mine. We're darting through the hallways of Moncha HQ and then ... it's like he goes dead. As if he ran out of battery mid-way through the chase. I'm both happy he can't give information about Jinx's whereabouts to the security team, and disappointed that he can't fill in more of my memory gaps.

The head guard frowns, but he has no more reason to hold us. As far as they know, there's nothing we could have done to alter the recordings. As far as *we* know, there's nothing we could have done. It's a mystery.

'We're adding a directive to these bakus,' he gestures at Slick and Petal, 'that if the stolen property is seen or talked about by you two then we will be the first to know. But things will be much easier if you simply cooperate with us and disclose any new information as soon as you know it.'

I resist the urge to scoff, disguising it instead as a cough.

'Understood?'

28

'We understand,' Mom says, through gritted teeth. 'Will you go now?'

The man fixes her with a disapproving glare but thankfully, he nods.

We breathe a sigh of relief once we're back inside our apartment and the door is firmly shut on the security guards. I feel like I'm standing right on the edge of the line between wired and exhausted.

'Eric doesn't have my baku,' I whisper, deliberately avoiding saying Jinx's name.

Mom pulls me close, kissing me on the forehead. 'No. But he still needs to answer for what his son did. Stealing your baku. If he wanted it back, he should have gone through the proper channels. And his son's actions ended up with you in hospital for a month. Plus, the nerve of sending his security team to interrogate us the night I get you back! Parent to parent, he needs to talk to me.'

We both jump as Petal starts shaking and vibrating, a strange sequence of lights flashing up and down her butterfly body.

'Time for an update, it looks like,' says Mom. 'I swear, these updates are getting more and more frequent ... they keep adding all these new features and apps to Petal. One day I'm worried I won't be able to keep up.' She gestures to her baku, who connects to the leash that snakes around her ear. Petal settles into a more comfortable position on her shoulder, and the flashing lights change to a single pulsing green to indicate her charge.

'Goodnight, Lacey. And don't worry. I'll get in touch with Eric and talk to him while you're at school.'

School. Profectus. I'd almost forgotten. I'm excited to go back and see my friends, to get back to normal and to focus on my goals. It will be different without Jinx, but I hope he's somewhere safe. I won't have to worry about him reading my thoughts any more. I won't have to hear his cheeky voice in my head, disrupting my train of thought. I won't have to keep getting into trouble because of things he did, not under my command.

I try and convince myself that is a good thing.

Who am I kidding? With Jinx gone, I feel like I'm missing a piece of my heart.

How am I supposed to live without him?

CHAPTER FIVE

W HEN I WAKE UP THE NEXT MORNING, relieved to find that I am in my own bed. It's still pitch-black outside. 'What's the time, Slick?' I ask my baku.

>>It's 5:05 a.m.

Oof, that's early. But I can't go back to sleep. I lie awake, staring at the ceiling, dwelling on snippets of dreams that seem more like memories. I take myself back to Moncha HQ and the fight with Carter. I can picture that much more clearly now: the large room where Carter was holding a caged Jinx, backed up by the fearsome security panthers. I had back-up too: Tobias, and the rest of my Baku Battle teammates Kai, River and Ashley.

I remember Slick helping me to free Jinx by removing the black mark on his paw – a device that disabled Jinx's movement. I remember holding Jinx in my arms and preparing to run away with Tobias and the rest of the team. But then he wriggles out of my grasp, and runs away.

The next memories don't make much sense. Running

through twisting hallways. Then, I'm standing on a street, in front of a house, but I'm indoors.

Then I'm outside again. I have an image of cats – not baku cats like Jinx, but real ones.

I wish I could understand what it all means.

At half-past six, I drag myself out of bed.

>>Want to know the plan for the day, Lacey?

There's no quip from Slick. No gag. No snark. Just my companion, my little level 1 beetle baku, doing exactly what he was programmed to do, obediently awaiting my commands, ready to help me – not only to tell me about my day, but to help me navigate my way through the world at large.

I give the slightest nod to Slick and he buzzes around me, projecting my calendar and scrolling through my messages and social media.

There are a bunch of overdue homework alerts, automatically sent through by Profectus, that threaten to overwhelm me; a notification about a single-line update to the baku terms and conditions; several news alerts about the latest antics of a celebrity which I'd previously subscribed to. I brush them all away, feeling an overriding sense of sadness. I miss Jinx's familiarity. I would take his quips and personality over Slick's efficiency any day. Jinx never laid out my schedule or reminded me about a Maths test. Those things might be useful, but they aren't what I want. I know I shouldn't be judging my new little baku. He's doing exactly what he was designed to do. He's making my life easier.

But I don't want a personal assistant. I want my friend.

>>With the bad weather in the forecast and traffic ahead, I suggest you leave for school twenty minutes earlier than usual.

I groan, but roll out of bed. I don't want to be late – in fact, I want to get there early so that I can meet up with Tobias and the rest of the team before school.

They're the only students at Profectus who know the truth: that Jinx was something more than an ordinary baku.

When I ask Slick to reveal the messages from Team Tobias, I'm bombarded by voicenotes and texts.

> ASHLEY: Hi Lacey! Tobias said you might not pick up these messages for a while but I hope you're okay . . . I was so worried when I heard you were in a coma. I've organized someone to take notes in all your classes so you won't miss a thing. Message me as soon as you're able!

> KAI: Lacey! OK, so, we didn't win the Baku Battles but thanks for making my last year at Profectus hella exciting. Catch ya when you're back.

River doesn't leave me a message, but instead sends me a series of videos of him running around, performing silly tricks with his frog baku, Lizard. He's letting me know he cares, but in his own unique way. My heart swells.

They're still my friends. I know that there are going to be

a lot of questions left to answer, and I'm going to need their help if I'm going to survive the upcoming scrutiny at school. Not only did I mess up the Baku Battles, but I've spent the last month in the hospital. Way to keep a low profile . . .

I throw on my school uniform after brushing my teeth and running a comb through my hair. I've given up attempting to make myself look any more presentable than that – everyone knows what I look like: my face has been emblazoned on the video screens in the arena, sweat dripping off my brow. But it still gives me a thrill to wear the Profectus Academy logo on my blazer. Profectus is the key to fulfilling my dream of becoming a companioneer. The state-of-the-art classrooms are ten times better equipped than at my old school; the professors are all Moncha employees imparting their knowledge; I can take classes in companioneering and coding and product design alongside normal ones like Maths and English and History and French. Almost every new companioneer hired at Moncha is a graduate of Profectus. Students vie from all corners of the globe for a place there.

And here I am, wearing the uniform.

'Mom?' I shout from my room. Then I turn to Slick. 'Slick, can you get a coffee brewed for me?' Everything in our Moncha-branded kitchen connects to our bakus – he could even make me some toast if I asked for it. But I'm not hungry just yet.

There's no answer from Mom – she must be getting ready in her room. I walk into the kitchen and grab my steaming hot coffee, prepared with an extra swirl of cream (just how I like it in the morning – Slick is good) and take a sip. Then I frown. Normally I can hear Mom bustling about in her bedroom, but it's so quiet, I could hear a hairpin drop.

'Mom?' I rap my knuckles against her bedroom door. No answer again. I push it open, but the room is empty.

'Slick? Send a message to Mom asking if she wants me to meet her outside.' Maybe she popped out for a minute.

>>I've just had her automated reply. She's at work, but she'll get back to you as soon as she's on a break.

At work? Already?

That doesn't make any sense.

Slick vibrates his iridescent wings.

>>I've just had another message through from Mom. It says: Sorry honey, gone in to work early! I'll see you after school.

Maybe she's gone in so early to try and talk to Eric Smith before her shift starts. 'I guess, send her a reply, telling her OK.'

>>Done.

'Then send a message to the Team Tobias group that I'll be arriving at school a little early.'

>>Done.

I hope my friends will show up and walk through the doors of Profectus with me. A show of solidarity. I feel very alone right now, with no Jinx by my side.

Outside, I see that snow has settled on the sidewalks, turning slushy. Living in Monchaville means we rarely have to deal with the normal hassles of living through a

Canadian winter. Monchaville is the nickname we give the part of the city that is funded and maintained by Moncha Corp. Monica Chan always wanted to give back to the city she was raised in, and to provide support for her growing number of employees. What started out as her buying her old condo tower turned into having Moncha-sponsored schools, a hospital, even a police force. It took the burden off an underfunded city council and promoted a sense of company love and loyalty that other big tech firms could only dream of.

>>On your left.

Slick warns me, and I step out of the way of a squirrel-type baku who sweeps over the sidewalk with his hard-bristled tail, brushing away the fallen snow and salting any ice below. The squirrel bakus (level 2s) are issued free of charge to work crews in charge of city maintenance.

Monica Chan seemed to have an instinct for how to build a community. It's one of the reasons she's my idol.

Monica Chan.

I have a jolt of memory and the strangest image pops into my head of a long-limbed, languorous creature draped around my idol's neck. The strangest looking baku. But how could that be right? Her baku is a cat model. I shake the image from my head. Right now, I'm concerned about how to get through the first day back at school after a month off and without my witty companion.

My feet carry me towards the Academy while my brain is in this daze. As I round the corner to the school, I see the familiar tail of Jupiter, Ashley's friendly spaniel baku, wagging at me. Ashley's fingers swipe furiously, seemingly in thin air – she must be playing a game projected by Jupiter. I grin widely. She's come to walk with me.

An alert from Jupiter makes her look up and she catches my eye, giving me a huge smile. When I get close, she links her arm through mine. 'I'm so glad you're okay! We were all so worried about you. How are you feeling?'

'A bit nervous.'

'Aw, no need to be, Lace! We're all here for you. And you're so smart, you'll catch up in no time.'

'Thanks. But it's weird not having Jinx,' I say in a low voice.

Ashley squeezes my upper arm. 'You still don't remember anything about that night?'

I shake my head.

'Don't worry, I'm here for you.'

'Thank you,' I manage to stutter out.

'We all are.'

We round the corner to see the rest of Team Tobias standing at the bottom of the steps to the Academy: Kai, River and – of course – Tobias himself. I can't help but grin as I see them.

As we approach, River's level 3 frog baku, Lizard, is doing somersaults on the wall. I sometimes wonder if River has altered Lizard's battery life to give him even more energy – or maybe River just generates so much power through his fidgeting that he keeps Lizard powered up, no matter what.

By contrast, Kai's husky baku Oka is much more still and

calm. But strength is visible in every inch of Oka's body, the same as Kai's muscle-bound body. It's amazing how much a person's choice of baku mirrors their personality.

No wonder Kai's eyebrows lift in surprise as he spots Slick on my shoulder.

'Lacey! You're back! Ooh, I wonder if they'll do a Baku Battle rematch now,' River says, rubbing his hands together.

Tobias gives River a warning look. 'What?' says River, throwing his hands up in the air. Then he looks at me. 'Lacey doesn't mind, do you?'

I shake my head.

'Seems unfair that you didn't get to participate in the final battle. There should be a rematch.'

I shrug. 'I think I've seen enough battles for now. I'll try for the internship next year.'

'As long as you're not too poor to upgrade your baku,' remarks Kai. His eyes slide over my beetle baku and he grimaces.

'Don't be so insensitive, Kai!' Ashley exclaims.

But Kai just grins. 'Lacey knows I'm kidding around. And you know you love me,' he says with a wink.

Ashley huffs, but there's a twinkle in her eye. Something has happened there in the month I've been away. My eyes drift over to Tobias, who I catch staring at me too. I look away, still unsure of what – if anything – is going on between us.

But surely there must be something if he visited me in hospital every day? We did kiss, once – but it feels like a lifetime ago after everything that's happened in between.

'Let's talk inside,' says Tobias. 'I'm freezing.'

I look up at the imposing Profectus Academy building, designed to look like the front of a gothic castle. It might be perfectly modern inside, but the outside is designed to intimidate and inspire awe. It works.

I focus my mind away from the cute boy and on to what classes I'll have first. As we climb the steps, I wonder who's taken over Companioneering now that Mr Baird is gone. Our principal, Dr Grant, fired him when she discovered he was a corporate spy for Moncha's biggest rival firm BRIGHTSPRK. I won't find out until this afternoon though. I have Maths first, then my coding class.

Slam! My foot hits against wood. We've walked straight into the doors to Profectus.

They won't open.

'Ummm . . . are we too early? Is school not even open yet?' asks Ashley. She turns to Tobias.

'No way, I've been here earlier than this a zillion times before,' he replies.

'Yeah, me too,' River says.

'In fact, isn't it part of the school's policy that the doors are always open in case we need access to the library or labs for our homework?' asks Ashley.

'Yup. Hang on, step back,' says Tobias.

We take a few collective steps down and then Tobias walks forward, Aero flying close behind him. The doors slide open for him and he walks inside.

'Must've just been a glitch,' says Ashley. She walks ahead

of me, Jupiter trotting at her heels, and passes through the doors without difficulty.

My stomach sinks, but I try not to think about it. As I walk back up the steps, my worst fears are confirmed. The doors won't open for me.

'Oh crap,' says Kai.

The doors open again as Ashley steps through to find out what's happening. Her face goes ashen as she realizes what this means. It's me.

I'm no longer allowed into Profectus.

'Come on!' says Kai. He grabs me under one arm, River grabs the other, and between them they hustle me into the building. I get through the doors. They don't slam shut. No alarm goes off. I wonder if I can breathe a sigh of relief.

But it's not to be. There's a flap of wings and the sharp tap of heels on the rich mahogany flooring. It looks like my entrance back into school isn't going to be as simple as I thought.

'Miss Lacey Chu? Can you come with me?' Dr Grant, our principal, does not sound pleased to see me. Last time I spoke to her, though, I was pretty rude. Maybe she just wants an apology.

'See you later.' I give Team Tobias a small wave, and they look at me with varying degrees of concern on their faces.

'See you in Gathering,' says Tobias, with a reassuring smile.

But the look on Dr Grant's face tells me that might be a long shot.

Slick has been unusually quiet, and I reach up to my

shoulder to make sure that he's there. I follow behind Dr Grant's neat beige block heels, shuffling along in my winter boots. *Just a little longer, and then things will go back to normal, I think. You've been away for a month. Maybe they've changed the settings on the door . . . or they need to do a new orientation . . . there must be an explanation for all this.*

She leads me into her office, shutting the door behind her. None of the secretaries lift their eyes up to greet me. It's as if they don't even see me any more.

'I'm sure you had difficulty getting into the school this morning.'

Heat rises in my cheeks. 'Yes, ma'am,' I stutter.

'While your friends might find it appropriate to drag you into the school, I'm afraid there's a reason that you weren't allowed in. As you know, Profectus has very strict rules. And one of those rules is that no student can attend without a level 3 baku.'

My chest tightens and I feel like I can't breathe. I'm transported back to the summer when my dream of getting into Profectus was dashed by a rejection letter.

But this is different. Profectus isn't supposed to discriminate towards its own students based on lack of funds – I should be offered a grant or scholarship or something. 'I . . . I was hoping that I could get an extension until the end of the semester? I'll try and get the money together to buy a level 3, I can talk to my mom . . . or maybe there's some financial aid from the school?'

I search Dr Grant's face for some sort of understanding. I

can't be the only student to have run into financial trouble. Plus, Profectus gives students money to buy new bakus all the time – for example, if they are destroyed in a Baku Battle. But there isn't a trace of sympathy on her smooth features, and her owl baku looks down his beak at me with a stern, cold gaze. It sends a shiver down my spine.

'I'm afraid that won't be acceptable. You cannot attend Profectus without a level 3 baku,' she repeats.

'But Slick can still pick up the homework alerts and—' There's nothing really that I can't do without a level 3 baku. The only thing would be the battles – which I wouldn't participate in now even if I were being paid.

She shakes her head. 'This is one rule that we cannot bend.'

The reality of what she is telling me is slow to sink in.

She signals to her owl baku, who blinks at me. Slick pipes up, having received a message from the owl.

>>I have your registration details for St Agnes. We had better walk quickly or we are going to be late to your first class.

St Agnes? But that means . . .

The Principal spells it out for me. 'You are no longer a student at Profectus Academy, Lacey Chu. I have to ask you to leave the premises at once.'

CHAPTER SIX

I DON'T EVEN HAVE TIME TO GO TO MY
locker or say goodbye to my friends. Dr Grant's owl baku
makes sure that I am escorted out of a different exit,
unable to return.

I'm too shell-shocked to do anything remotely rebellious.
It's only when I'm back out of the door (another door that
refuses to open for me) and in the frigid December air that
I think of all the questions I should have asked. *How is this
fair? What about my course work? Is this even legal?*

'Slick, call Mom,' I say, not wanting to waste any
more time.

>>Calling Mom.

His happy-sounding voice irritates me. He's not reading
my mood at all.

I wait on the steps, pacing to keep warm. After a few
agonizing seconds, Slick says, >>I'm sorry, I'm only
getting your mom's answering service. I've left a
message with Petal, asking for your mom to return
your call as soon as possible. In the meantime, we

43

should be getting to class. We've had an alert from St Agnes that you are in danger of getting detention if you don't show up to school soon.

'Call Mom again,' I say.

>>But . . .

'Call Mom again, Slick,' I repeat, more sternly. The beetle seems to flinch at my tone, skittering up my arm to hide in the hood of my jacket. But I can't bring myself to feel concern. All I want is for the baku to follow the orders I've given to it.

How ironic.

>>I'm afraid I got your mom's answer service again.

I groan. Mom always picks up when I call – even if I'm supposed to be in school and she is at work. This isn't a life-threatening emergency, so I hesitate to use our code – but it is getting close.

I don't want to leave the Profectus steps. I don't want to start school at St Agnes. I left that place behind. Going there would feel like a huge step backward.

But it's winter in Toronto, and there's no way that I can pace outside the school for hours. And there's always a chance that Slick will alert the authorities to my absentee status from school if I head to a café. He's such a goody-two-shoes. Jinx would never do something like that to me.

The pang of sadness hits me again. Where is Jinx? If he's not with Eric Smith or with me . . . I wish I knew how to get in contact with him. I feel like I need him more than ever. I wonder what he's doing now. He might have had a solution to this, one that didn't involve me sitting outside in the cold.

My next fear springs to life.

>>I'm afraid if we don't start moving towards St Agnes, I'm going to have to report you to the police as an absentee student.

I roll my eyes, and if he wasn't my only connection to the online world I might have squished that little bug in my hands. I don't want to get into any more trouble, so reluctantly I make my way down the steps and towards the school that I thought I'd left behind.

I wonder what they will make of my return.

The only saving grace is that Zora, my best friend, is a student there. Ultimately, she's the reason I get moving. At least she is someone I can explain the situation too – and with any luck, she'll have an idea for how I can get a level 3 baku again.

So far, Mom's prediction that everything will be all right today is not going to plan. I steel myself. One day at St Agnes. It won't be *that* bad.

As I pace towards my old high school, we leave the confines of Monchaville. It's a shift I can sense – as if it's something real and tangible. Even the air seems to smell different in the part of the city that is not under the control of Moncha Corp. A shiver runs through me that has nothing to do with the cold. Is it still Monchaville if Monica Chan is missing? Or is it now Eric-Smith-ville?

It's not fair that my biggest rival, Carter Smith, has been

living his life as normal for the past month after he tried to ruin mine. He tried, and maybe he succeeded. I don't have Jinx, I don't have a place at Profectus, my dreams of working for Moncha are shattered ...

It's two bus journeys and a short walk before I arrive at the St Agnes school gates. It looks so drab compared to Profectus Academy. There's no grandeur about the building design: it's a single-storey concrete block, wide and squat, with window frames painted in garish orange. There are no special classes here, no sense of ambition for their students. I feel a wave of revulsion as I walk down towards the entrance, even though I spent seven years passing through these gates. Seven years that I'd dedicated to finding a way *out*.

The doors to this school open without a single hesitation, and Slick chirps up as soon as we pass through.

>>We're a few minutes late but your schedule is downloading on to my system now.

These hallways are as familiar to me as the stairwells of my condo building, but I pause in the lobby to see where I'm supposed to head first. I feel so conspicuous in my Profectus uniform. Why didn't I think about going home to change?

Because you didn't think this was really going to happen, I remind myself.

I make a vow not to take off my coat, even though I know the overactive heating inside the building means I'm going to boil in about ten minutes. Better to boil than to advertise to the entire school that I've been booted out from the elite academy I'd given up everything to attend.

>>Your first class is Maths with Mrs Pendle, in classroom 24A.

I grimace. I don't know that teacher – so there's no hope of a friendly face up front. Still, I know where the classroom is, and without thinking about it, my feet take me exactly where I need to go. I follow the bland hallways lined with lime-green lockers until I reach 24A, staring down at the strange speckled linoleum floor. *Why do they make schools so hideously ugly?* I wonder. Is there some reason, some thought-process behind it all? If we were in Monchaville, I know that everything would have been thought out down to the tiniest detail. But here's it's just proof that students are not the main priority.

I'm procrastinating. I take a deep breath before opening the door.

The first face I see is Zora's. She's sitting in the front row, Linus on the desk in front of her projecting some pages from a Maths textbook. Her dark brown eyes open wide as she sees me.

'Lacey, what are you doing here?' asks Zora, standing up from her chair. Of course, everyone turns to look at me – which makes me want to turn around and run away.

Mrs Pendle looks up from her desk. 'Oh, Lacey Chu, is it? I wasn't expecting you quite this soon, I just got the notification . . .' She looks down at her baku, a hare model, who is tapping his foot impatiently. She gestures at a pile of chairs in the corner of the room. 'Grab a seat for now and set up at someone's desk. You can catch up on what you've missed after class.'

My cheeks burn as I'm forced to cross the classroom to the pile of chairs, convinced that everyone's eyes are trained on my back. There's an awkward moment as the metal legs catch and clatter together, and I almost find myself buried under the toppling chairs. I just about manage to stop them from falling, but so much for being cool and inconspicuous. I think back to my first day at Profectus, when *Jinx* had been the one drawing all the attention. I much preferred that to this option.

I drop the hard plastic chair next to Zora's desk as she scoots over to make room for me. Thankfully, everyone except Zora seems to drop their concentration back down to their work. She stares at me, and I stare back.

I know we're both thinking the exact same thing:

What on *earth* is going on?

CHAPTER SEVEN

MY TIME IN MRS PENDLE'S CLASS disappears in a flash of quadratic equations and formulae that I barely pay attention to. Thankfully this is one class that I could take in my sleep. We covered most of this in my first few weeks at Profectus, and Maths has always been one of my favourites amongst the 'normal' subjects. I think about how at Profectus I would be learning how to code battle strategies in Moncha's unique programming language – and then moving on to Industrial Design class, where we were going to use the Academy's own wind tunnel to test the aerodynamics of new baku prototypes.

St Agnes doesn't have a wind tunnel.

There's no state-of-the-art programming lab.

The gym is an ordinary gym, not a secret baku battling arena.

My heart rate rises as I think of all I'm losing out on if this expulsion is permanent. *It can't be. I have to find a way back to Profectus.*

I keep my head down, dodging looks from other students.

But I can't escape them completely. Slick crawls on my knee and projects a message on to my black Profectus-uniform trousers. Bakus aren't technically supposed to be active during class, but an enterprising St Agnes student had found a way around the block on external messaging in class. To get around it, messages are sent from baku to baku on a group school message board, rather than using names and profiles. A simple fix that the school's security should have picked up . . . but didn't. A loophole in the code.

If there's anything teens are good at finding, it's loopholes.

And messages are being sent to Slick already. There are lots of my former classmates here, people who have known me for a long time. Slick sends a steady stream of messages my way from those dying with curiosity about what must have happened to me.

They start out fairly normal:

Lacey, are you back permanently?

Has something happened to Profectus?

What the heck are you doing here?

But the longer I leave them unanswered, the more extreme they become.

Has Profectus burned to the ground? That's
the only reason I can think of that you've come
back here.

OMG. You've been expelled!

LACEY CHU WAS EXPELLED FROM PROFECTUS.

I let out a groan that makes Mrs Pendle almost drop her
electronic chalk. I snap my mouth shut and keep my eyes
glued to the top of the desk. Out of the corner of my eye,
I can see her glaring around the room but thankfully
she doesn't settle on me. I swipe my hand over the top of
Slick's wings, indicating that I don't want to read any more
messages. My stomach churns, knowing that the gossip is
going to spread around the school like wildfire. No chance
of my flying under the radar.

When the bell rings, I'm the first out of the door. I have
absolutely no worries about catching up with what's going on
at St Agnes and far more about what I'm missing out on at
Profectus. I need this school day to end so I can text Ashley
and find out exactly what's happening.

Zora scrambles out moments later to meet me. She grabs
my hand and grips it tight. Without saying a word (neither
of us want to talk about it with others in listening distance),
we march our way around to the one place that we know we
won't be overheard: the school library.

When we settle into one of the study booths, Zora

immediately grabs me into a hug. I embrace her back. I don't want to let her go.

'You're okay!' she says into my hair. 'I've been so worried about you. Sorry I didn't come and see you straight away last night but I was out with my parents and then they said you'd probably want to rest. How are you feeling? Are you totally better now?'

'I feel okay . . .' I say, with a shrug. 'Tired, but I don't know if that's from whatever kept me in hospital or what happened today . . .'

'They didn't let you back into Profectus,' Zora says matter-of-factly.

I blink rapidly. 'How did you know?'

Zora shrugs. 'I wondered about it when your mom didn't bring Jinx home. Without Jinx you don't have a level 3 baku any more. And isn't that one of the requirements?'

I nod. 'The doors wouldn't even open for me without a level 3. I thought they'd give me a pass since I was already enrolled . . . or maybe give me some financial aid . . . but nothing. I feel so helpless.'

'And you don't remember why you were passed out in the street? Or anything about where Jinx is?'

I shake my head. 'No,' I say, 'Slick doesn't have anything recorded in his memory either – it's like there was a glitch or something.'

'So what do you do now? Go to the press? The police?' Even though she's suggesting these things, I can see her fidgeting with the silver rings on her fingers – a sure sign that she is nervous about my response.

'Until I can remember more, there's not enough evidence to go to the authorities. Mom promised to talk to Eric Smith about Carter stealing Jinx. So, honestly? Now all I want to do is be able to go back to my proper school.'

Zora blinks at me, and I bite my lower lip, realizing how insensitive I'm being. St Agnes might not be *my* proper school, but it is Zora's. 'Oh my god, sorry, Z.'

She blinks again. 'For what?'

'I don't mean that St Agnes isn't a proper school . . .'

To my relief, she laughs. 'Don't be a dummy. Come on, I was almost as invested in you getting into Profectus as you were! It's always been *your* dream, not mine. I was just thinking . . . maybe there's a way for you to get a level 3 baku after all.'

I frown. 'What do you mean? There's no way that I can afford to buy another baku – let alone a level 3. Not unless you know a way to hack the lottery.'

'Ha, no. But you already turned a broken pile of smouldering metal into a fully functioning level 3 cat baku. Why don't you work on turning Slick into a level 3 over the Christmas holidays? We've only got another couple of days left at school, so you won't miss much. Then you can restart at Profectus in the New Year.' She lowers her voice. 'I know you don't want to replace Jinx . . .'

'I let him go,' I say, before I can stop myself.

'What?' Zora gasps.

Even as the words leave my mouth, I know them to be true. The memory is suddenly clear as day.

After leaving Moncha HQ, Jinx and I had run down twisting alleys, until we'd come to the gate of a local park, known for being filled with real, live, feral cats. I'd given Jinx a choice: to stay with me, or to go and be with his own kind.

He chose his own kind.

Emotions flood through me, a mixture of relief and sadness. At least now I know that Jinx is safe. Hopefully, he's happy too. He's found his place.

'I have to trust the old me that it was the right decision,' I say to Zora's still shocked face. 'But I like your plan for me to work on Slick.' The more I think about it, the better the idea becomes. The differences between level 1s and level 3s are mostly mechanical – with a bit of imagination and creativity, I might be able to turn Slick into some kind of super beetle.

My words bring Zora back to reality. 'I don't see why it wouldn't work,' she says, tentatively. 'Are you sure you're okay about Jinx?'

I pause for a moment, picturing his face – his shining dark eyes and pointed ears. But then I remember the flick of his tail as he ran to join the other cats. And I nod. 'I'm okay. But Z, I'm going to need your help if this plan is to work.'

Zora grins. 'I've tweaked Slick's code once before, so I have no problem with doing it one more time. And if this doesn't prove that you belong at your school, then nothing will.'

'I think it proves that *you* belong at the school too.'

Zora puts her hand on my arm. 'That's not what I want, and you know it.'

I stare down at Slick, ideas already crowding my mind for

how to change him to bring him up to a level 3. My brain itches to research it, my fingers twitching as if they have little minds of their own.

It's not Profectus, it's not Jinx, but it's something.

I can't wait to get started.

CHAPTER EIGHT

F OR THE FIRST TIME SINCE WAKING UP IN my hospital bed – maybe even for the first time since entering Moncha HQ for the final round of the Baku Battles – I feel back in control. I have a plan to get back into Profectus, Mom is going to talk to Eric Smith about leaving me alone, Zora and my Profectus friends are on my side *and* I think that Jinx is safe.

While I can't seem to control my memory, the fact that the Profectus plan includes companioneering makes me feel at ease.

Confronting authority figures with fierce security panther bakus? Not my style.

But building new features for a baku to take it from a basic level 1 to a kick-ass level 3? Now that's a project I can really dig my teeth into. I already feel the adrenaline coursing around my system, and I spend the rest of my class time at St Agnes daydreaming about exactly how I'm going to turn Slick into a level 3 baku. My mind is running through all the spare parts that I have collected from my time clearing up the arena and salvaging for Jinx. There's plenty that I can use.

As soon as classes end, I meet Zora and we race out of the school gates together and jump on the bus that takes us home.

Slick buzzes with incoming messages, so fiercely that I worry he's going to shake loose some of his connections.

I'm flooded with voice recordings and emojis and texts from Team Tobias. Ashley's are filled with urgency, starting from the moment that Dr Grant pulled me away.

ASHLEY at 8:28: What did Dr Grant want?

ASHLEY at 8:35: When are you coming to Gathering?

ASHLEY at 8:41: I'm really worried about you.

TOBIAS at 8:42: Just spoke with Ashley, said you didn't sign in. Hoping everything's OK.

RIVER at 9:09: WTF? What was their explanation about the doors?

KAI at 9:10: You OK dude?

TOBIAS at 12:49: The team just met for lunch. No one's seen you, the teachers won't tell us where you are, please text us when you can?!

TOBIAS at 1:13: We've been to Dr Grant and she said you've had to transfer schools? Let us know when you can. Missing you. Hope you're okay.

TOBIAS at 1:15: We'll get you back to Profectus, don't worry.

Tobias's final message brings the ghost of a smile to my face. I tell Slick to send back a message to my friends letting them know I've been forced to spend the last few days of term at St Agnes, but that I have a plan to get back as soon as possible.

Ashley is the first to reply:

Anything we can do to help?

I tell Slick to get Jupiter to give Ashley a big nuzzle as a thanks. Then I get a message through from Tobias.

TOBIAS: Hey – it was supposed to be a celebration of you coming back, but we're all meeting at Top's at 7. Please come ... I'd really like to see you. We all would.

My heart leaps at the text. Zora notices and quirks her eyebrow at me. 'Is that Hot Guy?'

'You know his name is Tobias,' I say, nudging her shoulder.

'Yeah, but I prefer to call him Hot Guy.' She winks. 'What's happening with you two?'

I shrug. 'I dunno. He's my friend . . .'

'A *friend* who visited you every day in hospital for a month. Sounds like more than a friend to me.'

A smile tugs at the corner of my mouth. 'It's all so confusing. We kissed . . .'

Zora shrieks. 'Wait, what? When did that happen? Why didn't you tell me? You have to tell me everything now.'

'No, wait!' I say, putting my hands up to halt her stream of excitement. 'So much has happened since then.'

'Yes, but now things are getting back to normal, right? So you can go back to . . .' She makes a smoochy face, and I grimace.

'I repeat: I don't know. Maybe. I hope so.' A blush rises in my cheeks.

'Then you have to go to Top's. You can't let Hot Guy slip away!'

'But the baku . . .'

'Slick can wait one more night. And you gotta keep me updated every step of the way, promise?'

'I promise,' I say. 'I'll send you a message after I've spoken to Mom okay?' I say to Zora as the elevator arrives at her floor. She nods. 'I'll be waiting.' She sticks her hand out to stop the elevator doors from shutting. 'I know you belong at Profectus, but I was happy to see you today. I've missed you so much.'

I smile. 'I wouldn't have survived the day without you.'

'Don't forget about Top's.'

'I won't!' I say with a groan. Then the elevator doors slide shut and I'm left alone in the hallway. Well, alone – apart from Slick.

>>Your Mom and Petal are inside, Slick informs me.

The information soothes the part of me that worried Mom might be still at work. I open the door and the smell of garlic bread baking in the oven hits my nostrils.

She smiles at me as I walk in, turning her head away from the pot on the stove, where she's stirring some pasta sauce. 'Hello, honey, how was your day?'

I jump up on to one of the stools, leaning my elbows on the counter. Slick scurries down my arm on to the countertop, beaming the time in front of me. 'Did you get my messages?' I pause, waiting for her outrage at my expulsion. 'You know ... about how I wasn't allowed in to school?'

Mom has turned back to the sauce now, and she doesn't react.

I continue babbling. 'It's okay though, because Zora gave me an idea for how I can get back to Profectus. But first, did you talk to Eric?'

I wait for Mom to answer, but she's still stirring.

'Mom?' I ask again, confused as to whether she's listening to me. Petal doesn't appear to be playing any music or anything to distract her. She taps the side of the wooden spoon against the edge of the saucepan, then turns around. She folds her arms across her stomach. 'What are you talking about, honey?'

'Last night ... you said you were going to call up Eric Smith.'

She gives me a totally blank look and shrugs. 'I don't know what you're talking about, Lacey.'

A chill creeps down my spine. Something is not right. 'But Mom – last night . . .'

She cuts me off. 'Lacey, I'm tired. I've worked a long shift and I want to have an early dinner and then go to bed. I've just got you back from the hospital. I'm sorry about your disappointment with Profectus but you're going to St Agnes, where your best friend is with you. It's all worked out in the end.'

'But it hasn't worked out!' I cry, flabbergasted that Mom would think it's okay for me to have lost my place at Profectus. My face heats up, rage coursing through me at her uncaring response. I take a deep breath and decide to switch tack. 'Don't you want answers too? Like about why I was hurt?'

Mom sighs. 'I'm just happy you're healthy again.'

'What about how Carter stole Jinx from me?'

'You've got a perfectly good, functional baku now, in Slick.'

'And what about what's going on at Moncha Corp? No one's seen Monica Chan in months . . . something's wrong, I know it is.' There's a memory lodged there, stuck in the back of my mind, and it won't budge. Something important.

Tears of disappointment prick in my eyes, but maybe I shouldn't be so surprised. Moncha Corp have given us everything – our home, Mom's job, my education. We don't know why I was injured, but I can see why Mom might not want to cause a fuss. We don't need a target on our backs.

The only reason I was fighting Moncha Corp was because of Jinx. They were after him, and I didn't want them to harm him. Now that he's safe, maybe I should give up too.

Mom presses her fingers on either side of the bridge of her nose. 'Monica Chan is a multi-billionaire. She has plenty of people looking out for her. She doesn't need rescuing by one fifteen-year-old. Leave the big problems to the big people, Lacey. You need to focus on you.'

Now tears spill out on to my cheeks, rolling down in thick tracks and gathering on my jawline. 'I can't believe it. You promised that you were going to help me.'

Our conversation happened only twenty-four hours ago. How could she have forgotten so quickly? It's as if everything has been wiped clean. Reset.

We're both distracted as Petal flashes, a series of lights dancing up and down her wings. Mom's listens to a message that she must be transmitting to her through her bone-conducting footpads and when she looks back at me, her eyes are blank. 'I have to finish cooking. This sauce is about to burn. How about instead, you tell me about your day? I want to hear about what homework you had, how your teachers were, how your friends are doing ... I do *not* want to hear another thing about Profectus, Moncha Corp or that old baku of yours.'

'I thought you loved Jinx too,' I say in a quiet voice.

'Jinx who?' Mom deadpans back to me.

That's when I can't take it any more. 'I'm not hungry,' I say. 'I'm going out.' I storm out of the kitchen, slamming my bedroom door behind me. I change out of my uniform in an angry huff, throwing on a pair of jeans, T-shirt and a soft fleece to go under my jacket. When I step out of our front door, I half-expect Mom to chase me, demand to know where I'm going, make me stay home.

But it seems like she doesn't even care enough about me to do that.

I press the button for the elevator, waiting there with my chest heaving. The longer I wait, the clearer it becomes that Mom isn't coming after me. The anger that has been building in my chest deflates. I just feel sad.

And then, the elevator refuses to come. I furiously mash the button, but nothing changes. It must be broken again.

I walk a bit further along the corridor and push through the door into the stairwell. It's a long way down – fourteen floors – and as I spiral down each set of stairs, I feel more and more alone.

I can't understand her change in attitude. *Maybe something happened at work . . .* maybe she had another visit from Eric Smith's security team and got spooked? I almost turn around and go back to ask her. But surely if it was something like that, she would have just said.

Rather than pretend like none of it matters at all.

It still matters to me.

And if Mom isn't going to help me . . . I'm going to need my friends more than ever.

CHAPTER NINE

TOP'S BUBBLE TEA IS A LONG WAY downtown, and I follow the directions laid out for me by Slick. I bury my hands deep in my coat pockets, huffing my breath out in front of me. I can't believe Mom's change in attitude, and I want Jinx more than ever.

A tiny mewl attracts my attention as I pass a deserted alleyway. I pause for a moment, squinting into the shadows. My heart leaps as I spot a pair of shining eyes staring back at me out of the dark. *Could it be?*

But as I step closer, the tiny fur ball darts away from me – a little ginger tom cat, not my rogue baku. A sweet cat all the same. I smile.

I hope you're living wild and free. It's my wish to Jinx. He wanted a life that was as close to real as possible – not chained to my side as a companion, not destroyed by Eric Smith at Moncha Corp. That's all I ever wanted for him.

My heart rate slows to a normal level for the first time since leaving the apartment. Now I just need the remaining gaps in my memory to be filled in, and I'll feel properly like myself again.

>>We're a bit early at Top's Bubble Tea & Baku Café.

I look up, surprised to see that we're outside already. I peer in through the window, but can't see my friends.

>>I've connected to the table reservation inside – we can go in and wait.

'Oh great!' I reply to Slick. When I get inside, I squeal with delight. I'd forgotten how cute it was in here. There are bakus *everywhere* – all specifically baby varieties such as kittens, puppies, lambs and baby rabbits. Originally it was modelled after cat cafés in Japan, where people could come and play with cute furry felines – perfect for those who weren't allowed pets in their high-rise apartments. There's a wide-open space in the middle of the café, for bakus to play in, and booths around the perimeter.

Top's Café allows people who don't have a baku yet to interact with different species and pick a favourite, or to experience a different level baku for a while. It's also a place where Moncha previews new baku models, so it's often crammed with Profectus students looking to get a sneak peek at what's coming next. The delicious bubble tea and selection of yummy decorated treats they display in a glass counter at the back of the room all help its popularity too.

I scan the room and feel a prickle of anxiety when I spot the striped tail of a tiger baku peeking out from one of the booths. I don't really want to talk to anyone else from Profectus – especially not Gemma, who is captain of Carter's Baku Battle team, so I quickly shuffle past. There's a booth reserved under Tobias's name in the corner, so I slide in, shifting a snoozing bunny rabbit baku off my seat first. Instantly it springs to life, and hops across the table towards me. I giggle and stroke its soft milk-white fur, then order a mango-flavoured bubble tea with extra tapioca pearls while I wait for the others to arrive.

Slick skitters around the table, projecting several options for me while I wait – an addictive jewel-swapping game, my social media feed, and the latest novel that I'm reading. But I wave it all away. Instead, I try to focus back on the missing memories. Now that I can remember saying goodbye to Jinx, I wonder if I can think back even further.

Something happened between Jinx bolting from my arms and us saying goodbye at the cat park.

We must have been in Moncha HQ, but there's a definite street in my memory, with houses – and a porch swing . . .

'Lacey!'

I'm snapped out of my thoughts as Ashley slides into the booth next to me. Kai squishes in beside her, and Tobias and River are opposite. Their bakus take up positions around the booth – and my eye is automatically drawn up to Aero, who perches on the ledge above us.

'You made it!' Ashley says, squeezing my shoulder. 'What a wild day.'

'I can't believe they've kicked you out of the Academy,' says Tobias. 'You okay?' His dark brown eyes bore into mine.

'Been better,' I say, with a shrug. 'These cute little bunny bakus are helping. And Zora and I came up with a plan to get me a level 3 baku.'

'Oh, that's great!' says Ashley. 'It's so unfair that they won't let you in. Anything we can do to help?'

'Just seeing you all is enough.'

'Well, we've missed you tons,' she says.

'It's not been the same without you!' says River.

Aero squawks behind Tobias's head, and he spreads his wing so that he can read a message. Then Tobias catches my eye. 'Hey, Lace, want to come with me to help me choose some snacks for the team?'

'Oh, uh, sure,' I say. Ashley and Kai make room for me to exit the booth, and Slick jumps up on to my sleeve before I follow Tobias towards the back of the café. The sweet, sharp smell of spun sugar and lemon icing makes my mouth water as we approach the glass-covered counter, staring at the little desserts all made up to look like different bakus. There's a fondant black cat that reminds me of Jinx, and I smile.

But the smile is nothing compared to the blush that rises in my cheeks as Tobias touches the back of my arm, his fingers lingering on my skin. 'Are you really okay? How are you feeling being out of the hospital?'

'I feel . . . pretty normal to be honest with you. But today has been strange. And even though my memory has been coming back in bits and pieces, I still don't really understand what happened to me after we were separated.'

'Okay, well, you take it easy. It was scary to see you like that. And I feel like . . .' He pauses, his breath hitching. 'Well, before all the stuff with the Baku Battles happened, there was something I'd been meaning to ask you. I wondered if

67

maybe you wanted to go out with me sometime?' He smiles. '*Without* the rest of the team, obviously.'

Now it's my turn for my breath to catch, but the answer is obvious – to me and him. I just need to say it . . .

'I thought I saw you come in here,' says another voice.

I close my eyes for a beat, hoping that I've imagined it. But I haven't, because Tobias addresses him first.

'Carter, we're kind of in the middle of something,' he says, his tone laced with annoyance. I finally look over at the guy who tried to steal Jinx from me. My long-term academic rival.

Son of Moncha's co-founder.

Carter Smith.

The expression on his pale face is especially smug today, even for him. His boar baku, Hunter, is at his feet, tusks glinting under the café spotlights. Such a menacing baku, especially compared to all the fluffy kittens and bunnies jumping around the café. 'Oh, I'm not staying long. My order was ready.' The lady behind the counter hands him the black cat fondant cake that reminded me of Jinx. He takes a deliberate bite of his head, his teeth getting covered in dark chocolate sponge.

I wish I was strong enough not to react, but I wince. He grins at me, cake all over his teeth.

'It's not over, Carter,' I say.

'What do you mean?' His eyes open wide in mock concern.

'You tried to steal Jinx from me. I won't forget that.'

'Oh yeah, I'm really scared. What are you going to do, tell on me? No one likes a snitch.'

'Come on,' Tobias says to me, in a low voice. 'Let's go back to the team.'

'Not really your team though any more, is it, Lacey? Now that you're back at St Agnes?'

'Leave it, Carter,' growls Tobias.

Carter holds his hands up in surrender, then laughs and walks back to his team.

'Don't let him bug you,' Tobias says.

'I'll try,' I say, although my fingers have tightened into fists at my side. I take a breath to relax. 'At least it's even more motivation to get back to Profectus as quickly as possible. Just to show him.'

'That's the spirit,' grins Tobias.

'Hey, team!' Ashley calls over to us from the booth. 'You should come back here – they're about to show off one of the upcoming baku models.'

Tobias and I exchange a grin, make a random selection of the cakes in front of us (they all look delicious) and head back to the booth. There, in the open play space, the café employees are bringing out the new baku models.

I reach out and grab Tobias's hand tightly.

He looks down at me in alarm. 'What is it?'

'That baku . . .' I can't speak any more. I can only point at one of the new models a Top's server is showing off.

Tobias traces the line of my finger. 'The baby sloth? What about it?'

I watch as the server leads the sloth around the room, its ambling gait drawing many sighs of admiration from the crowd. The baku halts in the middle of the room and shows off some of its unique functions – such as the ability to project a noise-reducing bubble and emit a soft lavender mist to help its owner relax and sleep on long journeys, in any environment.

My eyes widen, and my words come out in a jumbled stream. 'Oh my god. I think I know where Monica Chan is.'

CHAPTER TEN

TOBIAS DRAGS ME BACK INTO THE booth, and the others stare at me with a mixture of concern and fear. 'Aero, shield us.' His baku responds by spreading his wings in front of our booth, so that we're hidden from view and our conversation is muffled. 'What do you remember?' he asks, as I struggle to order my thoughts into understandable sentences. When I close my eyes, the dominant image in my mind is of a sloth – not a baby one like I've just seen, but a full-size one – hanging around a woman's neck.

I open my eyes again and swallow, hard. 'It's all coming back to me,' I say. 'We were fighting with Carter and the security panthers in the Team Happiness wing of Moncha HQ, weren't we?'

Tobias nods.

'I remember that clearly now. We'd just got Jinx back from Carter, but then he bolted. I chased him all the way down into the basement of Moncha HQ. He tried to stop me from following him, but I used Slick to get me through the doors – my friend, Zora, had programmed him with some extra special lock-picking technology. On the other side of that door was this strange place that was like ... a street, but a movie set of a street because we were indoors, and in one of the houses was Monica Chan. She had a sloth baku that seemed to be controlling her in some way, but she was lucid. She told me that Eric had his own plans to take full control of the company and that all he needed to do was to destroy Jinx and he would win. That's why he wanted Jinx so bad. That's why Carter took him.' It's all come back to me – the house, having tea with Monica Chan herself, the sloth, learning about how *Monica* was the one who created Jinx and as a punishment, Eric locked her away – a prisoner in her own company.

'An underground street, a sloth baku and a conspiracy theory?' repeats Kai. 'Sounds like a wild dream.'

I frown. 'It was real.'

'But how do you know? Your memory's been toast for over a month.'

Ashley puts her hand on mine and silences Kai with a look. 'Of course, we believe you.'

'So you actually met Monica Chan?' asks River.

'I did. I spoke to her. I even had tea with her! But she told Jinx and I to run away before security caught us. I was going to tell Mr Baird and go back to rescue her but then ...' Then I collapsed. And got hypothermia. And was in a coma for a month-long hospital stay.

And oh god, I've already wasted so many hours with

this stupid memory loss when we could have been rescuing Monica . . .

My voice quakes. 'What if she's still trapped in that place? Tobias, you said she hasn't been seen in weeks . . .'

'Hey, it's okay,' says Ashley, snuggling up to me. My cheeks are damp with tears. There's so much emotion rushing through me, my memory rising up like a tidal wave and bringing with it an ocean of turmoil.

'I'll go there,' says Tobias.

'Wait, what?' I splutter.

'I'll go to Moncha HQ. Tonight. I'll make my dad take me down to the basement, we'll find this underground house and we'll get Monica out.'

'Are you serious? You would do that?'

He nods. 'Dad is working round the clock at the moment. He's always saying I can visit whenever, even though I didn't win the internship, but I said no because I didn't want some kind of consolation prize . . . but now I will.'

'I'll go with you,' says Kai, puffing his chest out.

Tobias shakes his head. 'It will be better if I go by myself but Aero will live stream everything to the whole team,' says Tobias, addressing all of us.

Ashley nudges me. 'See? It will be okay. Tobias will find her,' she says.

I grab the closest napkin and Slick. One of Slick's appendages is like a pen, so I use him to draw out a map of what I remember. Every twist and turn I made following Jinx. Then I pass it to Tobias.

'You couldn't make this digital?' he asks.

'Hey, not everyone has a level 3 or above baku,' I quip back. Then I turn serious. 'Are you sure you're okay to do this?' Last time one of us went into the headquarters, we were attacked by menacing security bakus. Tobias might not be safe.

'Of course,' he says, his voice sombre. 'My dad will be there. And if what you remember is right, then they're keeping Monica against her will.'

There's no more reason to stick around at the café, and besides – for once, I want Tobias to leave as quickly as possible. We settle up the bill and scurry out, leaving our half-drunk bubble teas abandoned in the booth.

We say goodbye at the streetcar stop, Tobias heading over to Moncha HQ, the others going home and me back to my apartment building.

While I wait to hear from Tobias, I know I need to get back to tinkering. Companioneering. Fixing things. I need my hands to be busy. I need my mind to be focused on a problem that I can actually solve.

But I need to take it step by step.

And the first step while I wait to hear from Tobias is to fix up Slick.

CHAPTER ELEVEN

THE BASEMENT OF OUR BUILDING contains my sanctuary: a storage locker assigned to our unit that I have commandeered for my tinkering purposes. I've customized it to my exact specifications with shelving, storage boxes and hanging units, all secured to the cage-like metal webbing that surrounds the units. The other lockers hold rusted bikes and long-forgotten ski equipment. But my locker is my haven. It's filled to the brim with spare parts, wires, electronics, a scavenged 3D printer, an old-fashioned desktop-style computer for offline coding and, of course, plenty of mains sockets to power the equipment and leash up bakus to.

This is where I fixed Jinx from a hunk of rubble at the side of a train track to the fully functioning baku he became.

The locker's sanctuary is like a siren call to me.

I use Slick to unlock the padlock, then I send a message to Zora:

In the basement already. Top's was a bit more
eventful than we thought. More of my memory
came back! I'll tell you everything when I
see you next.

Once it's sent, I take a deep breath. Then I set Slick down
on the table. Time to get down to business.

>>Is there anything I can help you with, Lacey?

His tone is friendly but creepy. It's as if they've programmed
him to have enough care in his voice to provoke a positive
response in me, but not so much that I fall in love with him,
like I did with Jinx.

'Can you fetch me the standard level 1 scarab beetle
schematic?' I ask. Moncha keeps a basic diagram of all the
different types of bakus' circuitry on the cloud, in the interest
of complete transparency, so I figure there's no better place to
start than by looking at the basics of his functionality. That
way, I can see where potential adjustments or upgrades can
be made. I need an easy win right now.

There's a momentary pause, then Slick chirrups again.
>>I'm sorry, but I'm afraid access is blocked to
those schematics.

'What?' I frown. 'Can you repeat?'

>>Access to all baku schematics is now forbidden.
Instead, I've selected a behind-the-scenes tour
of a Moncha factory if you're interested in how
bakus work.

I wave the video away as he lifts his projector to start

76

playing. 'This doesn't make any sense? I've always been able to access schematics before. It's part of the Moncha terms and conditions.'

>>The terms and conditions are constantly updating in order to reflect Moncha's current policies.

'And when was the last update?'

>>27 days ago.

'But I didn't agree to it!'

>>Of course you did. When you woke up and leashed me this morning. I asked you if you wanted to see the changes to the Ts & Cs.

I wrack my brain for the memory and then it hits me: he did ask me. But he'd suggested that only a single line had changed so I didn't even bother to read it. I had just accepted it straight away. Like I normally did.

Always read the conditions of your contract. Mom's words echo in my brain. But I trust Moncha Corp implicitly.

You did *trust Moncha Corp.*

But you know better now. Especially with the security team showing up at our door, searching the apartment without our authorization.

And the founder currently MIA, last seen imprisoned in her own HQ.

I need to be more careful.

I drum my fingers against the desk. This is annoying. I didn't even think to print anything out. That would have been the sensible thing to do – to have a library of old schematics.

Slick lifts his wings. >>Zora has replied. She says she'll be down in fifteen minutes. she says she wants to hear EVERYTHING.

Now that I have Zora's answer, I don't need anything else out of Slick. I turn him upside down and lift up one of his left legs to find the 'OFF' switch. It's very fiddly and small, designed to make sure it can't be accessed accidentally.

>>Are you sure you want to power me down?

'Yes, very sure,' I mumble. I flick the switch, and – to my relief – the beetle's limbs go limp in my hand.

For a moment there, I thought maybe he would refuse to shut off. But that's a stupid and impossible thought.

I look up at the analogue clock on my wall – one of the little quirks of my favourite hideaway. I note the time, then grab a piece of paper to scribble down a message.

Z, JUST GONE TO FIND PAUL. BBS.

I stick it up with a small piece of tape, then I lock the cage with Slick inside. I traipse down through the maze of lockers looking for my favourite fellow tinkerer. Paul has been in the underground companioneering business for much longer than me (decades longer), and if there's anyone who might have a scarab beetle schematic tucked away in the corner of his locker, it's him. He used to work for Moncha Corp back in the day, but I'm not sure what his job was. He's a very private person, and I've never wanted to pry.

It's a bit eerie down here late at night, with only pale

yellow spotlights to guide me around the concrete and metal jungle, but it's my happy place. I like it best when I know there's going to be no one else around to bump into – no one carting down their skis or rooting around for their Christmas lights.

I can hear the tap of a hammer on metal and I pick up my step. He's the only other person who I know would be working down here at dinner time.

But when I get to his locker, it's almost completely dark. I press my face up to the wire mesh and peer into the darkness.

'Slick, turn on the light,' I say on autopilot, forgetting that I left Slick turned off in my locker.

Then, I scream and jump back. A face appears on the other side of the locker. A tiny little monkey face. I can't help but giggle as my initial fear dissolves.

'Hi George!' I say.

>>Good evening, Lacey.

'Hey, Tinker,' says Paul's gruff voice. 'Excuse George's behaviour – we don't get much chance for a bit of fun around here.' His face flickers into view as he turns back on the overhead light. 'It's good to see you. How are you feeling?'

I grin, glad for some laughter in what has been a stressful evening. 'I'm feeling much better, thanks, Paul.'

'Good to hear, good to hear. Nasty business, hypothermia.' That must be the official story that Mom has been telling people to explain my hospital stay. 'And where's that little cat baku of yours?' He looks down around my feet, searching for Jinx.

I feel my face burn, and I hope I haven't gone too red. 'Something happened ... I had to let him go ...' I mutter, shrugging my shoulders.

Paul raises his eyebrows. 'I see.'

There's a pause where he waits to see if I will explain further but one thing I love about tinkerers: they know how valuable secrets can be, and they don't press. 'So, what can I do you for?' he asks.

'I'm looking for some schematics of a level 1 scarab beetle baku. Do you have one printed out somewhere in those file boxes of yours?'

Paul's locker is even messier than mine – if that's possible. It's also *loads* bigger. Somehow he's convinced his neighbours to let him take over their lockers, and George will sometimes scope around to see if there's any unused space nearby. Sometimes I think he would take over the entire basement if he could – though I'm sure he'd let me use a corner of it. His dream would be a network of tinkerers, working towards their own personal goals, innovating and dreaming new technology into existence.

For a moment, Paul's face turns dark. 'Oh yes, I heard about that on the forums. The new terms prevent most people having access to the schematics online. The Monica I knew would never allow that to happen – I wonder what's gotten into her?'

I want to tell Paul everything – including my memory about Monica being kept in the underground city – but something stops me. I haven't had the best luck with adults lately, and I don't want to be disappointed by yet another. I want to wait until Tobias gets some more information. 'Um . . . the schematic?'

'Oh yes. Well, you might be in luck. I think I do have it somewhere. I've been meaning to sort my paperwork out for a while but it should be in the files out back. You can have a look yourself if you want?'

'Okay, great.'

He unlocks the door of his cage and gestures at the filing cabinet and piles of boxes behind him. There's a ton of paperwork to search through. Inwardly I groan.

But actually, I think he might be on to something. With absolutely everything stored on the cloud, it's possible that if the internet went down and all the bakus failed, we'd have nothing real remaining. Bakus are supposed to be more secure than most clouds. They're not solely reliant on the internet, or on mains electric power, like a normal phone. As long as there are human beings for them to leash to, bakus can exist. But what would a baku be without access to the Moncha databases, without the ability to communicate via satellite, without constant updating? Would they just slowly disintegrate, losing their ability to function? Or would they then be just the equivalent of robotic parasites, leeching off our natural kinetic energy?

It sends a shiver down my spine to think of it.

Something catches my eye and I send up a quick word of thanks that Paul is – while not exactly organized – thorough. There's a whole box full of level 1 baku schematics. Mixed in with the butterflies, dragonflies and the praying mantises, there's the one I need: the scarab beetle.

'Anything in particular that you're trying to achieve with that, Lacey? Maybe I can be of help in other ways?' Paul asks from his place at his desk.

'You probably can …' I hesitate for a second, and then I tell him part of the story – about how without a level 3 baku, I'm no longer able to attend Profectus, and so I had hoped to change Slick to suit.

The lines that criss-cross Paul's face draw deeper into a frown. 'Tricky. Hardest part's going to be the size difference. Level 3s are almost always bigger than level 1s, to accommodate the extra functions. That would involve completely overhauling the design of the beetle. Might even be beyond *your* companioneering skills to keep it balanced.'

My shoulders slump as visions of an ugly, oversized scarab beetle dance through my head. 'Is there any way that I can do it?'

Thankfully, Paul has a familiar twinkle in his eye that gives me a spark of hope. I immediately sit up straighter. 'Of course. Why don't I come down to your locker with you and we can examine the little beetle together and see what we can come up with?'

I grin. 'Thanks, Paul.'

He gathers up an armful of tools, and George nips around the locker, finding even more bits and bobs that we might need. He's strong for a lemur baku; I think about the power that must be driving the pistons in the creature's shoulders

82

and elbows, the strength of the material that must be used. Since he's a much older model, it's not obvious what level he is. I've never asked Paul – it seems like a bit of a rude question.

Once we get back to the locker, Zora is waiting for me outside, her hands tucked inside the sleeves of her sweater. She's not as comfortable down here as I am, and she looks visibly relieved as Paul and I approach.

'Hi, Zora. Haven't seen you down here in a while,' says Paul. George drops some of the gear at the entrance to the locker while I open it up.

Zora smiles at me. 'It didn't feel right to be here without Lacey. Now that she's back, I'm here to help her out.'

'She's going to need all the help she can get,' he says, gruffly. I swallow. I've only ever fixed; I've never created before. This is going to take every inch of my companioneering skill if I'm going to pull it off.

My eyes pass through the shadows and for a moment I have a panic that I can't see Slick on the desk where I left him, turned off.

But no – it's okay. I fumble for the light and as it flickers on, it catches the greenish-purple iridescence of his carapace. His legs stick up in the air, like the stamens of a flower, his wings spread like petals. He could almost be a flower in this position – albeit one that looks like it would eat little insects alive. A metal Venus flytrap. Maybe that could be my first range of bakus for Moncha Corp, if I become a companioneer. Carnivorous plant bakus.

Zora takes a step past me and sits down on my wheeled

computer desk chair, ready to get cracking on the code. In fact, she cracks each one of her knuckles and flexes her fingers in readiness.

Paul walks in next and picks the beetle up in his palm. 'Let's see what we have here. I haven't had a chance to look closely at one of the latest generation beetle bakus and I wonder what they've integrated into the level 1s now . . .' He puts a magnifying eyepiece to his left eye. 'Hmm, this is a bit strange.'

'What are you seeing?' I ask.

'I'm not entirely sure . . . hang on. George?'

Even though I'm sure that they don't have telepathic communication like Jinx and I did, George seems to know exactly what Paul needs. He brings him a tiny eye screwdriver, like one that would normally be used to fix jewellery. Paul starts digging around in Slick's body with the screwdriver and even though I'm not exactly fond of the little beetle, I tense.

But if there's anyone I can trust to be gentle with technology, it's Paul.

'Hmm. What do you make of this? There's some kind of . . . addition here.'

Paul pries open two of Slick's hind legs. I look down into the beetle's body. It takes me a few seconds, but then I see it. There's an appendage tucked away. Another retractable leg. Strange.

I frown, part of a memory coming back to me, as fleeting as a sneeze. Paul prises the extra appendage out of position. The 'leg' is filed down to a point. It's almost like a syringe . . .

There's a zap of movement, and the beetle suddenly comes to life. He flips over in Paul's palm. Paul yelps and closes his other hand on top of Slick.

'What's happening?' Paul asks. 'I thought you turned him off.'

'I did! When we walked in here he was silent. Maybe you flicked the switch by accident?'

But we both know that would be impossible.

The beetle flicks his wings, trying to wiggle his way out of Paul's grasp. A moment later, he's free and fluttering about the room. The scene is like something out of an old cartoon: I dive on to the desk to try to catch him but he darts out of my cupped hands; Zora launches herself at the wire mesh, almost face-planting into the twists of metal.

The beetle settles on a high shelf, just out of my grasp. He crawls backward into the shadow.

'Slick, come back!' I shout. 'Slick, to me!'

There's a moment's pause, and then Slick reappears, flying back down and landing in my hand, as if nothing happened.

>>How can I help you, Lacey?

'Tell me what that extra appendage is for?' I say, trying to use my most commanding voice.

>>I don't know what you mean.

I flip him over. 'This!' I say, pointing at the space where we'd seen the needle-like limb. But it's gone.

'What ... what's going on?' I ask Paul and Zora. 'Did he get rid of it somehow? Is this some kind of inbuilt security to prevent people from tampering with their bakus?'

Paul shakes his head, his eyes dark. 'Moncha would never do something like that.'

'But we didn't just imagine what was there,' says Zora.

We're all silent for a moment, no sound but a gentle buzz from the overhead lighting. It's broken by a series of electronic beeps coming from Slick.

He says: >>There's an update to my operating system. Please leash me as soon as possible.

He flies down into my palm. I eye him suspiciously, but everything looks normal.

I look at Paul and Zora. 'What should I do?'

'Maybe you'd better update before you make any changes? That might be why he's acting weird. Moncha are always trying to fix any bugs . . . no pun intended,' says Zora.

I nod.

But just as I'm about to leash him up, he buzzes with a message from Tobias.

TOBIAS: I'll be inside Moncha HQ in fifteen minutes.
Get somewhere private and I'll stream to you?

I turn to Zora and Paul. They don't know about Tobias's mission yet, so I make up an excuse. 'I have to watch this. Looks like we might have to give fixing up the beetle a rain check until tomorrow.'

Paul nods. 'I'll do a bit of research, see what I can find out.'

'Thanks,' I say, with a grateful smile.

'I'm not going to lie . . . Slick has spooked me,' says Zora.

'Might be good to figure out what's wrong before we tweak his code anyway. We don't want to make a mess we can't fix.'

I swallow. No matter how much I want things to go back to normal, it seems like all I'm able to do lately is create an even bigger mess.

CHAPTER TWELVE

WHEN I GET BACK TO THE APARTMENT, it's dark except for the strobing light of the television in the living room. I lean up against the doorframe, watching Mom on the sofa. She doesn't even lift her head to greet me. Petal slowly flies around her head, circling like a halo.

Instinctively I reach down and place my hand over Slick. I've trapped the little robot inside the zipped pocket of my fleece. I'm still wary of him. It's not just his strange behaviour in my locker that has me worried. It's something more bone-deep than that. A primal fear response that I can't explain.

I've seen the science-fiction movies. Read the books. But I've never feared a baku (except the security ones). They aren't scary metal humanoids with glowing eyes, or black boxes with an eerie electronic voice. They're cute companions. Friends. Helpers.

Or at least I thought so.

I turn my attention back to Mom.

I've always tried to be a good daughter, one that doesn't

cause too much fuss or worry – not after what Mom went through with Dad. I never wanted to be the cause of so much anguish. But I'd always assumed that if I needed her – really needed her – that she'd be there for me.

That she wouldn't sweep my concerns under the carpet, like she did this evening. Still, maybe there's a way to find out if she still cares.

'Hi, Mom,' I say, stepping out of the shadows. I walk over and kiss the top of her head.

She reaches up and strokes my hand. 'There you are, Lacey. Did you have a good evening?'

A small frown flickers between my eyebrows. Any other school night and I'd be receiving a lecture about storming out of the condo and disappearing instead of having dinner with her. At the very least I'd receive a stern look and a scowl. But her expression barely changes at all. I never thought that I'd be desperate to see my mom get angry, but I yearn for a reaction.

'I don't think I'm going to go to school tomorrow.' I test the waters, pushing our boundaries even further.

Those words do seem to have an effect on her and my heart leaps. She turns her head around, her spine straightening. She opens her mouth, and I swear she's about to tell me that there is *no way you're skipping school, young lady*. But then Petal buzzes gently, fluttering down to her shoulder and the leash. Mom's shoulders sag back into the deep cushion of the sofa. 'Well, I'm at work at six a.m. so I won't know. Just don't fall behind, sweetheart.'

I can't choke down my disappointment, but I don't want

to cry. What if Mom doesn't even react to that? She's not behaving like herself. Scratch that, she's not behaving like a normal human being.

The terror of that thought grips me, and my feet feel frozen to the floor. *What's happening?*

The fifteen minutes are almost up. Tobias is going to be live streaming, and I'm desperate to watch what he comes across.

I whisper a 'Goodnight' to Mom, who raises her head, smiles and says 'Goodnight' back. Her eyes drift back down to the TV, and I'm dismissed.

Feeling despondent, I head to my room. I sit cross-legged on my bed, take a deep breath, and take Slick out of my pocket.

>>Don't forget about the update.

There's no sign of him buzzing around like a mad beetle. He's back to acting like a normal baku.

'Fine,' I say, gritting my teeth at his incessant reminders. 'After the stream from Tobias. Can you project as widely as possible?'

Slick moves so he's on the edge of the bed, then he starts the live stream. In one corner, I see the faces of Ashley, Kai and River, who are also watching. They wave to me, but no one says a word. Tobias is streaming secretly, so we don't want to make any noise to give him away.

Tobias is walking down a nondescript hallway. I don't immediately recognize where he is in Moncha HQ, but I can only assume he's following my instructions.

'How was it you know about this place?' I hear a voice ask. Aero's camera pivots in the voice's direction, and I see a tall black man with short-cropped hair, greying at the temples. I recognize him from the photos I've seen in Tobias's home. It's his dad.

'Oh . . . I heard about it at school.'

'So you thought you'd come down here, gone eight o'clock on a school night?'

I don't have to wonder how Tobias is going to explain his strange request. His dad keeps on talking. 'I'm glad you're showing an interest, son, but the simple fact is, you're too late.'

They approach a door that I recognize. Through that door is the weird street where I found Monica. I hold my breath, edging closer to the live stream, so that I'm almost sitting inside it.

His dad opens the door. Aero flies through – but all his camera shows is a completely blank space. It looks like a giant aircraft hangar, huge and echoing and empty. 'I told you,' says his dad. 'We pulled this whole place down a month ago. We're replacing it with something even better, but that's classified.' He winks at his son.

My shoulders slump. The street with all the houses is gone. And if Monica was being held there against her will, she's not there now.

Our only lead disappears in an instant. Of course Eric was going to be many steps ahead of me – he's the head of a multinational tech corporation, and I'm just a teenager.

The transmission ends, with Tobias's final words ...
'Sorry, Lacey.'

In case I'd forgotten, Slick lights up with commands for me. >>Don't forget to update!

'I haven't forgotten,' I mutter. I fiddle with the leash at my ear, unhooking it so that it dangles down my neck.

Then, I lift the beetle to the leash. But just as we are about to connect – there's a crash against my bedroom window.

Standing outside with his face pressed against the glass is the last thing I expect to see.

It's Jinx.

PART TWO

JINX'S RETURN

CHAPTER THIRTEEN

I BLINK, UNABLE TO BELIEVE MY EYES. BUT AS his paw taps the glass again, I'm surprised to hear an impatient voice in my head.

>>Let me in!

I rush towards the window, fumbling with the latch.

'Oh my god, Jinx! Is that really you?'

I push the frame up, cold air and my favourite baku pouring through into my room. Seeing his sleek black body, pointed ears and mischievous face makes my heart leap into my chest. Since remembering that letting him go had been *my* choice, I'd resigned myself to never seeing him again.

And now, here he is.

He's come back.

The window drops and I open my arms to catch him in a hug. Instead, he darts forward, knocking Slick off of my shoulder. They tumble to the carpeted floor, a mechanical whirlwind. Jinx, master of the Baku Battles, comes out on top, of course. He pins Slick beneath his paws.

'Jinx?' I say. 'What's going on?'

95

>>Promise me you won't leash that bug until you've heard everything that I'm about to say.

'I ... I won't!' I stutter out. Reluctantly, Jinx releases Slick.

To the surprise of both of us, Slick is aggressive, flying directly towards me ready to leash up – without my permission. That scares me, and I grab him between my hands and grip him tight. I barely recognize this terrifying little bug any more.

I stuff Slick into the pocket of my fleece and seal the zip. Then I turn to Jinx, who is sitting on my bed, licking his paw without a care in the world, as if he hasn't just turned everything upside down by his reappearance.

I blink, convinced each time I close my eyes that he's going to be gone in the next millisecond.

But he's back.

My Jinx.

'You're here!' I exclaim.

>>And just in time. You can't survive without me, can you?

He hops down off the bed and sashays towards me. I stretch out my hand, tentative at first, and he bumps up against my palm, rubbing his head on my fingers. Then in a bounding leap, he's in my arms, the feel of his gentle purrs against my chest bringing tears to my eyes. 'Oh Jinx, I've missed you!' I say, into his soft electronic fur.

>>I've missed you too. He sounds as sincere as Jinx gets, but then he quickly turns serious. He slips out of my arms and sits facing me. >>Lacey, you can't install that update.

'Okay, I won't. But ... can I ask why?'

>>Normally updates are to make sure bakus have the latest apps, to fix any bugs in code, stuff like that, right?

I nod, unsure what Jinx is getting at.

Jinx's eyes flash. >>This time, the update isn't for the bakus. It's for the owners.

It takes a moment for Jinx's words to sink in.

'What?!' I shake my head as a chill shoots down my spine. 'No ... no, that's impossible.'

>>It's not only possible, it's happened. This has been Eric's plan all along.

'His plan? What plan? What does the update do?'

>>It's easier if I show you. His tail lifts and curls into a C-shape above his head, the projector opening. >>Do you remember Team Happiness?

I frown. 'That was the name for Eric Smith's personal team at Moncha HQ. Tobias's dad works in that group.'

>>I was able to download this from the Team Happiness server ...

'Still as good at hacking as ever then?'

>>Just watch.

He launches one of his apps, a baku-friendly version of the slideshow programs that used to be common for corporate presentations. It begins with a brief introduction from Eric, welcoming everyone to the launch of the Team Happiness update. Having his face projected large in my bedroom makes me grimace in disgust.

Thankfully, his face dissolves into a slightly distorted version of the main Moncha logo – a stylized M with a cluster of stars along one edge. It's the same logo that's above Tobias's front door. The same logo worn by the security team who searched our home. The 'Team Happiness' logo. Seeing it gives me even more chills.

I can touch the stars to unlock sections of the presentation. It's a very slick bit of technology, but I'm afraid of what I'm about to see. After a moment's hesitation, I reach out and touch the first star.

Eric Smith's voiceover fills the room. He explains that the Team Happiness update is a revolutionary new way to make a baku owner's life happier. By taking advantage of the incredible leash technology, a tiny tweak is delivered via the baku to the owner's mind that will ease anxieties and sadness. The presentation pitches it as a natural extension of the Moncha slogan: *Accompanying you to your happiest life ever.*

'But this ... this is essentially mind control!' I say, when I've picked my jaw up off the floor.

>>I know. That 'tiny tweak' is to the part of the brain that controls ambition. He thinks without aspirations, people will be happier.

'That can't be legal. No one would allow it if they knew!'

>>It gets worse. Jinx's tone is dark.

I gulp, and press the next star. It states that the update is ready to be beta-tested on real people. And who better to test it on than willing employees? After all, they've already agreed to be part of any and all Moncha experiments (or 'innovations' as the voiceover calls them) just by virtue of receiving a pay cheque once a month. Of course, this 'perk' is listed as one of the great benefits of working for Moncha – dressed up as getting access to advanced technology before anyone else. As employees, they get to be 'early adopters'.

>>What they don't realize is that that they've essentially signed up to be guinea pigs in Eric's grand plan.

The third star lists roll-out dates for the update – the first one was yesterday. But it's not the date that catches my eye. It's the name of the department. MONCHA TELESUPPORT.

Where my mom works.

I think about her strange behaviour today. How she'd flipped from super supportive to uncaring overnight. I think about Petal fluttering around her head with the flashing lights. The notification . . .

'Oh my god, Jinx!' I leap to my feet. 'Petal updated yesterday!'

CHAPTER FOURTEEN

J INX IS QUICKER THAN I AM AND HE DARTS
out in front of me, blocking the door. He arches his back,
hissing at me. I'm so surprised I fall back down on the
bed. He's never done anything like that before.

>> I learned that move from my time with my cat
friends. He slinks back into his normal form.

'I have to check if Mom is okay!'

>>You need to hear me out first. If she's already
updated, then there's nothing you can do. I'm only
sorry I didn't get here sooner, before she connected.

'But . . . we need to fix her!'

>>How? We don't know how to reverse the update.

'We can't stay here and do nothing!' I flail my arms, feeling
utterly useless.

>>We won't. That's why you need to listen to me.
- We stare at each other for a few seconds but finally I nod.

Jinx cocks his head towards me. >>She is okay. If
anything, the update is designed to make her feel
more content.

'Only because she can't think for herself,' I mutter, the sick feeling in my stomach and the acidic taste in the back of my throat not going away. The lump in my pocket buzzes, reminding me of the baku trapped inside. 'What about Slick? I'm not a Moncha Telesupport employee so I shouldn't have the update yet.'

>>Eric's made an exception for you. He wants you quiet and compliant now you're out of the hospital.

'Seriously?' I don't know whether to be flattered or annoyed that Eric still thinks I'm worth special consideration. 'But I need Slick for school! If I don't have a baku I'll be drawing more attention to myself and I really don't need that right now.'

>>I'm surprised you haven't destroyed him already. Jinx's voice is low, and the words are followed by an almost tiger-like growl.

'Destroy him? He might be just a level 1 but he cost me all my life savings!'

>>Even after what he did to you?

I frown. 'What he did to me? What do you mean?'

>>You don't remember?

'No . . .'

>>The night you left me at the cat park he shocked you through the leash. Then he unfurled a syringe from deep inside his casing. He injected you with something. I think it was to immobilize you so that Moncha security could find you and interrogate you — but luckily Tobias got there first.

A shiver crawls over my spine, a million ants dancing

101

across my skin. 'Slick ... Slick is why I was in hospital?' My baku brought me harm.

I think I'm going to throw up.

Even more pieces fall into place in my mind as the truth is revealed. 'So that's why that security team came to our apartment when I woke up?'

>>Yes, exactly. They wanted to finish their interrogation. They wanted to know how to find me.

Fear spikes inside my chest. 'Oh no, Jinx, if they find out you're here ... they'll hunt you down. I set you free because I didn't want you to get wrapped up in all of this.' I reach out to touch him again.

Jinx arches his back and pulls away from my hand.

>>What, and leave you to sort this mess out on your own? As if.

Jinx tails flicks at me, and I recognize the gesture. He's annoyed – but not at me, I think.

>>I admit, I was prepared to disappear into life with those real cats.

His voice is soft, wistful almost.

>>They welcomed me. They accepted me. And while you were in hospital, there was not much I could do. I checked by your window every now and then to see if you were awake . . .

>>But I knew Eric was up to something. As much as I wanted to just . . . be . . . I didn't want you to come to any more harm. I had to find out what he was planning. And now we know.

So you do care about me? I tease.

>>Yeah, yeah, don't get too emotional about it. I already said I missed you too.

'It's been so hard without you. Not being allowed into Profectus, this thing with Mom ... At least I know now that it was the update causing her to act so strangely towards me.' I sigh. 'And what about Slick? I need him so that I can act "normal". You can't be my baku because Eric Smith would find you in an instant.'

>>Maybe being trapped in your fleece for a while will do him some good, Jinx jokes. Then he is serious again. >>When you wake up tomorrow, block the bottom of your leash with duct tape so he can't connect. Charge him from the mains from now on. As long as he doesn't have access to your mind, it will be okay.

I nod, relieved that I won't be kicked out of a second school – this time for not having a baku at all. Then the weight of everything I've just learned threatens to crush me.

'But Jinx ... how do you *know* all this?'

>>I'm still able to access the private Moncha databases – like the ones I used to get you into Profectus in the first place. I was also able to wipe any mention of my location from Slick's databanks and the back-up in the cloud.

'Whoa,' I say, somehow unable to adequately express my awe at Jinx's capabilities.

>>Yes, whoa. But I can't stop the update from rolling out on my own. Now that he's done

beta-testing, the next phase will be to roll it out to all level 1 and 2 bakus.

My eyes open wide. 'But that would affect millions of people. Not just in Monchaville, or even in the city – in the whole world! So many people own a level 1 or 2 baku.' I chew on my lower lip. 'When will that be?'

Jinx shakes his head. >>I don't know. Hopefully it won't come to that. But the problem is Eric Smith. We're going to have to get Monica back in charge if we're going to have any chance of stopping Eric Smith before he can implement the next phase. We have to get her out of that creepy basement place. If we go there tonight, I can unlock the security door and—

I blink and can't help but interrupt him. 'But Jinx ... we can't.'

>>Why not?

He bristles his metallic fur.

'Tobias was just there. He streamed to me directly from the basement at Moncha HQ. Monica isn't there any more.'

He freezes. At first, I wonder if he's had some kind of short-circuit, because he's not even moving a tiny filament of fur on his body.

After a few seconds, he says: >>What do you mean, she's not there?

'I saw it on the live stream. They've torn the whole thing down.'

Jinx hisses. >>They must have moved her.

104

'But where?'

>>I . . . I don't know.

Jinx sounds totally confused. He keeps freezing in his movements, which I take to mean he's accessing data at such a fast rate, his electronics almost can't keep up. His next words confirm my suspicion.

>>I'm running through all the data I can mine from the Moncha cloud, but I can't find mention of anywhere they might have taken her.

Jinx hisses again. >>I thought it was a solid plan.

'What are we going to do? How am I supposed to go up against someone like Eric Smith? He's got all the resources on the planet . . . and he's already starting to manipulate people's behaviour. I can't compete with that. All I have is . . .'

>>Me, says Jinx. His hackles rise, sparking with electricity, as if he's trying to prove to me exactly what he can do. >>But we're going to need those friends of yours to help.

'What, Team Tobias?'

>>Yes, and Zora too.

'I'll call an emergency meet-up after school tomorrow. They'll come.'

Jinx nods. He stretches out along the bed sheets and then comes to curl up in my lap. I take a moment to marvel at just how *perfect* he is. If I hadn't seen his electronic insides myself, I might have mistaken him for a real cat.

I close my eyes, amazed that my friend is back again.

When I open them again, I look around my room. On the back of the door hangs my homework list for Profectus

Academy, colour-coded and tracked with what I like to call 'productivity stickers'. Zora had seen it and dubbed me 'such an engineer nerd'. Always attempting to organize things – to put things in their rightful place so that things – even my life – can run efficiently.

Turns out, life doesn't always like to be colour-coded, even if I use the shiniest stickers. Sometimes, the things you think you can rely on, the foundations upon which you build your life, end up crumbling away. Like my trust in Moncha Corp.

My chest tightens again.

Jinx's eyes bore into mine. >>Let's talk about it more in the morning. For now, you need sleep.

'There's just one thing I need to do first,' I say, getting to my feet. Jinx jumps up as if to follow me, but I shake my head. *Don't worry, I won't tell her anything.*

I slip out of my room, pad down the hallway to Mom's room, and slowly push open the door. I can just about make out her head on the pillow, a gentle smile on her face. Petal is on the pillow too, pulsating with a soft green light as she charges. I hope the update is giving Mom good dreams, at least.

I want to go to her – to give her a hug, to tell her that I love her and that I'm not mad any more: the reason we fought is because of the update. But she looks so peaceful, I don't want to disturb her. I close the door again.

Back in my own room, I am hit by a wave of tiredness. Without even getting up to brush my teeth or take off my clothes, I fall with a slump against the pillow.

'Thank you for coming back, Jinx ...' I whisper as I feel his weight move next to me on the bed.

He purrs gently, and I can feel my anxieties ebb away with his closeness. >>What else are friends for?

CHAPTER FIFTEEN

HEN I WAKE UP, I WONDER IF LAST night had been a dream. Until I look down at the foot of my bed and see a little black robot cat curled up at my feet, warming the blanket – a welcome comfort in the cold morning. I shiver, pulling the duvet cover up under my chin. I wonder why it's so cold – and then I see that my window is open a tiny crack. I must have left it a bit open when I let Jinx in. A bad mistake in the dead of winter, so high up in the tower that the wind whips around and into my room, making the papers on my desk flutter. Finally braving the cold, I make a leap to the window and lean on it to shut it.

'Jinx, what time is it?'

>>Don't ask me, I'm not some level 1 baku.

I groan, but since I don't have access to Slick, I'm lost for an easy way to tell the time.

>>FINE, it's 8.03 a.m.

'Oh, no!' Not only am I going to be late for school, but I've missed Mom. I quickly throw on my old St Agnes uniform and run to the bathroom.

>>Don't forget the duct tape!

'I won't,' I say, with a shudder. The update. The change in Mom's behaviour. I can't believe how close it came to being me too . . .

There's a roll of tape in our kitchen drawers, so I grab it after brushing my teeth. I place a small square over the bottom of the leash, and it's barely visible. Sometimes the simplest solutions are the neatest.

Back in my room, I pick my fleece up off the floor, holding it at arm's length.

I'm afraid of Slick, I realize.

Jinx may not be a normal baku, but he's never been as scary to me as Slick is now.

To my relief, the little beetle remains still as I unzip the pocket. He must be out of battery. But as I hold him, a series of lights brighten along the beetle's shell. >>I'm on very low power. Can I leash up to recharge and update?

I swallow, but guide him to the mains, where I plug him in.

>>I charge 45% less efficiently via the mains.

'I understand.' I plug him in anyway, and ask him to send a message to the Team Tobias group to meet me at my condo building after school. I don't know whether it will interfere with their training schedule, but they need to hear what I've learned from Jinx.

Tearing myself away from Jinx to go to school seems impossible, but he promises to be there when I return. I'm dreading my first few classes, as I don't share any with Zora – but I've sent her a message telling her to meet me urgently at lunch.

As it turns out, the morning passes in a blur. Even though just yesterday I was this strange and exciting anomaly everyone was talking about, today nobody seems to care.

Yesterday's news.

One thing Profectus and St Agnes students have in common: their ability to find new gossip to talk about.

Today at lunch, everyone is buzzing about the announcement from Moncha Corp that they're going to drop a highly anticipated new baku: a gecko. It's a level 3, so out of most people's budget. But that doesn't stop them from dreaming.

St Agnes students have either a level 1 or 2 baku. That means most people would be subject to the update. I look around at my fellow students interacting with their bakus and friends in the cafeteria.

The group in the corner playing games with a pack of cards projected by their respective insect bakus.

The kids teaching their butterfly bakus to copy elaborate new hairstyles from the latest celebrities.

The group with dormouse bakus like Linus, designing elaborate mazes for them to run through and filming it for the most views.

They all have dreams and ambitions of their own. Maybe not to be companioneers at Moncha Corp, but all equally valid and important.

Ambitions that shouldn't be *updated* away in the name of an illusion of happiness.

The gecko news is also big because Moncha Corp normally only reveals new bakus at their annual convention, held two days after Christmas. The announcement is like a little present for all of us Moncha fans, as anticipated as the Queen's speech on Christmas Day. Monica is the real Santa Claus for all of us tech geeks.

So if they were bringing out a new baku early, that could only mean one thing: that something even bigger and better is being prepped for Christmas. The school forums are awash with bloggers and students alike speculating about what it could possibly be.

But all I can sense is dread. What if it's the update? It eats away at the pit of my stomach. Plus, if Eric gives the speech, it will be the final nail in Monica's coffin. *He* will become the new CEO in the public's eyes, the face of Moncha Corp. I scroll through the tech sites, reading one opinion piece after another about how Monica's absence is a sign that she just doesn't care about the company any more. Some are wondering if she's sick or somehow incapacitated, but almost all state that it's only a matter of time before the impressive Eric Smith takes the reins.

I switch over to the Profectus channel at lunchtime. I still follow a lot of the Profectus students on my social media platforms – I haven't yet been barred from receiving the images and videos, which gives me a spark of hope. Maybe I haven't totally been wiped from their databases and I'll still have the ability to slot back into life at Profectus. Some people, like my friend Jake, stream almost constantly from school. It means I catch glimpses of Carter strutting around the place with his boar baku, acting like normal.

I'm on the outside, looking in, and it hurts.

'There you are!' says Zora, making me jump. 'What's so urgent? Did you fix what was wrong with Slick?'

'Not here,' I say. We leave the cafeteria, heading towards a stairwell at the far end of the school that hardly ever gets used. I set Slick to have a proximity alert, in case anyone enters the stairwell to interrupt us. He scurries along the floor, and I watch him closely. Between the syringe and the update, I don't trust him one bit.

But I *do* have to trust Jinx.

Just at that moment, I spot movement in the shadows at the bottom of the stairs. 'Look who's back . . .' I say to Zora. She follows my gaze, and she gasps. Her eyes light up at the sight.

'What? Are you kidding me? Jinx, is that you?'

He doesn't reply out loud, but slinks his body beneath her outstretched hand, allowing her to stroke him. 'Aw, it's so good to see you, buddy,' she says. Then she looks up at me. 'Why didn't you tell me? You can go to Profectus now, right?'

I shake my head, thinking how simple that would be. But the situation is way more complicated than that. 'Zora, Jinx came back because he had to show me something. And I want to show you too.'

Her eyes scan my face, and the smile placed there from Jinx's arrival slowly droops. Without any other explanation, I gesture for Jinx to show Zora the presentation he showed me last night.

112

Once it's finished, Zora is shaking. 'No way. This can't be real.' She chews on the ends of her braids, muffling her words.

'It's only my mom's department who have been updated so far,' I say.

>>For the moment.

Jinx's tone is ominous in my mind.

Zora's eyes open wide with alarm. 'Your mom? Is she okay?'

I shrug. 'She's not herself.'

'Are you sure it's the update? She *has* been through a lot too, you know,' says Zora. She stares at Jinx. 'Do you actually think that Moncha Corp have the technology to control people's emotions and the way that they act?'

She's more sceptical than I am.

'Trust me, Mom flipped from supportive to uncaring overnight. If you saw her – you'd understand.'

'It's . . . it's unbelievable.'

'I know. And that's why we *have* to have Monica back. She's the only one who can make sure that this gets properly sorted out. Eric Smith has no morals. We know that – look at his own son.'

'He's the worst.'

'I know. But his dad is ten times as bad. We have to stop him before the update spreads any further. I just hope that once we have enough proof and can go to the authorities, they won't shut down baku production for ever.'

A look of horror comes over Zora's face. 'They can't do that!' she exclaims, clutching Linus to her chest. 'Bakus are part of our lives now. They're as natural as . . . as phones or cars. They didn't ban the production of cars just because someone could crash one. They're just going to have to figure out how to regulate things better, that's all.'

'You're right,' I quickly reassure her. 'So are you okay to come over tonight?' I ask. 'Jinx has a plan and he says it needs all of us.'

'Of course I'll be there. Lacey, this is huge. I have coding club after school but I can skip it.'

>>No, tell her to come over after that.

I frown. 'Jinx says to go to your coding club as normal.'

Zora nods. 'Okay then, I'll be over before dinner. This is unreal.'

Jinx rolls his spine, a series of lights shooting across his fur. >>I'd better go before anyone else sees me. I'll meet you back at your locker, Lacey.

And just like that, he disappears back into the shadows.

The familiar nerves return as he leaves, but I squash them down. He's not leaving for good. He will be back. 'My old teammates from Profectus are going to be coming tonight too,' I tell Zora.

Now it's Zora's turn to look concerned. 'Are you sure that's a good idea?'

'What do you mean?'

'Well, didn't you say that your friend Tobias's dad works for Eric Smith?'

'Yeah . . .'

'So you mean to tell me that you think it's possible Tobias's dad works for Team Happiness but doesn't know what's going on or how the technology is being used? Of course he does!'

'Well ... maybe. But that doesn't mean that Tobias won't help us.'

'You're too trusting, Lace. That's always been your problem. You think that human beings perform like one of your builds, where everything is predictable. But you can't predict how Tobias is going to react when he finds out that his dad is involved this. I mean, think about it ... is Tobias really going to want to send his dad to prison, if that's what it comes down to?'

I frown. I hadn't thought about it that way. 'Maybe not ...'

'And it's his brother too, right? Who works at Moncha? I mean, we're talking about someone with *really* close connections to the inner circle. I wouldn't be so quick to give away all of our plans and secrets to him.'

I frown. The annoying thing is, Zora might just be right. 'But what choice do we have, Z? He's the one who can get us into Moncha HQ. Without his help, we're actually screwed. We might as well succumb to the update.'

There's a moment's pause. 'Well, would that be so bad?' mumbles Zora.

'What do you mean?' I reply, unable to keep my jaw from dropping as the weight of what she's saying sinks in. Suddenly, the stairwell seems to grow, the gap between us widening.

Zora sticks her chin out, more defiant now. 'I mean it. Maybe things would be easier if someone just made sure we were all happy with our decisions. I mean – look at my family. We're all related by blood and yet can we get on? Not at all. Do you know how many times I've wished for a way to make the fights with my sisters go away? If I got to keep Linus, keep my friends . . . what's wrong with being made to feel happy about everything else?'

'Maybe because you wouldn't have a choice about it?' I screw my face up into a scowl, crinkling my nose. I can't think of anything worse than not being able to have a say in my future.

Maybe I will make bad decisions.

Maybe I will take some wrong turns.

Maybe I *won't* always be happy.

But at least I will know that I have had the power to make the decisions along the way.

Zora shrugs. 'Who says we even really have a choice now? Do you think if I had a choice, I would've chosen to live with three older sisters and my parents in a tiny two-bedroom apartment? No . . . I would have chosen to be . . . I don't know, Tobias's sister or something, and live in a huge mansion. He seems to have a pretty sweet life. Or heck, how come Carter gets to have all his privilege and I don't?'

'So you'd rather just have someone else decide for you whether you were happy enough.'

She sighs. 'No, I'm not saying that. I'm just wondering if there might be a hint of possibility that there are *good* intentions behind this "Team Happiness".' She must take note of the horror on my face, because she shuffles up so that she's sitting next to me, and nudges my shoulder. 'Didn't they teach you to be open-minded at Profectus?'

'They did – but I could never be open-minded about that. Or at least . . . not if they did it without asking people first.'

'That's true. And pushing updates on Moncha employees just because they signed a job contract years ago is not fair. What they've done is not fair.'

'And I have to trust Tobias,' I say, in a small voice.

'I know you do. That's because you *lurve* him.'

'I do not!'

'You so do. Look, you only get that red if you're in the proximity of Tobias Washington. Or thinking about him.'

'If that was the case, I'd be permanently red-faced,' I say, with a grin. Zora bursts into a fit of giggles. 'He asked me out yesterday.'

'He did? What did you say?'

'I . . . I don't think I said anything!'

'Oh, Lacey,' she says, with an exaggerated sigh at my boy-related incompetence. We finish off the rest of our sandwiches and she links her arm in mine. 'You'll have to give him an answer another time. Don't leave Hot Guy hanging. But don't worry, I'll be there tonight. And always.'

CHAPTER SIXTEEN

W HEN I GET BACK TO MY BUILDING after school, Darwin – our porter – pulls me aside. 'Lacey, you have a visitor – but he wasn't on your approved list, so he's waiting around the corner in the lobby.'

I raise my eyebrows in surprise. It can't be anyone from Team Tobias – they're all on my list. I don't know who else would come and visit me.

I peek my head around the corner and my jaw almost drops in surprise. It's Jake Saunders, and his gorgeous chocolate brown retriever baku Vegas. Jake was one of my friends at Profectus – but we've never hung out outside of school. I didn't know that he even knew where I lived. He's one of the most popular and smartest students at the Academy, best known for running an underground betting app for Baku Battles. 'What are you doing here?' I ask, stepping into the hallway.

He comes up to me and embraces me in a big hug. I relax into it – I had no idea how much I needed that until he gave it to me. 'Hon, how have you been? I've been so worried about you since you didn't show up at school. Tobes told me that you'd been kicked out? That is seriously outrageous.'

I redden at the reminder, the humiliation of not being allowed back into school. 'I don't have a level 3 baku any more. This is my new baku, meet Slick.' Slick jumps from my pocket into my hand, and then down on to Vegas. They swap information, and then Slick is back in my pocket again.

'Oh cool – is that a scarab beetle?' Jake asks, politely. I know that he could never think that Slick is a truly cool baku. Maybe if he knew about the syringe . . . I shudder.

'Yeah, unfortunately,' I mutter, as he gives me a quizzical look.

'And you're good? I stopped by the hospital a couple of times but then things got a bit busy with the revised battles . . .'

'I'm doing okay. No lingering side effects.'

'And they still don't know what caused you to keep slipping back into the coma? I mean, I know hypothermia can be bad . . .'

I shrug in response, unsure of what to say. I almost think about bringing him into the fold but Zora's warning about who to trust springs into my mind.

'How are you otherwise?' he asks.

'I'm back at St Agnes where my best friend goes to school, so it's not all bad. And I'm hoping that I can get back to Profectus before too long . . .'

'Maybe we can start a petition! Or crowdfund your place

at the school! I could donate some of the proceeds of the gambling ring ... trust me, that would be a much better cause than what I was going to do with the money.'

'Oh, and what was that?'

Jake has a twinkle in his eye. 'A gambler never tells.'

'That would be great, but I could never accept it. I'll find a way back, I promise. So, Jake ... what are you doing here?' I ask, shuffling my boots along the ground.

'Can't I just have come by to check on a friend?'

I raise a single eyebrow in response, and Jake chuckles. 'Too clever for your own good, as always, Lacey. Okay, I did come here with a *slight* ulterior motive.'

'Oh, and what's that?'

'Well ... after watching the Baku Battles and seeing what happened to Jupiter and Aero and then Jinx ... I don't think the school has ever seen any repairs like it. Not unless the kids are super wealthy or have some major daddy connections, like that kid Carter. Those bakus on your team were utterly destroyed in the battles, and then they came back good as new.'

'Yeah ...'

His eyes bore into mine like laser beams. Jake has the ability to switch from the most laid-back guy ever to super intense – I suppose that's why he does such a good job of running the school's most illegal, and yet most participated in, activity. He knows when to turn it on and when to shut things down. Thank goodness he's gay, or else Tobias would have a serious rival for my affection. He's magnetic.

120

'The rumour mill at Profectus is a highly efficient and accurate one. I should know, I run it.' He winks at me. 'And it's obvious that the common denominator there is you. You must be one hell of a companioneer.'

I blush for real this time. 'I know a few things . . .' There doesn't seem to be any point in hiding it now. I'm not on any Baku Battle team.

'How?'

'I taught myself. I guess I've always wanted to go to Profectus and work for Moncha and so I thought I'd do what Monica did and learn as much as I could on my own.'

'Entrepreneurial spirit! I knew there was a reason I always got on well with you.'

'We definitely share that,' I say with a grin.

'Great. Well, you know how expensive the official vets can be, especially when it comes to fixing level 3 bakus and above.'

I can only imagine. The quote to fix Petal's bent wing for Mom was extortionate, so I'm sure for anything at a higher level, it would be much worse.

'Something's happened to Vegas's right paw. I don't know if he stepped on something or what – but he hasn't been moving properly. Can you take a look?'

'Oh, of course!' I immediately drop down to look at Vegas's paw. He lifts it up to me, and I can see that there are a couple of places where the components have been bent out of shape – and in fact, one of the screws is so worn down that it's almost destroyed. It's one of the common winter problems with ground-walking bakus in Canada. Because they put salt on the roads and sidewalks, some of that can get into the baku's machinery and erode crucial components. There are some little boots and coverings that you can buy to help with that – but of course, those cost money. I never would have taken Jake for someone to lack funds, but then again – some people are just a bit careless. I breathe a sigh of relief. This is a problem that I know I can fix. I've read up on it on some of the companioneering forums, and if I get stuck, I'm sure that Paul will be able to give me some advice. But I already have solutions swirling in my brain, and my fingers itch with the eagerness of getting on with solving the problem.

'Leave him with me. I promise that I'll get him fixed up, no problem.'

Jake's grin is so wide, I can't help but return it. 'That's great! Shall I drop him off on Friday after school?'

'Why not now?'

'Seriously? But you know I'll need him for tomorrow ...'

'You can just come and pick him up on your way in. If it's not too far out of the way, of course.'

'You think you can fix him overnight? Don't you have ... homework or something to do?'

I smile wryly. 'I'm at St Agnes now. Trust me, after the Profectus homework we've had to do ... this is like a walk in the park.'

'All right, smartie pants,' he says. 'I'll come by tomorrow morning. Thanks a bunch for this, Lacey. And let me know how much you want for it. You're doing me a huge favour here. If I put him in with a vet, he wouldn't be fixed for weeks. I wouldn't be able to do it until the Christmas holidays and the thought of being without Vegas for Christmas is just . . .' Jake shudders dramatically.

'Don't you worry about it. This one is on the house. Think you'll be okay without Vegas for one evening?'

Jake's eye twitches. 'I'll manage.' Still, he drops down and gives Vegas an enormous hug. The baku leans his head into Jake's shoulder, and I smile at the show of affection. That's one of the things that level 3's specialize in. I wryly think about my old plan to turn Slick into a level 3 baku. How would a beetle show affection? Maybe there are more reasons than just aesthetics that certain bakus are different levels.

'Catch you later, Lacey,' Jake says. He takes a few steps, then he spins around on his heel. 'This is just *bizarre*, walking away without a baku. What if I get lost on my way home? What if I need to contact someone?'

'Now you know how people used to feel,' I say, laughing.

Jake shudders. 'Literally, how did they survive? I'll be by first thing tomorrow. See ya!'

Even though it's only a tiny example, it reminds me of just how much people are reliant on their bakus nowadays. I would never want to take people's companions away from them. But we do need to find a way to make sure they're safe.

I gather Vegas up in my arms, so that he doesn't have to walk any further and risk more damage to his paw.

>>I'm at 3% battery, says Slick from my pocket.

123

'I'll plug you in as soon as we're downstairs.'

>>It would be much faster for me to leash as normal.

'We'll wait until we're downstairs,' I say again, through gritted teeth.

Once I get down to the basement, I search everywhere for Jinx – I'd hoped that he would be down here already.

But it's empty. I'm grateful that I have Vegas to work on, until the others arrive. I power him down with the switch beneath his ear, then set him up on my desk. I don't even need a schematic to figure this out – instead, I spend a good half an hour meticulously cleaning the components that make up his paw, wiping them down of dirt and encrusted salt so that I can see exactly where things have gone wrong. I carefully slide out the broken parts, then hunt through my drawers for replacements. It's the kind of fiddly, tricky and concentration-intensive work that I can lose hours doing, the part that no one seems to get or understand, except for other tinkerers. It can take a long time to do a job like this absolutely perfectly, but that's what I take pride in. I like to be meticulous.

And it helps pass the time until the loud snap of a camera shutter breaks my concentration.

CHAPTER SEVENTEEN

THERE'S A CACKLE OF LAUGHTER THAT follows the camera noise, and I look up sharply. It's only then that I realize how I must have looked: my head bent down low over an upside-down retriever baku, goggles on, hair tied back in the messiest bun ever and – worst of all – my tongue poking out from between my lips, which is a habit I have when I'm concentrating ultra-hard.

And now there's photo evidence of it. I groan. 'Thanks a lot, River,' I say, when I see his face.

'That's one for the history books!' he laughs.

River isn't the only one who's arrived. I roll back in my chair and see Kai and Ashley behind him.

'I'm not going to lie, I never thought I'd be back in this place – cool as it is.' Sarcasm drips from his voice and Kai crinkles his nose as he looks around my locker. I've learned to ignore his too-cool-for-school act, because I know that's exactly what it is . . . just an act. I give him an exaggerated eye roll as I approach the door, and he returns it with a big grin.

We cram into my locker, just as we did a few months back

when we were trying to fix Ashley's spaniel baku Jupiter. River jumps up to perch on my desk, sitting cross-legged. Kai has his arms folded, making his biceps bulge, leaning back against the wire frame of my cage and making a deep indent. Ashley stands next to him, elegantly cool in dark jeans and a chunky wool sweater. I swear she's leaning slightly into Kai's shoulder.

'Hey, Lacey!' Zora appears a split second after them and hesitates as she takes everyone in.

'Hey!' I leap to my feet. 'These are my teammates from Profectus – River and his baku Lizard, Kai and Oka, and Ashley and Jupiter. Everyone, this is my best friend, Zora, and Linus.'

She lifts her hand in a small wave. Linus wiggles forward, and there's a flurry of activity from the bakus as they share information with each other.

'Zora! I've heard so much about you,' says Ashley, who swoops over to give her a hug and bring her in. Ashley's warmth helps offset Zora's initial shyness, and it's not long before the two of them are chatting away.

Once Zora sits down at my desk in front of the old computer, she casts a glance my way. She tucks one of her long braids into the corner of her mouth, where she sucks at it anxiously. She knows what I'm about to tell them. I have to wait for Tobias to arrive, though.

'Up to anything over the Christmas vacation, Lacey?' asks Ashley, with a smile. A bow decorated with holly and ivy is wrapped around Jupiter's neck.

I shrug, unsure how to answer her question. Since Mom has been updated, I know Christmas is not going to be the same.

'Want to come shopping with me tonight?' she asks. 'They've got a late-night opening at the Eaton Centre . . .'

'I just can't wait for it to be vacation,' says River. 'Feels like we've been at school for years. The month after Baku Battles has gone so-o-o slowly.' Then he shrugs, with a wry smile. 'I guess, except for you, Lacey. You've been in a coma for most of it.'

'River!' says Ashley, as I wince.

'Thanks for the invite, Ashley, but I don't think I can come to the mall,' I say. 'Once Tobias is here, I'll explain everything.'

We chat for a few more minutes, before my ears pick up the sound of the elevator door ping. Tobias is finally here. He drags his beanie off his head, shaking the snow off his woollen hat. Little snowflakes stick to his dark skin, melting into tiny drips of water. He wipes his hand across his brow and grins at me.

Is it possible for someone to be any cuter? Even in a huge winter jacket, he manages to set my heart racing. 'Sorry I'm late.' He steps into the locker and closes it behind him. As he turns, he spots Zora. 'Oh, hey. I'm Tobias,' he says.

'I know who you are,' Zora says while wiggling her eyebrows.

The burst of laughter that follows breaks the tension, and my heart warms to have all my friends in the same room.

Tobias walks over to me and gives me a hug. 'So, Lacey, what's the big news?'

I take a deep breath, then take a conscious step sideways – taking me outside his grip. He frowns a little, but I need him to listen to what I have to say. What I'm asking isn't something he might want to agree to, and I don't want him to feel any obligations just because he asked me out. 'I've learned something since coming out of hospital, and it's not good news. I wanted to text you all to tell you straight away, but then I thought you might not believe me.

'Plus, I need know you're okay with keeping a huge secret. It might be risky. I'm asking you to put a lot on the line – to keep this secret from your family and other friends, and most of all, from Moncha Corp itself.'

Kai stands up straighter. 'Okay, you can't tempt us like that and then expect us to say no.'

River pipes up. 'How are you even going to stop us from listening to you and then spilling the secret anyway?'

Zora pipes up. 'I'm actually going to help with that.'

I look over at Zora in surprise. 'Just trust me,' she says, in a low voice. I gesture for her to go ahead.

She clears her throat, wriggling in her chair, trying to get comfortable with all of our eyes on her. 'I've developed a little tweak to the code of your bakus. It will obscure this conversation. You have to be willing to have it added to your bakus before Lacey can say anything. Otherwise, you have the choice to leave now. If you want to.'

'Seriously? You're threatening us with having code that, wow, we have no idea whether you even know how to

128

implement properly? What if you permanently mess up my baku? I just don't know if I can take that risk,' Kai says.

'I can promise you that it won't harm your bakus.'

Ashley looks up at Kai, his doubt spreading hesitation in her bones. But Tobias takes a step forward. 'Of course I'll let you implement a black-out code on Aero. Lacey trusts you, so I trust you.' He turns to me. 'But you shouldn't need us to prove our loyalty to you.'

'Yeah,' says River. 'You should know that we wouldn't betray you.' They're all looking at me.

'I promise, it's not you I'm worried about,' I say. 'The truth is, this is just too big, the consequences too huge not to take precautions. But I can't say anything more until you sign up for the code. If you want it, Zora is ready to implement.'

To my relief, Tobias steps forward first of all. Kai tuts, but his defiance seems to fade in the face of Tobias's leadership. I'm eternally grateful to him, and I hope that they all will understand once the truth comes to light.

Zora leashes Aero up to the computer, and Zora inserts the tiny tweak to his code. Once everyone has put their bakus through the process – and they all do – they turn and look at me expectantly. I shrug. 'We're still missing someone . . .' I say. I bite down on my fingernails.

'No, look, he's here,' says Zora, with a small grin.

On cue, Jinx leaps down from a shelf in a dark corner of the locker, right into the middle of all of us. Ashley squeals with delight, dropping down to embrace him in a hug.

Surprisingly, Jinx lets her, rubbing his spine up against her leg and sending soft vibrations her way.

Zora turns to me. 'Jinx came to me after school – and instead of coding club, I worked on coding this secrecy program instead. I only just finished in time or else I would have told you.'

'Thank you,' I say to her with a grin.

'Jinx! You're safe!' says Tobias. He kneels down, blinking hard as if he can't believe his eyes. But as Jinx flicks his tail and flashes lights on his body, Tobias's eyes light up. 'It really is him. I should get in touch with Mr Baird – he'd want to know.'

Jinx turns to Tobias and hisses furiously, his fur rising up into hackles. Tobias immediately throws his hands up in the air, backing down. 'Okay, not Mr Baird then?'

I shake my head. 'No way! No one else can know he's back. Eric Smith is still looking for Jinx – and plying a lot of resources behind it. His security team searched my apartment. Eric Smith wants Jinx destroyed.'

Zora pipes up. 'The code that you've just been given will prevent your bakus from transmitting any information about Jinx to the cloud, so that you can't inadvertently give away his position. It had nothing to do with us not trusting you – we just don't trust the prying eyes of Eric Smith.'

'And now I can show you why I asked you here,' I say.

'It wasn't just to show us Jinx is safe?' Tobias asks.

'I wish,' I mutter. 'Jinx, go ahead.'

He steps into the centre of the locker and projects the Team

Happiness presentation so we all can view it. This is my third time watching it, but it still doesn't creep me out any less.

There is silence in the locker as we cycle through the different parts.

When Jinx lowers the projection, Tobias stands up. 'I'm not listening to this. I'm going.' He strides out of the locker.

'No, Tobias, wait!' I say.

He spins around. 'My dad is not involved in that. That's not what Team Happiness is about. You're telling me there's some kind of sick plot to control people? That they might implement some kind of mind control?'

'I'm not telling you that they *might* implement it. I'm telling you that it's already happened. My mom was part of the beta test. She's been updated.'

Tobias folds his arms across his chest, his bottom lip jutting out. 'How can I believe you?' There's a tremor in his voice. 'I don't need this.' He walks off into the darkness.

'Tobias!' I say.

Ashley grabs my arm as I attempt to follow him. 'Let him cool off a bit. He'll come around, I promise. It's just a big deal.'

'A big deal?' says Kai. 'It's huge.'

I turn to all of them. 'We have to stop it from going any further. This can't be rolled out to level 1 and 2 bakus. I mean – my mom has already been changed. We can't let it happen to more people.'

'But how?' Ashley asks.

'Yeah, what can we do about it?' asks River.

'That's just it. We need to get back into Moncha HQ and find out where they're keeping Monica. She's the only one who can take back control from Eric and get him to reverse it.'

The cage door jangles, and we all look up. Tobias is back, his fingers wrapped around the metal webbing. He looks so sad.

'Lacey, I . . .'

'It's okay, I understand,' I say. 'It's a lot to take in.'

He shakes his head. 'Let me finish. I'm sorry for storming off. I still can't believe this is something my parents would be involved in, but your mom . . . she was so kind to me in the hospital. If something has happened to her – I want to be there with you.'

'There's a good man,' says a gruff voice from behind Tobias. Tobias almost jumps out of his skin.

I scramble up off the floor to see Paul's face staring at us through the wire. His eyes are dark.

I swallow, wondering how much he heard. By the looks of it – maybe everything.

'Everyone, this is Paul . . . he lives in my building.'

'So it's true,' he says. 'Team Happiness has been activated.'

My jaw drops. That's definitely not what I was expecting him to say. I move to hide Jinx instinctively, knowing that if Paul's here, his baku George can't be far behind. He grunts, acknowledging my gesture. 'Don't worry, George won't give anything away. I disconnected him from the Moncha cloud years ago.'

I start in surprise, but then I nod. Paul grits his teeth. 'Besides, I think I know where Eric would hide Monica Chan.'

My eyes open wide in shock. 'Where?' I ask.

'At the secret Moncha testing facility. Lake Baku.'

CHAPTER EIGHTEEN

'LAKE BAKU?' I ASK. 'WHERE IS THAT?'

Paul shakes his head. 'I don't know exactly. I've only heard rumours about it. Asking too many questions about it was one of the reasons I was forced to leave the main board of Moncha.'

'*You* were on the board at Moncha?' asks Kai, his nose scrunched up. I can see why he's sceptical. Paul is the definition of scruffy, with a white-speckled beard, oil-stained clothes and shoes with a hole in the top. He doesn't exactly look like a top-level business man.

'I was indeed, young man.' At that, his lemur baku George leaps into the locker and runs circles around Kai's husky baku, creating a small whirlwind that almost blows the husky off his feet. The display of strength from the baku is enough to make Kai reconsider his assumptions. Anyone who has such a high level baku probably once was high up at Moncha Corp. That, or extremely rich. And considering Paul lives in my building, it's doubtful that he is very rich.

'Do you know more about Team Happiness?' I ask him.

He nods. 'If you don't mind listening to an old man?' He raises an eyebrow at Kai, who stiffens in response.

I stand up and gesture for him to take a seat in my chair. 'Please, Paul. Tell us what you know.'

'I'll have to start at the beginning.' He presses his fingers against his brow, deep in thought. 'Oh, it must be twenty years ago now, I was running my own artificial intelligence firm, working on the self-driving cars you probably drove over here in.'

River bounces up and down on my desk. 'Yeah, we did come over in a self-drive! Cool!'

Paul looks up at him and nods. 'I was invited to attend an angel investor meeting where a young upstart named Monica Chan demonstrated the first ever baku, Yi. I couldn't believe my eyes. I knew from that moment on, I had to be a part of her company. I couldn't believe such innovation and skill had come from someone so young. Actually, you remind me so much of her, Lacey.' Paul fixes his gaze on me and I blush furiously. He's made comments like that before but I never realized how close he was to Monica herself. If I'd known that, I wouldn't have been able to stop asking him questions – but that might have been precisely why he didn't tell me.

'I joined her board of directors right from the start, helping out with the financial side of the business, gathering investors and making sure Monica developed a sustainable business plan.'

I can't believe I'm learning so much more about my

favourite tinker. We've had an unwritten rule not to ask too many questions, but I've always been curious. Then a thought strikes me. If Paul worked at Moncha from the start, maybe he knew my dad? I lock that thought away as Paul continues to talk.

'I always believed in what Monica wanted to achieve. She was smart – and not just in companioneering. She knew the dangers of their technology if it fell into the wrong hands. She drew up an agreement to make sure control of her company was handed over to an independent board of directors if she ever retired or was absent for a long period of time. But her co-founder, Eric Smith, was also smart. Monica might have been the CEO of Moncha, but he had plans of his own. It was all to do with the leash.'

Instinctively, my hand goes up to the leash at my ear – covered in duct tape now.

Paul's brow furrows, casting a dark shadow over his face. George comes over and curls his tail gently around his neck. Paul reaches up with his arm and scratches the baku's head. They have such a natural connection; it's something I always envied before Jinx came along. But the look on his face sends a chill down my spine.

He clears his throat before continuing. 'The leash is the connection between baku and human. It uses the owner's own kinetic energy to provide power to the bakus, revolutionizing the concept of battery life. But Eric saw the potential for even more uses for the leash. He pushed for his own lab and team, dedicated solely to the study of leash technology. Nothing they did could be released to the public without Monica's approval, of course. But that didn't stop him experimenting. That man had quite a few wacky, ambitious ideas and often needed to be reined in.

'The craziest of Eric's ideas was a way to make people happier by figuring out a way to tweak ambition and desire. He thought that if people no longer had any wants, if they didn't feel like they were lacking something, missing something ... then they would be happier – and more productive at their jobs, of course.

'You have to understand, we were living in an age of intense envy, where social media was a highlight reel of the most golden and shiny parts of people's lives, everything viewed through a filter. It was cited as the cause of skyrocketing levels of depression, anxiety and other mental illnesses across the generations. He wanted to reverse that process via the leash. If we could be satisfied with our reality, then as a society we would be more content, or so he thought.'

'This is just like in the presentation,' I say to the others, who nod.

'Presentation?' Paul asks.

'Jinx stole the internal Team Happiness presentation from the cloud. That's how we knew about the update to begin with.'

Paul sighs. 'It seemed so far-fetched to the board at the time ...'

'But now he's done it,' I say, darkly.

'So it seems,' replies Paul. 'And since bakus are so prevalent ... it will be very hard to stop him without Monica's cooperation.'

I screw up my nose. 'This is like super-villain level disgusting.'

'Agreed!' says Zora, emphatically.

'So why do you think she's at this Lake Baku place?' I ask Paul. 'What is it exactly?'

'Lake Baku is Moncha's top secret baku test centre. Access was restricted to a very limited group of employees. Even as a board member, I couldn't find out exactly where it was. That was, until I saw that Moncha Corp had made a huge purchase of land. I think Monica took inspiration from other business leaders in the past for that, like Walt Disney who bought hundreds of acres of land in Florida to have plenty of room to build his theme parks but also to keep advertisers and other rival businesses away. In Canada, one thing that we don't lack is space. Once I saw that invoice for the land, I started asking questions about it. I heard the name Lake Baku, started putting two and two together ...

'Then I was pushed out of the board before I could investigate any further. Demoted. They used my injury as an excuse,' he gestures towards his missing lower arm, his sleeve pinned up over the elbow. 'But I know it was because I got too curious. Some people were sent to live up there – to run the experiments and test the bakus. People ... who were never heard from again.'

My heart stops. 'Do you think my dad could have been one of those people?' It comes out as barely a whisper.

Paul turns to me, his eyebrows knitted together in a frown. 'Oh, Lacey, it's been a very long time since I worked at Moncha. But I did know your father. He was a great engineer, and I was as surprised as anyone when he disappeared. All I know is that Lake Baku would be the perfect place to hide someone like Monica from public view.'

I blink, finding it hard to process the information. I've always been good at compartmentalizing – something I've learned from the laser-like focus I've acquired from spending so long as a companioneer. Jinx leaps up on to my shoulders and nuzzles my neck, calming me. Instinctively, I bury my hands in his electronic fur. *My dad . . . Jinx . . .*

>>It's going to be okay. But we need to focus on Monica.

Jinx is right. Getting Monica back is the best chance I have of reversing the update to Mom's brain. I take several deep breaths, then stare around at the people in my locker – the team of teens and one old man who are thinking about how to find the founder of one of the biggest tech companies in North America.

'Wait, I know where that is!' says Tobias, breaking the stunned silence brought on by Paul's appearance and revelation.

Paul raises a single bushy eyebrow. 'You do?'

'The moment you said it, the name rang a bell. I've never actually been there, but I've seen it marked on this old map of the area on the wall of my dad's office. I used to study it when I was younger. It's in the Muskokas, near where we have our cottage. Aero, pull up a picture of my dad's map.'

Aero spreads his wings out so wide, they almost reach end to end in my locker. The others gather round his wingspan as a photograph of a map of the Muskoka region, north of Toronto, is prominently displayed. Tobias uses his fingers to zoom in. 'Look, we have a cottage here, on a private lake.'

'Dude,' says Kai, impressed.

'Lake Washington,' reads out Ashley. 'You're so fancy you have your own lake named after you!'

A blush rises in Tobias's cheeks, entering his hairline. 'Yeah, but at what cost, right?' he mutters darkly. 'Anyway, Lake Baku should be . . .' He moves the map with his fingers. 'There.' He zooms in, where sure enough, there are the words LAKE BAKU in tiny print.

'Find her, Lacey,' says Paul. 'Bring Monica home. That's the only way you'll be able to save Moncha Corp – maybe even the world – from Eric Smith's update.'

CHAPTER NINETEEN

PAUL LEAVES US THEN, SHUFFLING BACK to the elevators to head up to his apartment. He looks tired, worn down. But he promises to look through his old files to see if he can find any paper copies of the agreement that Monica had drawn up in the event of her absence.

It frightens me what the implications of that are. That we might need legal back-up. It all seems way above my pay grade. And *definitely* above my school grade.

The atmosphere inside my locker is a state of shock. 'Now we know about Lake Baku, we have to check it out straight away,' I say.

'It's all private land up there,' says Tobias. 'There's a ton of security.'

My shoulders slump with disappointment.

'So what are we going to do?' asks River.

'That part's easy,' says Tobias. We all turn to look at him expectantly. 'Like I said, my cottage is on that private land. My parents always throw this massive pre-Christmas party and I was going to invite the team anyway . . . so I'm sure I can convince them to invite you and Zora too,' continues Tobias, unaware of the thoughts running through my brain. 'We leave on Friday, straight after school.'

'Friday? That's still two days away.' My mind races. *Who knows what might happen in two days?*

>>Tobias's party sounds like the best shot we've got, says Jinx.

'We can't go any earlier. We can't skip school,' Kai says. He might give off a tough-guy attitude, but even he values his place at Profectus.

'Neither can we,' says Zora to me, gently placing her hand on mine.

'We'll leave on Friday,' Tobias reconfirms. 'But we'll only have a couple of days to look for Lake Baku – then it's Christmas Eve and you'll all have to go home,' continues Tobias. 'It's tight timing but . . .'

'No, that sounds like it will work,' I say. Then I turn to Zora. 'Do you think your parents will let you?'

'Are you kidding?' Zora replies. 'If you can make it happen, Tobias, I'll be there.'

'Right. And you, Lacey?'

At first I'm hit with an almost uncontrollable urge to yell at him: MY MOM WON'T CARE; HER BRAIN HAS BEEN TAKEN OVER BY THE UPDATE. But I force myself instead to take a deep breath. The reality of what we've been told hasn't yet sunk in for Tobias, the way it has for me: the fact that my mom's mind has been altered. Instead, I just nod.

'Great. I'll message you once it's all confirmed.'

Slick buzzes up against me, butting up against the duct-taped end of my leash. I jump out of my skin and bat him away.

'Whoa, what's wrong with your bug?' Kai asks.

'He wants to update me,' I say. 'But not only that ... Slick is the reason I was in the coma. After I let Jinx go, he shocked me and injected me with something that affected my memory. Jinx saw it all. Eric Smith's orders.'

'Seriously?'

'That's unbelievable!'

'No way!'

There's a chorus of shocked protestation, and they all turn to stare at the beetle.

Tobias is straight there, pulling me into a hug. 'It's all right, Lacey. We're going to find a way to stop this and get all these bakus back to normal.'

I smile up at him, but then that smile dips into a frown. 'I feel like I've dragged all of you into this when you could be living your own lives and focusing on school ... not this kind of end-of-the-world, conspiracy-theory, bakus-turning-on-humans stuff.'

He grabs my hand, and warmth floods my body. 'We wouldn't be here if we didn't want to be. Stop worrying, Lace. We're going to find Monica.'

'Thanks, Tobias.' I reach up and kiss him on the lips, bolder than I've been in the past. Heck, if I'm thinking about taking down the founder of the biggest tech company in North America, shouldn't I be brave enough to kiss the guy I have a crush on?

He starts as if surprised, but then gently leans into the kiss. There's a chorus of groans from the audience that makes us giggle – it's affectionate, I know. 'Can I take that as a yes, then?' he whispers.

'Sure,' I say back, with a small smile.

Kai throws his arm around Ashley's shoulders and pulls her close. Even their bakus walk side-by-side, haunches bumping into each other.

Once everyone has gone, Zora turns to me and gives me a high five. 'Nice move, girl! Looks like the key to breaking your shyness is to plot to save the world.'

I grin, poking my tongue out at her.

'And the code worked perfectly,' she continues.

'With you at the computer, I wouldn't expect anything less.'

'Damn right!' she says. 'Want to head upstairs with me? I have to grab some pjs and my toothbrush from my apartment first.'

I side-glance at Vegas, who I know is lying under a blanket in the corner. 'I've just got a few things to finish up here, but I'll meet you at mine?'

She gives me a sceptical glance, but then nods. She knows that sometimes I just need some time to myself to decompress.

When everyone has gone and the basement is quiet again, I let out a deep sigh of relief.

Jinx hops up on to the desk. >>At least we have a plan.

Hopefully Tobias can get you to his Christmas party at Lake Washington.

'Yes, and then we hope Paul's right, and Monica is at this Lake Baku.'

I pick up Vegas from underneath the blanket and lay him gently down on my main work table. Even though he's a robot, I can't help but want to treat him with gentleness and kindness. I still feel like I'm reeling from learning so much about – and from – my friend the tinkerer, but nothing helps focus my mind more than companioneering.

'Jinx, can you pull up the schematics for a retriever baku?'

>>Here you go.

I smile at him gratefully. He's able to circumvent the new rules and access the correct files on the cloud.

After double-checking my work on his paw, I can see that there's not a lot else wrong with Vegas. There's just some other ordinary wear and tear that might turn into a bigger problem later on down the line. I want to return Vegas even *better* than Jake could have imagined. Anything to distract myself from what I've learned tonight, and the fact that we can't leave for two more days.

I think back to what Paul said, about how I reminded him of Monica in the early days.

Would Dad be proud of me?

I drop the tools, shaking the thought from my head. I can't stop thinking about Dad. He left us – and even if it wasn't voluntary, it's been a decade since we've seen him. The chances of finding him now? It has to be next to impossible.

My focus has to be on Mom. We need to find a way to reverse the update. And to do that, we have to find Monica Chan.

>>I think you've done all you can. Jinx gestures with his paw to Vegas.

I nod and close up all the open casings, giving him a final polish with a fine microfibre cloth. He looks perfect. I grab Slick from where he's charging on the mains beneath the desk, before turning the lights off in the locker.

We head upstairs and find Zora waiting in the hall outside my apartment door. She puts her arm around my shoulder and guides me in. I feel bone-tired.

Normally when Zora sleeps over, we'd watch an episode of our favourite show, *Outerlands*, and our bakus would fetch snacks from the kitchen, but tonight we're just too tired. Just as we're about to climb into bed, there's a ping from Tobias. Slick reads it out to me.

> TOBIAS: Hey Lacey. Checked in with my mom tonight. She says I'm fine to add a couple more people to the guestlist. Looks like it's on. A car will pick you up early Saturday morning. Be ready – and bring lots of winter gear.

Zora and I high-five. It's really happening.

Mission: rescue Monica Chan is on.

CHAPTER TWENTY

I SET SLICK TO WAKE ME SUPER EARLY IN THE morning to make sure that I catch Mom before she leaves for work. Zora groans in the bed next to me as Slick's buzzing makes the sheets vibrate.

I'm almost too late – she's headed out of the door at 5.45 a.m. My eyes are bleary with sleep, but I manage to stumble from my bedroom door as I hear the chain being lifted on our front door. 'Wait, Mom, can I talk to you for a second?' I blurt out.

'Oh sure, honey,' she says, pausing beside the door. Petal flutters by her ear, no doubt alerting her that if she doesn't make the bus within the next ten minutes, she's going to be late for work. I feel a surge of anger towards the delicate butterfly baku, before I remember that it's not really her fault. It's Eric Smith's.

'Tobias invited me to spend the first few days of the Christmas vacation with his family up at their cottage. Is that okay? I'll be back on Christmas Eve.'

'Oh, that's okay. I forgot to tell you that I'd actually agreed to work over Christmas this year.' She leans forward

147

and kisses me on my dumbstruck cheek. 'It's beyond busy at the office but I'm loving it. Are you home for dinner tonight? Get some take-out if you're home before me. Also, I've been doing a clear-out, so can you take the bags in my room to the garbage chute before you leave for school?'

Then Petal buzzes in her ear and she's out of the door.

Fury writhes through me, then disbelief, sadness and finally – acceptance. There's no way that Mom would work over Christmas voluntarily. This is the update at work, and it's made me more determined than ever to put a stop to it.

It's still early, but I'm so wired by Mom's reaction that I know there's no way I'll be able to get to sleep again. Zora's still fast asleep, and it's hours until I have to head to school. I decide to fulfil Mom's request and take the garbage out. I realize that I haven't been into her room since the update. I wonder if anything has changed there.

At first, when I open the door, I'm relieved – there isn't any huge sign of her change in personality. She hasn't swapped her colourful comforter for something plain and boring, for example. There are still photographs of the two of us on her dresser, and her make-up is neatly ordered underneath the mirror. I run my finger across the edge of my favourite photo – it's of the two of us when we first moved into the apartment. There's no furniture in there yet, just piles of cookbooks all around us. I'm sitting on a pile of them like a stool, and Mom has her arms wrapped around me. Zora's mom had taken the picture, after arriving in a whirlwind with a tray of baked goods, her children – including Zora – in tow.

We look happy in that moment, our grins wide, eyes shut as we hold each other tight, even though I know that so much must have been going on for Mom during that time. Does she still wonder what happened to Dad? Did she stay in Monchaville because she thought that would keep her close to him – or did she have no other choice? A single mom, with no money and big dreams of becoming a chef but no way to go about it. Monchaville was a security net so wide, it was impossible to miss.

Impossible to say no to.

There's another photograph next to it. One of my dad as a young man. He's wearing a white lab coat, and at his feet is a beautiful German Shepherd baku. The silver frame is tarnished in a couple of places – and when I pick it up, I realize it's browned in exactly the places someone would hold it in their hand. Mom must hold this photograph all the time.

The thought fills me with sadness.

I tear my eyes away from the photograph and spot the black garbage bags in the corner of the room. I pick up the first one and grunt at how heavy it is. I immediately drop it back down on the floor.

>>Holy bakus, what has she got in there, a ton of bricks?

Jinx slides in through a small crack in the door, jumping up on to Mom's bed and not offering to help me at all.

'I knew I should've got a stronger baku – then you could have lifted this to the trash chute for me.'

>>I'm your companion, not your slave, he says, licking his paw.

'One thing you have right – I have no clue what she has in here that weighs so much.'

I feel awkward about opening the bag – Mom and I have always respected each other's privacy. She doesn't poke around inside my basement locker, allowing me to keep all my weird and wacky treasures – as long as I'm not doing anything *too* illegal, she's happy to mind her own business. As a result, I almost never go into her room, unless she's specifically asked me to. If I didn't want my mom to snoop on me, I wasn't going to snoop on her.

But this is stuff that she wants to throw away. So there can't be any harm in looking. Also, I have this aversion to throwing potentially useful things away (Zora says one day I'll be found buried under a mountain of useless electronic equipment). Maybe there's something in the bags that I can salvage for use in the locker. I'm sure I heard a clink of metal when I put the bag down.

I untie the top of the black bag and peer in. 'Wow, this is weird,' I mutter, half to Jinx and half to myself.

Jinx is there in a flash, his natural curiosity getting the better of him. He scurries into the top of the bag, then drags something out between his teeth. He drops it at my feet. >>What's this?

'Oh, that's one of my mom's old cookbooks.' I frown. It's

strange that she wants to throw it away. This is one of her oldest ones, filled with Post-it note flags and annotated with little tips and reminders in her neat handwriting.

I reach into the bag and pull out more. The clink of metal I heard turns out to be several of those giant old metal-ring binders clashing together. Not at all useful for my tinkering. But I've never seen them before. Inside seems to be a collection of stuff from before we moved into the apartment – bills, old bank statements, and, most shockingly of all, an acceptance letter to a culinary school in Montreal.

It's dated from a few months *after* we moved into Monchaville. I don't understand. That would have meant that she applied to the school while she had a job working in the Moncha telemarketing department. I can see that they've offered her financial aid as well, as a result of being a single mom. But why wouldn't she have taken it? And why has she decided now is the right time to throw it all away?

It *has* to have something to do with the update. But for the first time, I feel uneasy. Not going to culinary school – not following her passion – must have been a decision that Mom had made earlier on in her life, long before there was any update. Maybe she is happy where she is? I'm beginning to realize that not everyone is like me – so desperate to follow my dreams no matter what the cost.

If the update can take away the petty stresses, make every day feel like it's worth it, put a smile on my mom's face – maybe, just maybe, it isn't so bad after all?

I shake the thought from my head. Because my eye has

caught on something else: letters between my mom and dad from before I was born. I can't believe she's throwing them away.

The letters are old-fashioned and sweet – she would treasure these, not want to get rid of them. *This must be the update at work.*

>>It's even worse than we thought.

I nod to Jinx. I skim through the letters, feeling like I'm intruding on something private between my parents, but also desperate to see something concrete of my dad. I read about how he yearns to be an engineer, wanting to make a difference in the world. Always pushing himself to work harder. I rub my fingers against his old engineering ring, which I wear on my thumb. It's a Canadian tradition that newly qualified engineers wear an iron ring on their pinkie finger (but his is too big for mine). The story says that the iron came from a collapsed bridge. It's worn as a reminder, a symbol of the responsibilities of an engineer to their work.

No wonder Mom thinks that I take after him.

It only makes me wish I knew him more. Paul's suspicion echoes in my ears. *Maybe the same thing which happened to Monica happened to my dad years ago.*

Eric might have perfected the art of 'disappearing' people long ago.

I always assumed that Dad had just left us. Abandoned us with no hope of return. And if Mom had had any suspicions there was more to the story, she'd never shared them with me – until recently.

There's one more thing I find in there. A little analogue watch, with a leather strap. You don't see many of them any more. I wrap it around my wrist, pleased with the retro look.

I take the plastic bags but I don't bring them to the garbage chute. Instead, I decide to store this stuff in my locker. Who knows if Mom really means to throw it all away? Plus, this is *my* history as well as hers. Maybe looking at it is upsetting, and the update is telling her to get rid – to purge herself – of any sort of negativity. But I don't care. I haven't been updated yet. I want to cling on to these little slices of our history, even if it makes me sad.

Tears begin to roll down my cheeks. Jinx comes up to me and nuzzles his way beneath my arm. I hug him tightly to my chest.

We're going to get my mom back if it's the last thing we do. And there's someone who might be able to fill in some more of the blanks. An adult who once offered me so much help.

'Jinx – do you how I can get in touch with Mr Baird? Don't worry – it's not so I can give you to him!' I quickly add, remembering his reaction when Tobias mentioned our old teacher. 'I think we might need his help with this.'

Jinx flicks his tail. >>I'll see what I can do.

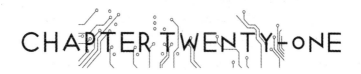
'ZORA, LOOK AT THIS.' I SHOW HER THE contents of the black bags.

'Wow, she was going to throw this all away? This update really is no joke.' She hadn't seen the consequences of the update first hand, but now she's getting the idea.

I shake my head.

She breathes out a long, ragged breath. 'Well, only two more days of school. Then we'll be on the hunt for Monica. Don't worry, Lacey. We'll get your mom back to normal.'

Slick buzzes, and even though it no longer makes me jump out of my skin, I still wince with a touch of fear. >>There's someone downstairs in the lobby to see you.

My eyes widen. 'Oh, that must be Jake! I'd better go down and meet him.'

'Want to catch the bus together later?' Zora asks.

'I'll meet you at school,' I say. 'There's something I have to do first . . .'

Zora raises an eyebrow at me. 'You're not going up to try and find Lake Baku on your own, are you?'

'No, nothing like that. I *promise*.'

'Okay, good. Because we're a team in this, remember.'

'I won't forget,' I say with a grin. 'Thanks for staying with me last night. See you at school.'

I wave her off, then head down to the basement to collect Vegas before meeting Jake in the lobby.

'Lacey, thank you *so* much. He's back to brand new again!'

'My pleasure! He's a great baku.'

He takes in my plain clothes for school. 'So, still not allowed at Profectus, huh?'

I shake my head.

'Well, if you need anything, ever, just call me. I owe you one,' he says.

'Thanks, Jake.' I have a feeling I might need him even sooner than he expects.

It's still early when I leave the condo, but I don't feel like going back upstairs. It's early enough that the streets are still quiet except for the keenest of commuters. It's not rush hour yet.

I walk until I pass the threshold of Monchaville, heading towards downtown. When we're no longer on streets guarded by 24/7 baku surveillance, Jinx feels more comfortable to be at my side, and I catch sight of the black cat baku streaking along ahead of me. He's waiting at a streetcar stop, and when I reach him, I put Slick in my pocket. Now Jinx and I look just like everyone else – owner and baku, happily coexisting.

Other people's bakus are *slightly* more helpful than Jinx, though – of course. I'm the only one waiting at the streetcar stop because Jinx wasn't kind enough to inform me that the next one wasn't due for another ten minutes. Across the street from where I'm standing, waiting and shivering, I can see into the window of a local coffee shop chain, busy with people sitting at tables, sipping their winter-themed spiced lattes. No one is waiting in line – the bakus are doing that, while the people chat and catch up with work. I wish I could send Jinx to get me a hot drink, but somehow I don't think he'd take too kindly to that request.

My eye catches movement on the roof, where I see a couple of stray cats staring at us, their ears twitching. But when I blink to check again, they're gone.

Thankfully, it's not too long until the streetcar pulls up and I'm able to jump on board. Jinx pays my fare, and we settle into a seat next to a woman with a super-cute Maltese terrier baku, all fluffy and white. His innovative fur has spread apart on his back so she can watch a video on her commute. It's an episode of a popular reality television show – bakus and their owners compete in tasks to see who is most 'in tune' with each other.

Jinx and I would totally rock that show.

The streetcar pulls up at a stop outside the old warehouse on West Queen West, almost as far down the street as you can go. But whereas before there was the BRIGHTSPRK logo discreetly on the door, now there's nothing. The windows look boarded up and broken. The whole place feels deserted.

Jinx leaps from my shoulder up to the windowsill. My

156

breath catches as he balances on the thin ledge, but he manoeuvres with effortless grace. Once again, the detail in his craftsmanship absolutely astonishes me. He disappears through a hole in the window, gliding around the broken glass so that he doesn't scratch himself.

I hang around outside, burying my mittened hands into the depths of my puffer jacket, my breath freezing around my nose. Sometimes I can't believe how cold it gets in this country, and I hope that Jinx isn't long.

It only takes a few seconds before his face reappears again.
>>They've gone. There's nothing here any more.

'Is there anything online that might tell us where BRIGHTSPRK have gone, or how to find Mr Baird?'

>>Derek Baird has disappeared off the Moncha system grid since giving up his owl baku, and he doesn't seem to have picked up a BRIGHTSPRK halo.

'That's because *no one* uses those,' I scoff.

>>He did say he would have to go into hiding once his secret came out. I bet Moncha want him punished for corporate espionage.

'That makes sense.' I remember how shocked I was when I found out my former companioneering teacher had been a mole for BRIGHTSPRK the whole time he had been working for Moncha Corp. But also I can't help my disappointment. Monica had trusted Mr Baird enough to contact him when she attempted to escape from Eric. He couldn't help her then. Now when she needs him again, he's gone into hiding.

Jinx pulls up a bunch of news stories, projecting them

towards me, showing me scary headlines of what's happened to those suspected of spying. Moncha persecutes them with the full strength of the law. Monica might be okay with people messing with her source code once they own a baku, but she definitely doesn't want them getting their hands on her new proprietary technology.

'Can we talk about this somewhere else? We've still got ages until we need to head to school and I'm freezing.'

>>There's an old public library not far away.

'Okay, great, let's go there.' Anything to get warm. Jinx leads me further uptown, to a pretty building that once belonged to the university. It's now one of the public libraries in Toronto – and they're open twenty-four hours a day. There are way more libraries in the city now than ever before. That was a Monica Chan initiative. She thought it was important for people to have a place to go where they could be with their bakus but also read books.

'One thing I've learned is that you can have access to all the information in the world (as bakus do), but if you don't know how to research then that information is useless. You have to know the right questions to ask. And libraries can teach you how to ask those questions.' Monica Chan said that in one of her television interviews.

Thankfully the heating works inside the library and it's lovely and cosy, kitted out with plenty of comfortable sofas. There are stacks with a constantly shifting rotation of books out front, and huge numbers of other books behind, accessible by baku only.

We find a secluded corner and huddle together. The disappointment of not being able to find Mr Baird sinks into my bones. He was the only person who had been willing to help us before. 'I don't understand why he would have to go into hiding? BRIGHTSPRK were the ones who made him go undercover. Shouldn't they be protecting him?'

>>Maybe putting him into hiding is part of their plan. Have him lie low until the storm passes.

'Well, are there any other BRIGHTSPRK offices nearby where we can leave him a message?'

>>According to my research, there's one north of Bloor Street. But there's no Mr Baird registered as working there. And look at this. He projects a few news stories and a complicated-looking graph. >>This is a live stream of their latest stock price. It's tumbling. No one is buying their halos.

Why would they? I think. Halos are like ... the anti-baku. They're cold and uninteresting, just circles of metal that are worn around the wearer's head in a circle, from ear lobe to ear lobe. Some of the halos are so thin as to be invisible, whereas others can be customized in different colours. They're so very ... functional. It was a gamble for BRIGHTSPRK to offer something so unobtrusive, and so far – it looks like they've failed.

>>They probably can't afford another scandal right now.

'It did seem like Mr Baird was working on his own for a long time. Maybe he couldn't find the support he needed in house.' I chew my bottom lip. 'Doesn't change the fact that we might need all the help we can get at the end of all this.'

There's a little buzz in my pocket. It's Slick. >>According to my Maps data, if you leave now, you will arrive at school on time and won't risk a late detention on your final day before vacation.

'All right, Slick,' I say, standing up from the comfortable sofa.

I look around the library. *Jinx*, I say in my head so that Slick can't overhear. *Do you think that we should look up Lake Baku while we're here?*

>>No — you heard what Paul said. If our search is flagged to Moncha then we'd be in big trouble. They might move Monica before we have the chance to find her.

I look around. All the librarians have little mice bakus, to scurry around the library finding books or restocking the shelves. Even though we're not in official Monchaville, Moncha's influence is everywhere throughout the city. I desperately wish that Mr Baird had left a way for me to get in touch with him.

But since he hasn't ... it looks like me, Zora and Team Tobias are on our own.

PART THREE

THE CHRISTMAS PARTY

CHAPTER TWENTY-TWO

S ATURDAY MORNING COMES, AND ZORA is a nervous wreck on the car ride up to Tobias's family cottage. We're both bundled up in our warmest winter gear. I even dug out a pair of snow pants from the back of my closet that I'd bought second-hand for an ill-fated ski trip last winter.

'I'm not sure this is a good idea,' she says to me, as the driverless car Tobias provided for us speeds along the highway. 'I'm not like you, Lacey – I don't know these people that well, and they're all from Profectus . . .'

'You have no reason to be intimidated – you're a better coder than any of them!' I say.

'It's not just that. I mean, look how far we're driving! Out in the countryside where there might be bears and wolves and stuff? What if we get snowed in? What if I need an emergency energy drink? I can't just pop out to the store. You know I'm a city girl.' She picks at the edge of her nail anxiously. Her eyes dart around the inside of the car, taking in the swish leather interiors, the baku resting places, the giant panoramic windows that show the Toronto cityscape rushing by.

I remember the first time I sat in one of Tobias's family cars. They're top-of-the-line and I doubt Zora has ever been in anything like one before. Linus seems comfortable enough though, nestled into a cosy hole lined with soft microfibre fabric designed to polish baku fur. 'Are you sure that I can't code from home?' she continues. 'This thing can turn around and take me back, right?'

I reach over and grip her hand. 'Zora, remember the update? I need you on this. Right on the front lines. And anyway, I promise you there aren't any wolves up there.'

'Oh yeah? And what about bears.'

I shrug and she starts to make 'Oh hell no,' sounds.

I laugh. 'I've reminded Tobias to stock up with all the top-of-the-line energy drinks.' Something about coders and Red Bull. It's like part of their DNA.

She exhales deeply. 'Okay, if you say so. I guess it will be cool to see the Washingtons' cottage. I bet it's enormous. And Hot Guy has a brother, you say?' She waggles her eyebrows.

I giggle but shush her. I'm not sure if these cars record our conversations but the last thing I want is for Tobias to get wind that we're talking about him and his brother behind his back. His brother is such a touchy subject for him. I still don't feel like I know enough about that relationship – only that the competitiveness between them is extreme.

Zora doesn't stop. 'If he's half as fine as Tobias then maybe this weekend won't be so bad after all.' She grins, but then her face turns more thoughtful as she looks out of the window.

'What is it?'

'You're still *sure* we can trust him on this?' Her deep brown eyes turn to bore into mine.

'Yes, I'm sure,' I say, a little bit annoyed that this is coming up again. I trust Tobias with my life. He was the one who rescued me from the cold. He's the one who showed up every day to visit me in hospital. He's the one who came up with the plan to get us all to Lake Baku. Just because he flipped out for a moment when I suggested his dad might be involved doesn't matter. I have to trust him.

'It's just that ... you know me. How I see things. Something doesn't quite add up in how easily this plan has come together.'

Zora has a point. She does have one of the best analytical minds I know.

I shrug. 'I don't know what to tell you. Maybe everything is coming together for once. And really, what's so out of the ordinary? I mean, all we're doing as far as anyone else is concerned is joining Tobias and his team for a little vacation. His parents host a pre-Christmas party every year.'

'I hope you're right,' she replies, looking doubtful.

The rest of the journey disappears in a flash; the once nightmarish Toronto traffic, eased by the introduction of driverless cars, gives way to long, empty country highways as we wind our way further north, deep into cottage country. We pass by signs for summer camps, partially obscured by

165

ice. Everything is a winter wonderland – pine trees draped in snow as if they are wearing thick fur coats.

After a couple of hours, we take a small turn-off, so discreet that I never would have noticed it. There's no signage of any kind.

I keep my eyes peeled for any hint of the high-tech 'security' that Tobias mentioned. I wish Jinx was in the car with us, but as we don't know what security measures are in place, we decided it was too risky. How he's travelling – or how he's going to get past security – is beyond me. But I trust Jinx.

Then, there's no more time for thinking. Zora and I both gasp at the same time.

The cottage comes into view – but 'cottage' hardly seems like an appropriate word to describe it. Mansion? But it's not like the mansion that Tobias lives in on Companioneers Crescent. Whereas that is a traditional building, all columns and red brick and big bay windows, this is an opus of glass and wood. Somehow, it's designed in a way to complement the scenery all around, the pine trees seemingly blending into the architecture, the wooden beams painted a warm grey to match the bedrock of the Canadian Shield. Multi-tiered decking (all cleared of the snow) wraps around the outside of the building, the banisters themselves then all wrapped with greenery and bright red ribbons for the Christmas season.

'That must be a nightmare to heat,' is all that Zora mutters, but then she catches my eye and we burst into laughter. As we draw closer, we can see that the interior is filled with fairy lights and there's a giant Christmas tree decorated in white and gold beside a huge stone fireplace, with a chimney of grey and white brick that stretches up two storeys. 'Are we travelling to some sort of Christmas movie set?' Zora asks.

I don't know how to respond. I knew that Tobias's family was wealthy – his dad is in the upper echelons of Moncha Corp, after all – but I had no idea that there was *this* much of a disparity between my family and his. I cringe as I wonder what he must think of my crummy condo building and the locker that I spend most of my time in. I mean, my locker is probably smaller than any of the bathrooms in this place. Once, I might have found that inspiring – look what I could achieve if I worked hard enough at Moncha! But now I'm wondering whether the 'utopia' that Monica provides at Monchaville is really everything I've grown up to think it is … or whether it's just another way to placate us just enough so that we don't question the disparity at work. Would the other perks of working for Moncha – the affordable housing, the community amenities, the super clean sidewalks and access to healthcare and good schools and plentiful food – would all that offset the lack of privacy and personal freedom?

And now I get to spend a few days with my boyfriend's impossibly rich and talented parents, who may or may not be involved in Eric Smith's sinister plans. Joy.

However, my eyes light up when I see Tobias standing at the top of the stairs, waiting for us in the warm glow of the front porch. The car pulls around the semi-circular driveway and I get out, waving. But the guy at the top of the stairs doesn't wave back. And then my stomach drops. Now that we're closer, I can see that it's not Tobias at all. That becomes especially obvious when his baku slides out from behind him: a gorgeous black jaguar that looks as if it should belong on a security team – but it's obviously his personal baku.

'Oh my days. Lacey, is that Tobias's brother?'

My cheeks redden with embarrassment as I realize that I was creeping on my boyfriend's brother. But Nathan is undeniably attractive. I take my time getting out of the car, grabbing my backpack from the trunk with deliberate slowness. I pull my hat down low over my forehead, hoping it covers up the fact that I didn't even brush my hair this morning – that's how early we left. Also, the longer I take, the more I hope Nathan will just get bored and leave us to it.

No such luck. I glance up and I can see he's still standing inside the doorway, staring down at us with a look of mild amusement. I curse under my breath, wondering where Tobias and the rest of the team are – to save us from Nathan's scrutiny.

'Slick,' I say, quietly under my breath. 'Send a message to Tobias that we've arrived.'

>>Right away.

Zora, by contrast, is totally star-struck. If she were an anime character, her eyes would be literally bulging from her head. I take the stairs slightly behind her. When we get to the top, though, Nathan addresses me first. 'So, you're the famous Lacey Chu,' he says, stepping out ever-so-slightly so that he blocks the doorway. I wish Jinx were here to fire a little quip into my ear and relax me. I've only got Slick riding on my shoulder, and Linus is tucked into the hood of Zora's jacket. Our bakus pale in comparison to his, and he knows it.

'Hi,' I say, barely choking out the word. Our breath streams out in front of us.

'Well, come on in,' he says, finally stepping aside – but not before giving me an up-and-down appraisal with his eyes. 'It's cold out there. You must be pumped to be here for the convention.'

'Convention? I thought it was a pre-Christmas party?' Zora asks him, her voice betraying the same curiosity (and alarm) that is running through my head. The annual Moncha convention is scheduled for December 27th, as it is every year.

'Didn't you hear on the news?'

'We didn't listen to any on the way up . . .'

'Oh, and I suppose your bakus are too low level to be programmed to give you any breaking news updates.'

I frown. If it was news to do with Moncha Corp then I've definitely set Slick to notify me. He's been silent the entire trip.

Nathan doesn't seem to miss a trick, examining our faces with the continued expression of bemusement. He might look like Tobias from afar, with his close-cropped black hair and rich brown skin, the same tightly muscled body, but he lacks Tobias's natural warmth and kindness. Nathan

169

seems harder around the edges, his jawline sharper, his temperament more quick to laugh, maybe – but I sense that his jokes are on the cruel end of the spectrum. He looks like he not only doesn't suffer fools gladly, but that he'll gladly point out all that fool's faults and not let him (or her) make up for it.

As someone who can sometimes be a fool, it sets me on edge. I instantly dislike him – and it's not just because of the stories Tobias has told me. He seems to relish holding this news over us.

Somehow, Zora seems to be immune to this. Her eyes are still starry as she looks at him. 'So what's going on with the convention?' she asks, pulling her hat off from her head now that we have moved inside the lobby and running her hands over her braids to smooth them out.

'It's been moved up. Now we're going to hear all about the new development on Christmas Eve instead.'

My stomach drops.

'So you'll be here to watch it all,' Nathan continues. 'And not even from the sidelines. The biggest surprise is that Eric has decided to move the announcement here. You girls are going to be right in the heart of the action.'

'Wow, cool,' says Zora. But all I can think about is: what if he's planning to announce the update roll-out at the convention?

Zora nudges me and I remember myself. Nathan doesn't know the real reason we're here. So it would be weird of me not to be excited about this too.

'Oh, uh, that's awesome,' I say, scrambling to make up ground.

Nathan's eyes bore into mine, but thankfully we're saved by a familiar voice.

'You're here!' squeals Ashley. I look up to see the whole team gathered at the railing of a mezzanine balcony above our heads. I grin widely at the sight of them.

Tobias is the first one down the stairs. He rushes over and pulls me into a big hug. 'Sorry we weren't here to meet you,' he says, casting a sidelong glance over to his brother. 'I set up an alert to notify me when you arrived.'

Even though he spoke in a low voice, so that only I could hear him, his brother picks up on it. 'Oh yeah, about that. I thought you would be too busy showing your other friends around so I rerouted the alert to come to Shasta here.'

Tobias glares at his older brother, and I swallow hard. Even though what Nathan has mentioned sounds like such a small thing, it would actually be quite a big deal to hack into the notifications system and switch the permissions around. I'm torn between being impressed and weirded out. Why does he care so much about being first at the door to meet us?

'Well, I'll leave you kids to it,' Nathan says. 'Nice to meet you both.' He winks at Zora (who turns into a puddle on the cottage lobby floor) then clicks his fingers at his baku, who turns around on a dime and follows her owner out of the door.

The tension in the air when Nathan is gone finally releases

and it feels like the first time I've been able to breathe. I look at Tobias, and he can tell that I have a million questions.

'Not here,' he says, answering my first unasked question. 'Follow me upstairs.'

Without any further delays, we head up to the mezzanine. After a quick round of hellos, it's all action stations. Zora and I barely have time to gasp at the beautiful interior before we're ushered into a room that seemingly has no windows at all. 'This is our media room,' says Tobias. Now it begins to make sense – there's a row of comfy sofas and a large blank wall at one end – probably the screen for a projector. 'It's totally soundproof and we can get alerts if anyone is approaching. There's no way that we'll be overheard in here.'

'Okay, brilliant,' I say. 'So what's this about the convention?'

'I know,' says Tobias. 'To be honest, it's thrown everything here into complete turmoil. You should have heard my mom. I almost never see her angry side but she was *fuming* last night. I thought she was going to make us cancel this whole bloody visit up here. Luckily I managed to convince her that maybe having a few extra hands wouldn't be the worst thing in the world ... so apologies in advance if you get roped in to some tasks that you weren't expecting.'

'I've already been made to cut more Christmas cookies than I ever thought I would in my life,' moans Kai.

'You shouldn't have been so good at it, then!' says Ashley, laughing.

'It's not my fault I have such delicate hands,' he replies primly.

Sounds like they've all been having a good time – when what we really need to do is work out how we're going to find Lake Baku.

'Don't worry,' Tobias says, as if he's reading my mind. 'I have a plan.'

CHAPTER TWENTY-THREE

EVERYONE IN THE ROOM LEANS FORWARD, sitting up straighter after lounging on the squishy couches, suddenly alert. This is what we're all here for.

River shifts so that Zora and I can sit down, and we form a semi-circle around Tobias.

Aero spreads his wings and the map shimmers into view. 'This is where we are,' says Tobias. We all lean forward. The cottage is perched right at the edge of a long, thin lake, labelled as Lake Washington.

River lets out a low whistle. 'This is like billionaire cottage country,' he mutters. He's not far wrong either. All around the lake are cottages marked with the names of the richest people in the country. Monica Chan and Eric Smith both have cottages on the map.

'Why is it called Lake Washington if everyone has a cottage here? What makes your family so special?' asks Kai.

'My mom found this place. It was just a bunch of rundown old shacks around the lake before. She designed all the buildings and turned them into luxury cottages.'

'Holy cow – your dad is a top companioneer at Moncha and your mom is an elite level architect?' says Zora. 'Impressive.'

'Thanks,' he says. He looks awkward at all the attention on his family, so I reach out and touch his arm.

'Where's Lake Baku?' I ask.

'Here.' Tobias zooms in on the map, flashing me a grateful smile. Just to the west of Lake Washington is a much smaller body of water. It does appear to say 'Lake Baku', in very teeny tiny writing. Tobias must have really studied this map closely – and thank goodness for his prodigious memory. 'It's about two kilometres from here, if we cut through the woods.'

'The woods?' asks Zora, her voice sounding sceptical. 'Are there like . . . wild animals and stuff in there?'

'Well, it's winter, so there won't be many wild animals. But there will be a lot of snow. Thankfully I think we've got enough winter gear in the basement for all of us. Ever been cross-country skiing before?'

Zora and I exchange a look. We might both be Canadians, but we've never really had much experience of life outside of the city – and apart from a few large parks, there's not a lot of green space. Zora's family has never taken her skiing, and although I went to the Blue Mountains last year with Mom, it was kind of a disaster. The best thing about that trip was warming up at the lodge at the end and having a hot chocolate with extra whipped cream.

She's a coder and I'm an engineer. Neither of us are exactly the typical 'outdoorsy' type. But I grit my teeth. I know I will do whatever it takes.

Zora shakes her head vigorously at Tobias. 'I've never even been on a pair of skis before.'

'Cross-country skiing isn't too difficult to get started ... But I do think we'll need a team based here, in the cottage, to help guide us and keep things on track in case something goes wrong at Lake Baku. We don't exactly know what we'll find there.'

Zora raises her hand. 'I'll volunteer for that.'

River does as well. 'Me too, man. I'm not really one for the old Nordic style, if you catch my drift.' He gives us all an exaggerated wink and Ashley tuts and rolls her eyes. Zora raises her eyebrows in alarm.

'He's being a jerk,' says Ashley. 'Nordic style is just another name for cross-country skiing.'

'Oooh, okay,' says Zora, looking relieved.

'So that's sorted. You two will be running point from here, inside the media room. We'll all stream directly from our bakus to the big screen here.' Aero squawks, and there's movement from the far end of the room. The wall opens out to reveal a floor-to-ceiling television screen. 'Then Lacey, Ashley, Kai and I will head to where we think Lake Baku is.'

'Awesome. I can start work coding up some trackers so that we can all make sure we know where we are – in case you need to split up.' Zora's in her element now. She moves to the table in the middle of the room. Linus plugs into the huge screen, bringing up Zora's preferred coding platform. Then, Linus projects a keyboard on to the surface in front of Zora, and her fingers soon send code flying across the screen.

River comes and sits next to her. Within seconds, they have recent satellite imagery of the region up on the big screen. Zora zooms over to where Lake Baku is indicated on Aero's map. 'Huh, this is strange,' Zora says.

'What is it?'

'Look – the area where Lake Baku is on your old map . . . it's completely blurred out on *this* map.' She types a string of code. 'Sometimes this can work to layer old images on top of the blurred one to try and get it to be unblurred . . . nope, no luck. We're not going to get anything new out of the satellite imagery.'

'Well, Paul did say it was top secret.' I exhale deeply. 'Okay, so the convention is scheduled for two days away. When can we get going to Lake Baku?'

A smile tugs at the corner of Tobias's mouth. 'Are you ready to go now?'

CHAPTER TWENTY-FOUR

OWN IN THE BASEMENT OF THE cottage, there's so much sporting equipment it looks like a branch of a mountain equipment store. There are pairs of skis in all sorts of shapes and sizes but I head towards the shape of skis that look familiar to me from my brief time on a mountain.

'Uhh, those are downhill skis,' says Tobias, gently guiding me away. He points instead to some skis that are tall, long and skinny. 'These are for cross-country.'

I grimace. They look intimidatingly long. How on earth are you supposed to turn in those?

'Don't worry, if you can't get used to it then Oka can help to pull you,' Kai says. I check his face for sarcasm or mockery, but it seems to be a genuine offer. His baku is a husky, after all. Maybe additional horsepower is one of the additional benefits of having a level 3 baku.

'Thanks,' I say.

'Come on, let's find a pair of boots that fit you,' says Tobias, dragging out a box of slim boots, much less cumbersome than downhill ski boots, from beneath the bench.

'Holy cow, that's a lot of spare equipment,' I say, when Tobias happens upon boots that are a perfect size for me.

He grins. 'We have a lot of guests who come up here; we like to have a range of equipment so no one is left out.'

'Benefits of the super-rich,' mutters Kai. But he does up his boots with expert flair, as if this is far from his first time.

Ashley seems comfortable too, selecting her skis with an expert eye.

'Have you done this before?' I ask Ashley.

'Yeah, my family have a cottage in the Gatineau, near Ottawa, where we go skiing sometimes too. Nowhere near as nice as this place, of course.' She winks at me.

'Are you going back there for Christmas Day?'

'If I'm no longer needed here,' she says, with a firm nod.

Her determination warms me. We're all in this together.

Tobias speaks up. 'We'll use Aero as a drone, to help guide us. He's got the map and coordinates set on his internal guidance system. I'm not a hundred per cent convinced that we're going to find anything – I've been out that way before, and I've never seen anything that could remotely be considered a test centre – but we'll see what we find.'

Hearing Tobias's scepticism makes me cringe inside, and long for Jinx. I need a supportive ear right now. Presuming he was able to find a way through the security, he should be back in touch again soon – but I have no way of knowing whether he'll be successful. I just have to trust him.

'Oh, Tobias, are you taking your friends out for a little jaunt? Don't forget to be back for the party later.' We look up to see Tobias's mother standing at the top of the basement stairs, dressed in a chic white sweater and long cream trousers, contrasting beautifully against her dark skin. She looks like a supermodel rather than someone's mom.

'No problem, Mom. We'll be back to help set up.'

'Thank you, sweetheart.'

Tobias gestures at me to follow him. My breath immediately hitches in my chest. In all the frantic worry about the convention and finding Lake Baku, I'd forgotten I would be meeting Tobias's parents. It's especially awkward because I'm still not sure what we are – boyfriend and girlfriend? Just friends with potential for something more if life goes back to normal?

One thing's for sure: he won't want to date me if I end up updated.

All these thoughts race through my head even as my feet carry me towards Tobias and up the stairs to meet his mom. Thankfully, she gives me a warm smile that makes me feel a lot more at ease. We step out into the gorgeous atrium, and Tobias puts his hand on the small of my back.

'Mom, this is Lacey.'

'Nice to meet you,' I say, extending my hand. 'Thank you so much for inviting us up to your cottage. It's absolutely beautiful.'

She clasps it in both her neatly manicured hands. 'My pleasure. And so pleased to meet you, Lacey! We've heard a lot about you from Tobias here.'

Immediately I blush. I can't believe that Tobias has told his mom about me. She doesn't let go of my hand, even as she continues talking. 'And I take it you've recovered completely? Tobias told me about your hospital stay. So brave going back out into the cold now. You take care of her.' She directs that last part at Tobias, while patting my hand gently.

'I will, Mom,' he says. 'But we want to get out while the snow is still fresh . . .'

'All right, I get the hint.' Before unclasping my hand, she pulls me in a bit closer. She smiles at me with her perfect, sparkling white teeth. 'And don't worry, Lacey, I'll make sure you have a front-row seat to the action for the convention.'

I stifle the wave of fear that comes over me and manage to stutter out my thanks.

'Well done,' whispers Tobias to me as we head back downstairs to the basement. 'My mom can be kind of . . . intense.'

I shake my head. 'She's amazing,' I say, and I mean it. I think about all the buildings she's designed, all the impressive homes she's built. Has she ever had her ambition curbed, or was she allowed to pursue her dreams? I doubt that she would allow it. It makes me sad for my mom. She let go of her dreams, and now she's paid the ultimate price for it by being updated out of her ambitions.

Tobias helps me do up the fastenings on the ski boots. They have a thick sole with hard pieces of plastic against the toe, which I assume will click into the bindings. He measures a couple of skis against my height, handing me a lightweight pair. 'These should work.'

'Great,' I say, with far more confidence than I feel.

When we're all geared up and ready to go, Tobias addresses us as a group. 'This is the scouting mission,' Tobias says. 'We have a rough idea of where Lake Baku should be, but we don't know what we're going to find. Set your bakus to record the whole time.'

I nod and move Slick up to a special baku pouch in the hood of my jacket, so that he can record things more easily. We throw our skis over our shoulders and march outside.

>>The temperature is -8°C, Slick chirrups in my ear as we step outside.

I zip my jacket right up to my chin, then pull a bright red knitted hat with a bobble at the top over my ears. We step into the skis and almost straight away I wobble on the narrow surface. Tobias grabs my arm to steady me and hands me a couple of poles. 'This will make it easier.'

And it does. We arrange ourselves in single file to leave the cottage, Tobias, Ashley and Kai all carrying large backpacks filled with supplies, drinks and extra layers in case we get cold. I've been relieved of needing a backpack this time, concentrating instead on my cross-country skiing technique. Once I get the hang of it, pushing out one leg and sliding the other to meet it, it becomes much easier – almost fun. I follow in the tracks laid for me by Tobias, and my skis run smoothly in his path. It's not long until my body warms up enough that I drag the hat from my head and stuff it into my pocket. My cheeks feel rosy with warmth, and I find myself smiling despite myself.

The beauty of having a cottage – even a fancy one – is that within a few paces we are almost completely engulfed in the Canadian wilderness. Snow balances precariously on branches making snow ghosts of the trees, the ground all around us sparkling and shimmering, carpeted in unbroken white. There are tracks in the ground from deer and birds braving the winter, but mostly it's a serene and unspoiled place. The only sound comes from the heavy breathing of my companions and the crackle of ice breaking as the temperature warms up ever so slightly.

That is, until the snow beneath my feet appears to vibrate. Alarmed, I ask Slick to connect me to Zora. 'Are you seeing this? What's happening? Do they get earthquakes in this part of Canada?'

'See, this is why I didn't want to go outside!' I hear her voice in my ear, and it's immediately comforting. 'You okay? You sound like you're panting. And don't worry – no earthquake activity in your area.'

'Of course I'm panting, this cross-country skiing thing is hard work!' The snow vibrates even more fiercely now, and it's accompanied by the sound of a loud engine. 'Oh, not an earthquake after all,' I say.

'Turn your video so I can see,' says Zora in my ear.

We all come to a stop as the roar draws closer. I turn around, adjusting my hood so that Slick – and therefore Zora – gets a better view.

There, on the fanciest snowmobile I've ever seen, is Nathan. Sitting behind him is a girl in a faux-fur hooded jacket and big sunglasses, gripping tightly to his waist. There's a compartment for both their bakus underneath their legs, and the machine appears to glide across the snow with effortless grace – almost like it's hovering over the snow rather than sliding. He skids up beside us, sending a shower of snow over our heads.

'How quaint – enjoying your cross-country outing?'

'Leave us alone, Nathan,' says Tobias, through gritted teeth.

I have a sudden fear that Nathan is going to follow us through the woods. There's no way we'll be able to find Lake Baku if that is the case.

To my relief, the girl behind him has other plans. 'Come on, Nate, I thought we were going somewhere we could be alone?'

'Don't worry; we're not staying long. Just wanted to say hi to my little bro. Don't get into any trouble, now.' With that, he revs his engine, spraying us with snow again, and then he disappears in the opposite direction.

I breathe a sigh of relief. 'Who was that girl and how do I kill her?' says Zora in my ear, making me giggle. I feel bad for Tobias, though, having to deal with such a show-off older brother.

'Was that one of the new hovercraft-snowmobiles? So cool,' I hear Kai whisper to Ashley.

I turn to Tobias, trying to catch his eye, but he studiously avoids my gaze, his jaw set in a firm line.

We get moving again, at first travelling along what looks like well-used paths, following close to the shoreline of Lake Washington. But on Aero's signal, we deviate deeper into the forest, Tobias forging ahead to cut the track.

Aero stops after we've been skimming through the forest for about half an hour. 'We'd better be getting a hot chocolate after this,' grumbles Kai, from behind me.

I'm glad that we get to stop, my breath coming heavier now, leaving my throat in streams of steamy air. We've had a couple of fun downhill slides and tiresome uphill slogs, where I've had to turn my skis into a V-shape and make my way up in a cumbersome manner. I haven't got the hang of it, and it takes me twice as long as everyone else. I feel drained, and I'm grateful when Ashley passes me over some hot tea in a flask.

Tobias calls Aero down from the branch, and he lands on his arm. I take a moment to marvel at the incredible engineering of the eagle baku. I'm amazed at how well he is able to function in the extreme cold. It's as if Moncha Corp have thought of everything. Even the precipitation doesn't bother him. They would need so much testing to make it work.

Lake Baku.

They'd need that kind of extensive practice ground. It makes total sense, even though I wouldn't have thought about it in a million years.

'That's weird,' says Tobias. 'According to the map, we should be able to see Lake Baku right now.' We take a

185

moment to look around but the scenery hasn't changed from the thick line of forest spreading off into the distance. There's certainly no sign of a lake or of any buildings that could be the secret home of Moncha Corp's experimentation.

'This is ridiculous – there's nothing here!' Kai rips his hat off his head in frustration.

Tobias frowns, his brow furrowing in frustration. 'But this is exactly where the map says . . .'

'You mean the map that no longer exists, that you have dragged up from your baku's memory files? Maybe that was just a decoy . . . or a plan that never made it into existence? Like old blueprints for something that was never actually made. I mean, Lacey is the only one who saw the street beneath Moncha HQ. When you showed us the live stream, it was totally empty.'

'It existed,' I say, through gritted teeth.

'I believe you,' says Ashley, scowling at Kai.

>>It's okay. Let me handle this.

A slinky black figure leaps out from the underbrush and bounds over until he's sitting on my skis. 'Jinx!' I say.

The sight of him lifts all of our spirits, and I can feel that the group's mood vastly improves. Even Kai has a big grin on his face. Now that Jinx is here, it feels like the impossible has a chance at being made possible.

And that's exactly what he does for us.

>>It took me some time to bypass the security to the area. But I got the idea from Paul's baku George.

I disconnected from the Moncha cloud completely. But
you have to see this — come with me.

He flicks his tail and moves towards the thick line of trees.
But there doesn't look like there's a way through for us – not
with our skis. I unclick myself from my bindings and try to
follow Jinx. But the trees are so tightly packed, I can't find a
way through. I hesitate.

>>What are you waiting for?

I can't even see him any more, the trees are so thick, it
seems impassable. 'Hang on, let me see if I can get around . . .'

But the snow here is so deep, I sink down almost to my
knees as I try to take a step forward. I hear a snort of laughter
from Kai, and I hate to think how comical I look trying to
plough my way through the snow. He reaches out a strong
arm to me, and I gratefully use it to lift myself back on to the
path. Jinx is frustratingly out of reach.

>>You can make it through.

'I can't! There's no way.'

>>Send Oka and Aero through the trees — and tell
them to keep their cameras on. Watch on Jupiter.

When I relay this command from Jinx, Kai and Tobias
both look at me with scepticism. 'Slick is the baku who
should go through there – Oka is huge, he's not going to fit
through the trees.'

'I think . . . I think we have to trust Jinx,' I say.

'Okay,' Tobias nods. 'Aero – go meet Jinx.'

We all cringe as Aero obeys the command, expecting him
to crash into the branches. His alerts are going wild, warning

187

Tobias not to go in that direction. Yet, the bakus obey any order that their owner gives, so Aero behaves without questioning. I can't bear to look, so I watch the feed stream from Jupiter's back.

But there's no crash. Aero swoops straight through the trees.

And the feed from his camera goes completely blank. We lose sight of the eagle baku completely.

'What's happened?' says Tobias, panicking.

'Oka, go after him,' says Kai almost immediately. The same thing happens – Oka runs at the line of trees but passes through them safely – and disappears from view.

>>Now you'd better follow us, don't you think? There's a tinge of amusement in his tone.

He doesn't have to ask me twice. Feeling bolder than I have done in months, I stride through the path I created in the snow, but then I keep going, walking *through* the trees. I close my eyes, expecting to end up with a face full of bark. But I don't. I move swiftly through to the other side.

I hear the clicking of bindings, Tobias, Kai and Ashley obviously desperate to follow.

And I can't wait for them to arrive. Because what I'm looking at is almost unbelievable.

I'm staring at an enormous curved wall, as tall as the eye can see. It stretches on for miles either side of us. How could we have not seen this, from the road, from the windows of Tobias's house …? I reach out, until my fingertips almost touch it, but they don't – hovering just above the surface.

'Whoa,' says Tobias, as he pulls up behind me.

It looks like we've found Lake Baku. There's just one problem.

I place my palm down flat on the opaque wall. It's solid. There's absolutely no way through.

CHAPTER TWENTY-FIVE

'EXPLAIN TO ME AGAIN,' ZORA SAYS, after a long pause. She exchanges a look with River. We spent a couple of hours at the wall, trying and failing to find a way in. Now that we're back at the cottage, we're relaying the story to Zora and River. They believe us, but they're struggling to understand what it was exactly we saw.

Because it sounds totally fake. Like we've decided to play an elaborate practical joke on the two who had been left behind.

It doesn't help that we don't have any proof. The moment we stepped through that illusion barrier of trees, the cameras on all our bakus stopped working. We can only relate what we've seen with our own eyes, without any video evidence.

'We found Lake Baku,' says Ashley.

'It's a friggin' enormous dome,' says Kai.

'But we can't see what's inside the dome,' I say. I alternate between elation and fear, my emotions swinging wildly. I can't believe we've found Lake Baku. That means Monica might be close by . . .

My teeth chatter with nervous energy, and I find myself pacing around the room.

Zora and River blink almost in synchronicity, staring at us in turn. 'So just over there, there's a big dome?' River asks. He points in the direction we walked, where all that is visible is a blanket of trees.

'Yup,' Kai replies. 'And it looked like it could cover a huge surface area. So, who knows what is inside it?'

'Did you see anyone around?' Zora asks.

'No one,' I reply. 'But this has got to be the right place. Why else would they go through so much trouble to hide it? All that technology used to disguise it . . . All we have to do is figure out a way in before the convention.'

'So . . . before tomorrow?' says Zora.

'Um, yeah. Before tomorrow evening at least.' I glance over at Tobias, who still hasn't said a word. He's stroking Aero's back, lost in concentration.

A little face wriggles its way up out of my jacket.

'Jinx!' Zora squeals. I grin – his presence is reassuring, to the others as much as me. 'But . . . how is it safe for him to be here?' She looks up at me.

'He's disconnected himself from the Moncha cloud – for now, he can't access it, but they can't access him either.'

Jinx squirms all the way out and leaps from my arms, then dashes over to where Zora is sitting down. He and Linus curl up around each other and my heart warms.

'And we have to get through the party first,' reminds Ashley.

'That's right. We need to give Jinx a makeover ... in case Eric recognizes him,' I say.

>>A temporary one, says Jinx, in a warning tone.

'You'll just have to stick close to people so you blend in with the other bakus.'

>>Don't you worry about me. I can blend in when I need to.

I grimace. 'Yeah, right.'

>>I can! But in the meantime, I think you're going to need this . . .

He flicks his tail, this time in the direction of the television screen, and immediately a picture of the dome is displayed on the screen. Both Zora and River lean back in their chairs. 'Whoa,' they say, at the same time.

>>I know, I'm brilliant, says Jinx.

Jinx, why didn't you show this to us earlier?

>>I quite enjoyed watching you all try to explain it.

I stick my tongue out at my annoying friend.

'So it *is* real,' says River, rubbing his hands together. 'Now we can get to work on figuring a way into that place.'

'You weren't joking after all,' says Zora. 'It's exactly like you said ... it's huge.'

'Looks like there's a door here of some kind ...' River says, manipulating the image.

'What, where?' asks Kai. I look up sharply too. We definitely didn't see a door when we were on the ground.

192

But River zooms in on the edge of the photograph that Jinx has taken. There's a very thin line down the edge of the dome, almost like a distortion.

>>Ah, good. If we get close enough then I'll be able to access the security and shut it down for a few minutes while you pass through. It's not too sophisticated.

'How can you do that if you're disconnected from the Moncha cloud?' I ask Jinx.

But it seems like Zora's way ahead of me. 'If none of the satellites are able to see it, and the maps and GPS and everything go all skewy and you say that there's some kind of illusion barrier on it ... that must mean they're blocking any sort of signal from entering.'

'That sounds right,' I say.

'Well, that will also mean that they're blocking any signals from coming out, too.'

'Okay ...' I say, not following Zora's logic.

But River does. 'Oh, right! If there are no signals going out, then that means it will be difficult to have some sort of alarm. All the security will probably be hard-wired somehow.'

'And hard-wiring can be hacked.'

>>Exactly, says Jinx.

Not for the first time, I'm glad there are much smarter people in the room than me. There's no way I'd be able to do this on my own.

'How did I not know about this?' Tobias's eyes are wide, his voice quiet. He's said very little since we returned from

Lake Baku. 'I've been along that trail more times than I can remember. I thought I'd explored all around here. But we never went in that direction. It was always impassable ... blocked off. I never thought ...'

>>It's not his fault, Jinx tells me. >>It was designed that way. Designed so that no one would be able to find it — no baku GPS would ever lead there. in fact, as you saw, everything is designed to lead away from there.

I swallow, glancing at Tobias as he struggles to process the information. It's looking more and more likely that something seriously shady is going on. I know the feeling. I'm struggling too. But while I have the benefit of distance, Tobias and his family are directly involved.

His dad, who he idolizes.

His brother, who he competes with.

Does his mother know too? She's an architect. Maybe she helped to design Lake Baku?

'Hey, Tobias,' I say. 'Can you show me where the bathroom is?'

'Oh, sure ...' He answers as if he's in some kind of trance, and I can see the others' eyes following us as we leave.

'It's just down here,' he says, but I don't walk with him. Instead, I take his hand and lead him in the opposite direction. We walk towards the vast pyramid-shaped window, which looks out over the lake. There's soft snow falling outside: serene, beautiful and calming.

'Are you okay?' I ask him, when we're out of earshot of

the others. We lean against the window, our foreheads nearly touching.

'Do you think ... do you think my whole family knows the truth and they've just been keeping it from me?'

'I don't know,' I say, honestly. 'But if they do know, they probably want to protect you. Let you focus on your studies while you're at Profectus.'

'But what if they're just waiting to see if I'm worthy of knowing?'

I put my hand over his. 'You're amazing at everything you do, Tobias. You don't know the extent of Eric Smith's manipulation. They might be desperate to tell you everything, but they can't.'

He pulls away from my touch, his hands closing into fists. 'What if I'm not good enough to join their inner circle, Lacey? I already lost the Baku Battles.'

'That doesn't mean anything ...'

He stares at me. 'What if I become one of the employees who are "updated", just like your mom.'

I pause for a moment. Then I shake my head. 'You don't have to worry about that.'

'Why not?'

'Because *no one* is going to be like that,' I say fiercely. 'We're going to make sure of it. No matter how clever or how ambitious or how ordinary anyone is – no one deserves to have their choices taken away from them. We're going to stop it.'

Aero shimmers with a notification. 'Oh my god,' says Tobias.

'What is it?' I ask, alarmed by his state of panic.

'I didn't realize how late it is. We'd better get ready for the party. If we don't . . . my mom will make sure we're not alive to see tomorrow.'

CHAPTER TWENTY-SIX

'I S THIS THE ONLY THING YOU BROUGHT TO wear?'

Zora picks a black corduroy pinafore dress up out of my suitcase, wrinkling her nose as she holds it out, as if it smells.

I grab it out of her hands. 'Yeah, what's wrong with it? With my maroon sweater underneath? I thought it might look cute ...' I hold it up against myself and stare in the mirror. Zora and I are in one of the numerous bedrooms in the cottage, balancing on the edge of a massive, bigger-than-king-size bed. The style is definitely winter country charm, with furry blankets and plaid-covered throw pillows neatly stacked across the bed.

>>Ah, what every fifteen-year-old girl wants . . . to look like a five-year-old at her boyfriend's parents' Christmas party. Jinx leaps up on to the covers next to Zora. They both tilt their heads to one side at the same time, judging me.

'All right, I get it!' I say, and throw the dress over Jinx's head. He leaps out of the way just in time.

197

Then I sigh and sit down next to Zora. 'What am I going to do? I have no idea what to wear to a full-on, formal Christmas party.'

'Don't worry, I'm not exactly prepped for this level of ...' She gestures around us. 'What do you even call this anyway? Richness doesn't seem to cover it. Wealth? Glamour? Extravagance? At least I'm not the one who's trying to impress the parents. Although Tobias's brother is fine *as*.'

I drop back on to the bed, my head bouncing against the fluffy mattress. Everything is so luxurious and comfortable. But still, I groan. 'Don't remind me.'

'Ladies, I think I might have a solution.'

I sit bolt upright again, and turn to the voice that has just appeared in the doorway. It's Ashley, and over her arm are several sparkly, shimmery dresses. Jupiter comes bounding in, and he leaps up on to the bed, so that all our bakus are sitting together in a row.

I stand up and take a few dresses from Ashley's overloaded arm, admiring the richness of the fabrics. Already I can see they're far more appropriate to wear to this Christmas party than anything Zora and I would have, even in our wardrobes back home. Even Z, who isn't the most fashion-forward individual, gasps as she looks at what's on offer.

'Where did you get all of these?'

Ashley cringes. 'Would you think less of me if I told you I brought them myself? I'm horrible at knowing what to wear so I always bring a ton of options.'

'What, you mean these are all yours?'

'Yep. And I know you're a lot taller than me, Lacey, but I think we might have something that can work. Some of my midi-dresses would probably look mini on you!'

I shrug. 'Anything has to be better than what I have to wear!'

We take turns trying dresses on – some are ridiculously short on me and some look just plain ridiculous, but it turns out there is a midi-dress that suits me: a silvery A-line with a hem that hits Ashley mid-shin and me just above the knee. It has whisper-thin spaghetti straps that make me feel self-conscious about my bony shoulders, and even though it's cosy and warm inside the cottage, I'm worried that I'm going to be cold.

'I'll be right back.' I take myself away into the bathroom, shutting the door behind me. I lean down on the marble countertops, the cool surface chilling my palms. It feels nice. I stare up at myself, through a layer of make-up thicker than I normally wear – expertly applied by Ashley. Zora has braided my dark hair back off my face, a few wispy strands of baby hair slipping out at my temples. My unruly eyebrows aren't tamed, but the cat-eye flick that Ashley has given me accentuates the shape of my eyes. She's put a touch of glitter at the corners, highlighting the sparkle in my dress. It actually looks pretty.

I wish I could enjoy it.

>>We'll get in the dome tomorrow — don't worry. Step one is done: Find Lake Baku. You should be happy.

I almost jump out of my skin – I hadn't realized that Jinx had slipped into the bathroom alongside me. He looks so strange in his new skin, like an avatar gone wrong. River – who is surprisingly creative – has changed the colour of his black metallic fur to that of a silvery-grey. When other people look at him, they see him as a different cat baku. An ordinary one.

>>You couldn't have thought of a more original code name than Whiskers?

'Whiskers is cute!' I say, quickly trying to rearrange my expression.

>>And I look like I'm made of tinsel. He bristles his back, raising his shiny new silver hackles.

I can't help it; the image immediately makes me snort with laughter. Jinx shoots me a piercing glare, but I can't stop – instead, I scoop him up in my arms and twirl him around the bathroom. Jinx always knows how to make me smile, even when I'm feeling down.

'At least we match,' I whisper to him, as I bury my face into his soft electronic fur. 'And if I didn't know it was you . . . I'd be fooled. You look exactly like any other generic cat baku.' No wonder he hates it so much.

>>Take it back!

I laugh. 'Okay! Not generic then. You still look handsome. Just . . . with extra sparkle.

>>Better.

He jumps out of my arms and sashays towards the door.
>>Come on, we can't stay in the bathroom for ever. Let's get this party over and done with.

My thoughts exactly.

CHAPTER TWENTY-SEVEN

'WOW, LACEY, YOU LOOK AMAZING!' says Zora, as I step out of the bathroom. 'I don't think I've ever seen you in a dress like that before!'

'Beats the pink frilly dress I wore to junior prom, doesn't it?'

'You're telling me!'

She's standing halfway behind the wardrobe door, hiding most of her front, so I can't see what she's wearing. 'What about you?'

She steps out reluctantly, wearing a dress the colour of sunsets and autumn leaves – so incongruous in this Christmas season but against her dark skin it pops like fire.

My jaw actually drops, and it takes me a few seconds to recover.

'Doesn't she look great?' Ashley says, beaming with pride. She looks gorgeous too, in a pale blue mini-dress, her blonde hair in soft waves.

'Zora, you look like … like actual flames! Linus, take a

picture.' Linus snaps a photo as Zora strikes a pose. 'I should send this to your sisters!'

'You dare!' Zora shrieks.

'They'll go nuts,' I explain to Ashley's confused face. 'They're always trying to get her to dress up in beautiful dresses and she always refuses.' Then I look over to Zora, raising my eyebrow. 'Hmm, what makes you so keen to do it this time?'

Zora's lips scrunch up into a pout. 'None of your business,' she says, with a laugh in her eyes.

'Yeah, right! She has a crush!' Then immediately I realize that she must be dressing up for Nathan ... and the realization deflates my excitement. Luckily Zora doesn't notice as she's too busy throwing a pillow at my head. I duck, and Ashley giggles uncontrollably. Then she looks down at her watch and exclaims in surprise.

'We'd better get down to the party – people are going to be wondering where we are!'

'Let's go,' I reply. *Do you think I look ready?* I ask Jinx.

>>As you'll ever be. I'll roam the perimeter, but if you need anything, I'll be there.

Thank you.

I know the finishing touch that is missing, though. Slick. He's plugged into the mains, charging in secret so that no one asks why I don't have him leashed up. I swallow, steeling myself before picking him up again and placing him on my shoulder.

>>Anything you need from me, Lacey? Are you sure you don't want to update? he asks again.

He sounds so innocent, but I can't help the little shiver that runs through me.

I have an urge to see Tobias and find out the game plan. This kind of partying, networking, whatever it is – it's so not me. I want to be somewhere quiet, where I can work on the plan for tomorrow, where I can tinker with something, do something with my itchy hands. I wring my fingers together, flexing and bending them, until Zora notices and reaches out to grab one of them. 'You need to act normal,' she whispers to me. I catch her eye and nod. 'Normal' is not 'normal' for me, but I know that I can act it for a day.

And Jinx will be in the room too, in his strange disguise. Not too much can go wrong with him there.

We step out on to the landing, and immediately we are hit with a wave of noise. It's surprisingly loud for a party made up only of people talking, and my anxiety rises as I realize just how big the crowd is.

>>The more people there are, the easier it will be to blend in — and you'll be less likely to bump into Eric or Carter Smith.

That's true, I think, grateful for Jinx's grounding words.

A string quartet plays a fancy version of 'Jingle Bells' and is only just audible above the noise of the chatter and clinking of glasses. From the mezzanine balcony, we finally get a view of the whole party. And *what* a party. Bakus and people mix, along with flutes of champagne that sparkle with their contents. The lighting is warm, twinkle lights draped wherever there is space, creating an atmosphere that looks as if the party is surrounded by stars.

I scan the crowd. Then, I drop my eyes. I realize that I've been looking for Monica. A part of me still believes that maybe this is all a mistake – that she's not being imprisoned against her will any more, that someone *else* from inside the company could have freed her – that all of this doesn't have to rest on the shoulders of me and my friends.

Alas, there's no sign of her.

'Holy bakus,' Zora says from beside me.

I'm awed too. This must be the biggest gathering of level 4 and 5 bakus that I've ever seen. I wonder if some of these are even another level above what I even knew was out there – some of them are so incredible. In the middle of the party is someone with a full-sized *horse* baku – so incredibly impractical, unwieldy, but also amazing. I wonder if they could ride it off into the sunset? It's certainly an attention-grabbing accessory – people are gathered around them to take a look.

For the most part, though, the bakus are more 'traditional' but still jaw-dropping. There are plenty of big cats roaming around at foot-level, and lots of exotic creatures like monkeys and a fair few large reptiles. A few birds are circling around, taking a video of the crowd. I'm sure this is going to make the gossip blogs go wild.

Through the chaos, I try to pick out the people that I'm looking for.

My breath hitches as I catch sight of Eric – his red panda baku draped around his neck.

204

>>Breathe, Lacey.

But what if he recognizes you? This is too dangerous. We should leave.

>>We should stay. He knows you are here. It will be far more suspicious if you don't make an appearance with Slick.

I tear my eyes away from Eric, and instead, I find Tobias – his golden eagle standing out above even the incredible level 4 and 5 bakus of the rest of the crowd. Aero is one of a kind.

'Might as well join the fray, huh? Those hors d'oeuvres look amazing,' says Ashley.

And they do. There are trays of miniature Christmas food from around the world being passed around, from little Yorkshire puddings filled with roast turkey and gravy, tiny slices of Tourtière, bowls of poutine with cardboard forks and Nigerian meat pies stuffed with potatoes and carrots and minced meat. There are little mince pies as well (the British kind, with preserved fruit and sugar), and Christmas cookies galore on an elaborate buffet table at the back.

My mom would have died and gone to cooking heaven if she could have been here. Or maybe not any more . . . I want her to be back in the state of mind where she could enjoy this type of feasting again.

We walk down the stairs and, as I move my way through the crowd, I hold my breath. I know it's stupid, but I feel so small and out of place, it's like I don't even deserve to breathe the same air as these people. I'm sure that I recognize a lot of them from my school textbooks and from the documentaries

I've watched about Moncha Corp – and isn't that the mayor? And even the prime minister over there? Oh my god, I'm at a party with the leader of the country, on Christmas Eve Eve. I have to pinch myself.

>>I can tell you who any party guest is, says Slick in my ear.

'What?' I whisper to him.

>>One of the prerequisites of accepting an invitation to this party is that you enable yourself to be identified. So I have a list of everyone here and I can name them for you.

'So who is that over there?'

>>Canadian prime minister Mr Alain Cartier.

I breathe out through my teeth. I was right. 'Wow. Neat trick, Slick. I suppose that must be helpful to all these people so that they don't forget the name of someone important.'

Once again, I lift my head and see Aero on the far side of the room. I want to get to Tobias, to have him see me in my pretty dress. He's never seen me in anything like this before, and I have butterflies of excitement in my tummy.

I spin around to walk in his direction – and too late, Slick chirrups a name in my ear.

Too late, because I know exactly who I'm walking towards – I don't need the baku to fill me in.

>>Stay calm, Lacey. Remember, he doesn't know that I'm here. I hear Jinx's voice, and I take several deep breaths.

Then I hold my head high as Eric Smith approaches. His suit is perfectly designed to integrate his baku, so that his panda's red, bushy tail with a triangle of white at the end curves over the lapel of his jacket, tailored to be there. His eyes appear to light up as he sees me, which makes me feel nervous. I have to control my expressions, though – I could quite easily feel a sense of awe or admiration but the overriding sense is of disgust. *Remember what he's done, Lacey.* I just wish I didn't get so overwhelmed by the awesome tech.

'Lacey,' he says, pausing in front of me. 'What a surprise to see you here – I didn't realize you were still in such close contact with your classmates after you unfortunately had to leave Profectus.'

I swallow, carefully maintaining eye contact even though I want nothing more than to run away. 'Thankfully my invitation to Tobias's annual Christmas cottage celebration didn't require having a level 3 baku,' I reply.

His eyes tighten, losing some of their pleasure at my sass. 'Ah yes, and is that him?' He gestures to Slick, who is sitting docilely on my shoulder.

'Yes – a level 1 scarab beetle.'

'An excellent choice. And have you been keeping him up-to-date?'

I nod automatically.

'Good, good,' he replies. The tension in his shoulders drops, and he grabs an hors d'oeuvre from a passing tray. 'Got to make sure you never miss an update or else you risk that little baku malfunctioning. This is much better for you – I'm sure you will be happy this way. Enjoy the convention, won't you?'

He moves on, swept away by the crowd, who are all clamouring to meet him. Well, in the way that posh people clamour – slowly circling until it becomes appropriate for them to swoop in. These kinds of parties always give me the creeps. It seems like lots of people are having interesting conversations, but then you look and see that both parties are actually looking *behind* their heads, over their shoulders, to see if there's someone they could possibly have a more interesting conversation with. It's all so inauthentic and fake.

The visible sigh of relief at having Eric believe I've been 'updated' fills me with a strange warmth of pride. Eric Smith is still afraid of me. Eric Smith, acting CEO of Moncha Corp, is afraid of *me*. A fifteen-year-old. A nobody – just somebody who happened to have my eyes on him at the wrong (or the right) time. I straighten my spine. It's going to take more than a dodgy update to keep me down.

But behind Eric is someone standing there, who only has eyes for me. Not Tobias – unfortunately, the eyes are nowhere near that kind. Instead, they're looking at me with an expression of disdain and vague amusement.

Carter Smith.

Jinx is in my head again. >>Keep your cool. He's going to look to get a rise out of you, but he won't be able to because you're supposedly updated, remember? Just pretend that you are perfectly happy and content where you are. Bore him with whatever you have to — talk about St Agnes.

Got it.

208

I try not to change my expression from calm and serene. I know I must look like a spaced-out weirdo – but Carter's opinion is one that I really could not care less about.

His boar comes snuffling up first, and I try my hardest not to recoil.

'Lacey ... enjoying your few days mingling in the big leagues?'

'Yes, thank you, Carter, it's lovely to be here,' I say, my tone bland.

He tilts his head and pouts in mock pity. I try not to change my expression. 'All this must be way over your head now, mustn't it? It's a shame for you – if you hadn't been so intent on getting that mangy cat baku of yours back, you might have actually had a shot at working in Moncha HQ. My dad was impressed by you, for whatever reason. And yet you threw it all away and now you'll just end up working in the call centre, like your mom ... "Hello, Moncha customer service, how can I help you?"' he says, in a mocking tone.

I grit my teeth and shrug. *Try to remain serene,* I remind myself. *You are happy and content. You have no ambition. Carter's words cannot bother you.* 'And what's wrong with the call centre? I get to help people who are having trouble with their bakus ... it sounds like the perfect job to me.'

I wonder if I might have overstepped the boundaries of believability, because he leans in close, his eyebrows pulling together in a deep frown. I fight to keep my expression neutral, even though it's hard with his bony face so close to mine. 'Wow, we really did get to you, didn't we?'

His frown now pulls at the corner of his mouth. He seems almost ... disappointed.

'And school is great, it's nice being back at St Agnes,' I natter on. 'Don't you sometimes wish you could be back there too, without all the pressure of life at Profectus? It's like, I can actually go to my classes and yet still have a life. It's nice. Do you want to hear what some of your old friends are up to?' I try to wrack my brains to think of who *were* Carter's friends at St Agnes – I'm not even sure that he had any. But thankfully, I don't have to make up any stories.

'Oh god, no,' he says, suddenly all of his scepticism disappearing. Then he laughs. 'As if I would want to know about life at St Agnes? Who do you think I am?' He leans forward, his face agonizingly close to mine. I almost break character, but I manage to keep it together. 'And to think ... Dad is going to roll out this update to all level 1 bakus tomorrow night.' He waggles his eyebrows. 'Come on, Hunter. Let's not waste any more time here.'

>>Good job, says Jinx as soon as Carter moves on.

'Thanks,' I mutter, and I shudder with disgust, now that I'm able. *So now we know. Eric is rolling out the update tomorrow.* I need to tell the team about what I've just heard. I catch sight of Zora's bright red dress, so I rush towards her, heedless of who I'm pushing out of the way.

But as I draw close, I spin around on my heels and head in the opposite direction. She's deep in conversation with Nathan and I know she'll kill me if I interrupt. Everything about her body language screams that she is into him, and in a way, I am happy for her. But there's another part of me that's scared for her. I don't know what Nathan is really like, but Tobias hates him – and that doesn't bode well for her.

But then I forget about Zora and Nathan, because Tobias is in front of me.

His eyes light up as he sees me, but then his brow creases in worry. 'Everything okay? You're sweating.'

'Just ran into Carter and Eric Smith,' I say, wiping my brow. He winces. 'How did that go?'

'We were right, the update is being launched at the convention tomorrow.'

Tobias whistles through his teeth. 'Geez. And Carter just told you that outright?'

'He believes Slick updated me, and that I no longer have any ambitions for life beyond St Agnes and a call centre.'

'They must be more stupid than we could have imagined if they believe that.'

'They're cocky,' I say. 'But we're smarter than that.' Finally, I take in how smart he's looking. He's not wearing a tuxedo, but he is looking more dressed up than I've ever seen him – he's wearing a blazer with a mandarin collar that has a thin strand of gold piping down the edges, which matches Aero's metallic feathers exactly. There's a patch on his shoulder where Aero can 'clip' in, so that when he leashes up they become one in-sync machine. But then I notice something troubling. Tobias has a frown etched across his brow, and he looks as if he has a shimmer of sweat on his forehead too. He also hasn't noticed anything about what I'm wearing. Maybe that's okay – I'm not so vain that I expected to be showered in compliments – but he's normally so observant. 'Are *you* okay?' I ask.

He smiles at me, but it seems strained. 'Yeah, fine. Just find it a little strange to be here with everyone. And I'm worried about tomorrow. Whether we can get into the dome, what we might find there, and whether we're going to need outside help ...'

I put my hand on his arm. 'But who can we trust?'

His frown deepens, this time in annoyance. 'I have no idea. But I'm still worried that we won't be able to help Monica. Lake Baku ... the way it was disguised ... this whole conspiracy might be so much bigger than we think. What if we need more time?'

He's echoing all the concerns that I have, and I know that they are all legitimate. But now it's my turn to be the strong one. Tobias is used to being the leader, the decisive action man – but even the strongest people need support. I'm learning that now. 'We'll do this,' I say.

'Will we?' he asks.

'Don't worry. I have faith in us. We're a strong team – the strongest, remember? We would have totally won the Baku Battles ...'

'Yeah, that's right, we would have.'

I search his face, worrying at my lower lip. I wonder if he wishes he had never met me – that I'd never found Jinx and gotten into Profectus and on to his team. I've turned his entire world upside down. Before, his concerns were about earning his place in his family – now they're about saving the world.

There's a tinkling of glasses and we turn our attention to the stairs, where Tobias's parents are standing at the very top, champagne glasses in hand. 'Hello, everyone,' says Tobias's dad, his voice rising above the crowd. 'Welcome to our annual Christmas party. We are honoured to have so many of you here today, and *especially* honoured that this year we are going to be hosting the Moncha convention at Lake Washington. I'm sure you are all buzzing for that – so make sure you don't drink too much champagne and miss the real festivities!'

There's a tinkle of laughter after which Tobias's mom takes over.

'The convention is going to start tomorrow evening, at around 7 p.m. It will be broadcast live around the world – and we're expecting to break records with viewing numbers! We've always known that this is an important time for our brilliant company, and we are so grateful to be involved. In fact . . .' She gestures out into the crowd. There's a rustle of movement, and I stand on my tiptoes to try and make out what's going on. I don't have to wait long to see – Nathan steps up on to the steps. 'We are so proud as parents to have our son working for Moncha Corp, at the top level, on some of the most exclusive projects.'

'Thanks, Mom,' says Nathan, bowing his head with humility that I'm sure not used to seeing from him. 'As someone who has a little insider knowledge, I'm sure

Mr Smith won't mind me teasing that we have a hugely exciting announcement to make tomorrow. Something that is going to make a lot of people's lives a *lot* better.'

Tobias's palms tighten into fists beside me, and his whole body tenses up like an electric band being pulled to full stretch.

'We truly believe that Moncha continues to make the world a happier place, and we are proud to be a part of it,' continues Tobias's father.

'Now, let's eat, drink and be merry. Happy Christmas Eve Eve, everyone!' His mom raises her glass, and we all follow automatically. There's a universal clink, and the chatter resumes to full volume.

'I have to go,' says Tobias. 'I'll catch up with you later.'

And then I'm alone in the party.

PART FOUR

LAKE BAKU

CHAPTER TWENTY-EIGHT

THE NEXT MORNING, WE'RE UP EARLY TO head back to the lake. Zora and River install themselves in our 'mission control' room, and I stride confidently towards the skis. But Tobias stops me with a touch. He seems back to his old self, his head held high.

'Not that way. Today, we're not wasting any more time.' He leads us from the basement into the garage, where there are four gleaming hovercraft-snowmobiles.

'Wicked!' says Kai.

'I thought we'd take the fast route,' says Tobias.

'This is amazing!' Ashley clambers on to the nearest machine, pulling a helmet down low over her ears.

It *is* really cool, but I don't have a clue how to use one of these.

Jinx reads my mind. >>Don't worry, Lacey, I got this.

He's returned to his normal black colour now, having shed his silver skin. He crawls into the baku compartment where he plugs into the machine. The engine revs, and Kai lets out a loud *whoop*! I straddle the padded leather seat, gripping the handlebars – but it's Jinx who is going to be doing the driving. I'm just along for the ride.

It's a lot easier to find the way this time, and thrilling. The snowmobiles hover over the snow, smooth as silk, and the cold wind rushes past as we zip through the trees. The machines are pretty nimble, and Jinx is an expert driver.

As we approach the lake, it's hard to believe that the forest in front of us is an illusion. Even when Tobias sends Aero to fly high above the dome, his video feed shows only miles of trees.

It's disconcerting.

But still not as disconcerting as the actual dome. Once we pass through the barrier, we're face to face with a giant opaque wall, so tall you can't see the curve from the ground. The only place someone could build something so huge is out here in the wilderness.

I put my hands up against the wall. *Are you inside, Monica?*

>>We'll find her. And if we don't, we'll keep searching. We'll help your mom . . . and stop Eric in his tracks.

His voice sounds so fierce, it gives me courage.

'So, how do we get in?' Kai asks, ever the practical one. He bangs his fist against the wall where we had seen the crack in the photograph and I cringe – what if it was electrified or sets off an alarm or something?

Tobias obviously feels the same way, as he barks out, 'Dude. Stop.'

Kai shrugs, giving us his best 'And?' expression.

>>Follow me, says Jinx, using his speaker so everyone can hear.

We watch as Jinx darts along the edge of the wall, staying close to the perimeter. Every now and then, his tail reaches out and touches the wall, sending electric sparks flying up the surface.

'This doesn't make sense,' mutters Tobias from behind me.

I reach out and grab his hand. Something was off with him last night, but I've put it down to nerves about what might happen today. I know the feeling. My stomach is tight and even though the journey on the hovercraft-snowmobiles was so much faster and easier than the skis yesterday, I'm fuelled by fear of what might happen if we don't do this on time. We even had to skip out on an incredible breakfast that Tobias's mom was laying out for us.

Jinx stops, which breaks me out of my thoughts. Now that he's done with sending electric shocks up the wall, the outline of the door is much more visible. There's even the dark outline of a security panel. Finally, a breakthrough.

>>The security on this wall is shockingly lax. I bet even your beetle could break in.

'Why is that?' I ask him. It seems surprising to me that Moncha would have gone through all the trouble of building this secret place, and then not bother with top-notch security.

>>Well, I guess it wasn't supposed to be anything nefarious originally — just a testing facility. They

219

didn't expect anyone to find it. Why do you need to lock something that nobody can find?

'Wait, so it's not locked?' asks Kai.

>>No, it is locked. Still, that shouldn't be a problem for us. Like I said, even the beetle could do it. In fact . . .

He flicks his tail, sending a directive to the little baku on my shoulder. Slick crawls down my arm, then takes a flying leap on to the door. The sticky suction pads on his appendages immediately grip on to the door, where he scrambles over to the lock mechanism. He works his magic, sticking one of his pin-like antennas into the lock and whirring it around with expertly programmed efficiency. Zora programmed this lock-picking capability to help me get into my locker when the padlock stuck. She is far too clever for her own good.

A minute later, and the door pings open.

>>As far as I can tell, this is a completely closed system. The easiest way to make sure that no one can find out about it is to make it as discreet as possible. It would take huge amounts of electricity to sustain this dome. I assume anyone suspicious about it would think the houses around Lake Washington were using the power.

Tobias frowns. 'But we have solar energy at the cottage.'

>>Exactly, says Jinx.

'What do you mean by huge amounts of electricity?' I ask.

>>Just look.

He head-butts the door, which swings open.

There are no words.

I stumble as I step through, barely catching myself on the edge of the dome.

By stepping in, I've gone from winter wonderland outside to an eerie permanent summer, a fake sun in a clear blue sky and not a breath of wind chill to stir the pleasantly warm temperatures.

What is this place? I'm in awe. 'Oh my god,' I say out loud.

'Lacey? Lacey, what is it?' asks Zora, in my ear.

I take a few more steps forward, moving away from the door so that the others can enter in beside me. There's a succession of gasps and a couple of curse words as they follow me through, as the rest of my friends struggle to process what we're seeing.

Ashley reaches out and grabs my hand, Jupiter wagging his tail beside her.

'This place is unreal,' she says. 'Look over there!'

I follow her gaze. We're standing at the top of a grassy hill, giving us a fantastic view of the interior of the dome. Everything under the bubble is green and fresh, the trees full with leaves that whisper gently in the light, warm breeze. There's grass underfoot, and bursts of colour from spring flowers growing nearby. My brain is struggling to take in what I'm seeing, having some sort of understanding-disconnect after coming from a world of frost and snow and bare branches. The forest continues all the way down to the shores of a beautiful lake, so still that the water shimmers like diamonds in the sun. I don't even know how to swim but I want to dive in – it looks so inviting. There's a wooden plank dock anchored in the middle of it, and I have an image of us all diving and jumping off into the water, spreading our towels out on the dock and watching the fish swim underneath us. It would be idyllic.

'Can we stay here for ever?' jokes Kai. Even Oka looks happy, rolling around in the grass. 'If we could have a winter without a winter, that'd make Canada practically the perfect place to live.'

'But Kai – aren't you on the ice hockey team?'

'Yeah, so? Doesn't mean I don't prefer to sunbathe!' He stretches out his arms, basking in the weird fake light.

'Can you even get a tan from a sun that isn't real?'

'Even better – warmth without the cancer danger!' He fist pumps the air and I roll my eyes. Still, I can't help but smile as we shed our jackets. There is something oddly satisfying about this place. It makes me feel . . .

It makes me feel happy.

Instantly the thought sends a shiver down my spine.

CHAPTER TWENTY-NINE

I T'S CHRISTMAS EVE, NOT THE MIDDLE OF *the summer,* I remind myself. *This is just . . . a movie set. An illusion. None of it is real.*

I wonder if this too is part of Team Happiness. It's unbelievable what Eric Smith has been able to achieve.

I grit my teeth and concentrate on the mission. Find Monica Chan. Stop the update from happening. Fix Mom.

And Dad? says a little voice in the back of my mind. I grit my teeth, trying to hold back all my swirling emotions.

'No one is going to believe this,' says Kai. We haven't dared to move yet beyond our viewpoint on the hill. There's just too much to take in.

Past the tree line, there are facilities to test every type of baku. There's a vast turf arena, ringed by a racetrack, for testing the speed of the bigger bakus. There's a section that's completely covered in sand, with rolling dunes like in the Sahara. Even in the sky, there are suspended hoops – like an aerial assault course to test the bird bakus.

We'd need months to explore it all. But what we're most

interested in is at the far end of the lake, where we can see the roofs of little cabins, half-hidden by the trees, clustered together almost like a village. A single-track path runs down the middle of them. 'That must be where they'd keep Monica,' says Tobias. He reaches out and grabs my hand. My pulse starts to race, and I don't know whether it's from his touch or from the adrenaline of finally being in Lake Baku, with the possibility of finding Monica.

Tobias's eagle lands in front of us and spreads his wings out wide. He projects a 3D topographical map of the area that he's created by doing a brief fly around the dome. What a beautiful, useful baku he is. *And he was probably tested right here.*

That gives me pause for thought, too. As far as we can tell, there are no other bakus in the vicinity. If this were still being used for its primary purpose – as a test centre – there would be hundreds of different baku variations here, running around under the fake sunshine. But it's deserted.

So why is it still up and running? My suspicion rises, and I hope that means we're on track to find Monica.

'We're here.' Tobias points to a small rise at the edge of the dome. I dare to turn around. Behind us, through the open door, the ground is totally white with snow. Here, we're standing on grass. I tilt my head up, but I can't see evidence of the dome – even though I know it's there.

'This is the biggest building.' He points to a house at the very far edge of the lake, a cabin made of pretty mahogany logs, tipped in bright red at their edges. It could have been plucked from a catalogue of picturesque country cottages. With a pinch of his fingers, Tobias zooms in. He's every inch the leader in this situation, taking control of us just as he did in the Baku Battles. 'That's where I think Monica will be.'

>>I agree.

Jinx continues to use his speaker, so the whole group can hear.

>>Also, according to my analysis, it's the cabin that's had the most activity, which would fit in with the timeline of Monica having been moved there recently.

Tobias continues. 'We'll have to skirt around the outside of the village to stay out of sight, but I don't think that will be too much of an issue if we stick to the tree line.'

'Should've brought some different shoes,' says Kai, gesturing down to his unwieldy winter boots.

'At least they're not as heavy as ski boots,' Ashley replies.

'Yes, but hardly sneaking around material.'

'Do you think anyone else lives here?' Ashley whispers. 'What if there are guards in the other buildings?'

My fingertips tingle with fear and anticipation. I remember what Paul said, about employees who were sent to work here and then never returned, but I can't afford to get distracted. Monica is the goal.

Getting her back would fix everything.

Jinx swirls in between my feet, with as much nervous energy as I have. *Jinx, what's wrong?*

>>I don't know.

225

He speaks just to me this time.

>> I think Kai might be right, things do feel too quiet. I expected there to be much more security than this.

Maybe it's not a priority for Eric? I muse. I mean, he's about to do his first big solo announcement at the convention and then he's only a step away from taking control of the company. Once that happens, he won't need Monica. It will be much harder for her to regain her position if she resurfaces. So maybe he's powering down the security at Lake Baku, concentrating on moving logistics over to Lake Washington?

Jinx nods. >>That might be correct. I've checked and a lot of energy has been directed towards the Washington cottage.

I grit my teeth. We have to stop him.

'We've had a lot of luck so far, so let's run with it,' says Tobias. 'But I think our best bet to cover as much ground as possible is to divide and conquer.'

'Ash and I will go around the lake to the right,' says Kai.

'Good,' says Tobias. 'Lacey and I will stay left, and keep to the tree line for as long as possible. Remember, document everything that you see. Take pictures with your baku. Oh, wait! We can't send messages to anyone outside of the dome. One of us should stay at the entrance and keep Zora and River up-to-date back at the cottage.'

'I'll stay,' says Ashley. 'I can serve as a lookout too.'

'Perfect. We can run this exactly like one of our team plays. We're good at this, remember? According to Aero's inbuilt GPS guidance system, it will take us about thirty minutes to reach the furthest cabin. Remember, in and out is the key. Meet back here in two hours maximum. Any danger, any issues – or if you've been at the lake for longer than an hour and a half – you get back here immediately and get outside the dome. We just have to check in as often as possible – understand?'

'Got it, boss,' says Kai.

'Ready,' says Ashley.

'Remember the objectives: get to the log house, find Monica Chan, get out of the dome. Quick and easy.'

Kai disappears off, crouched down low, Oka by his side. Ashley takes up position by the door, and Jupiter leaps out into the snow to send a message back to River and Zora that we've made it inside.

Tobias grabs my hand, interlacing his fingers with mine. He's putting on a brave face, but he must be as thrown by all this as I am.

>>Let's go, you two. This way.

Jinx flicks his tail, scampering down the woods. With a quick wave goodbye to Ashley, Tobias and I follow him down towards the lake.

CHAPTER THIRTY

WE LEAVE OUR BULKY JACKETS bundled by the exit to the dome, freeing us to move around more easily. We scramble down the hill towards the buildings, staying in the shelter of the trees. Sweat trickles down my back – I'm regretting the choice of thermal leggings and top, but then I never would have guessed we'd be travelling into the middle of summer.

We pause a few metres away from the closest house, crouching down low, hiding ourselves in the foliage. 'I didn't think it was going to be like this,' Tobias says.

'Me neither.'

'Do you think ... if they're capable of building such an advanced testing centre ...'

'Who knows what else they can do?' I finish.

He frowns, and a shudder runs through his whole body. I don't know if I should feel grateful that he's so comfortable showing off this kind of vulnerability, when I'm so scared too. Surely one of us should be strong? Then it's my turn to shake myself. Of *course* it's okay that he's scared. I'm glad that he can show me that.

Together, we can be each other's strength.

'Okay, according to Aero, there's no sign of movement inside this building. I think we can continue to the next one. But let's stick to the trees.'

I nod. We crouch down low, scuttling underneath branches and using leaves for cover.

Jinx darts to one side.

>>Lacey, stop!

But his warning comes a moment too late. I step forward and cry out in pain, jumping back as I'm stung by an electric shock.

'Lacey, what's wrong! Are you okay?' Tobias catches me as I stumble.

He moves past me.

'No, don't!' I say. He snaps back too as he receives the same shock.

'What the hell?' he cries out.

'Jinx?' I ask.

He steps up and places his tail through the air in the vicinity of where we got zapped. >>It's a vast electric fence. Looks like it blocks access from the backs of the houses into the trees.

I wonder – is that meant to keep people like us out, or to keep the inhabitants in?

'So this means . . .'

>>We can't sneak around the back.

'You mean we have to walk through the town?'

>>Looks like it.

'Yo!'

The voice makes us both jump out of our skin, and even Jinx springs up on all fours, his hackles raised. We spin around, and to our relief – it's Kai.

I drop my hands down to my knees, trying to return my breathing to normal.

'Oh, thank god it's you,' says Tobias.

'I see you two have discovered the electric fence too. Damn thing nearly shocked me to hell. Three times.'

>>He had to be shocked three times before he realized it wasn't a fluke?

'He's not the brightest . . .'

'Hey!' says Kai, but he gives me a big grin. I'm glad he's here. And I'm glad Oka is here too.

'So, we're going to have to go through the centre of the village,' says Tobias. He frowns. 'We move quickly, keep to cover as much as possible. Got it?'

Kai and I nod.

'If there's any sort of alarm system then it would have been triggered by now. But to be on the safe side, let's assume that we're going to get caught at any moment. Therefore, the plan still needs to be to find Monica as quickly as possible.'

We scamper towards the first house, Jinx leading from the front so he can guide us around the electric fence. Once there, we hide in the shadows of the roof overhang, our backs to the clapboard wall. It's eerily quiet. There are cottages on either side of the road, porches with swings facing each other. 'Oh my god,' I whisper to Tobias and Kai, even though there doesn't seem to be anyone around here except for us. 'There are shops here. Look at that. That one is a convenience store.'

The sign above the store reads POPPA JOE'S, like we've walked on to the set of some old-time movie.

'Come on,' says Tobias, swallowing hard. 'This place is giving me the creeps.' We move from the shelter of one porch to the next, checking for movement, but there's no sign of life from any of the houses and streets – no twitch of the curtains or light bulbs turning on.

Kai is bolder. He peers in one of the windows of the cottages. 'Looks to me like no one is home.'

'What if it's just guards waiting for us in the house at the end? What if Monica's not there? What if we're too late and they've moved her already?' I ask, not really speaking to anyone in particular – just voicing all the fears that are running through my mind.

'No,' says Tobias, yet he is wringing his hands together, still so jittery. 'She's gotta be here.'

'What's got your panties in a twist?' asks Kai, his face screwed up into a ball.

'Shut it, Kai!' snaps back Tobias.

'Hey, hey, guys, let's cool it,' I say, standing in between them as they square up to each other.

'You've been a jerk since we got here, T. It's like whenever Nathan is nearby you get a giant stick up your butt. I thought having a year without him had loosened you up but you're just as kiss-ass as you've always been. You're terrified of him!'

'I am not! Leave Nathan out of this.'

'Look!' I say, grabbing them both by the hand. 'This is a tense situation. But let's do what we came here to do and then get out of here. You two can sort out whatever this is then.'

There's a beat as they square off against each other, but then Tobias nods and Kai backs down. I breathe a sigh of relief. But I also exchange a worried look with Kai. So, I'm not the only one to notice a difference in Tobias's behaviour since we've been at the cottage.

'Come on, the quicker we move ...' Tobias drops my hand, his jaw tight from the confrontation. He steps out of the shadows and strides down the path, not hiding at all any longer. Kai and I jog to catch up with him. We end up jogging all the way to what we hope is Monica's house, heedless of any alarm that might be raised.

Even close up, it's breathtakingly beautiful – much more so than the others we've seen, which are more typical, neat clapboard style. The dark painted logs gleam in the sunlight and there are hanging planters overflowing with colourful flowers. There are two huge bay windows in the front, although they're currently shuttered – strange for this time of day. There's nothing to indicate that it's occupied. But according to Aero's data, there's someone inside.

'Ready?' Tobias asks, as we climb the stairs to the front door. Kai tries to peer through the shutters, but he shrugs. Nothing there. I nod.

Tobias reaches out and jiggles the handle on the door, but it doesn't budge.

'Locked,' he says, with an exasperated sigh.

'Maybe we can break a window?' suggests Kai.

But I've noticed something else. There might be a handle, but there's no keyhole. I place my hand on the door itself, and give it a hard push.

It swings open. It wasn't locked after all.

And I gasp.

Because there she is. Standing in the hallway of the cottage as if she's been expecting us.

Tobias sighs with relief. I look up at him and his whole face lights up, as does mine. I'm so grateful to see her alive, and apparently healthy. She even still has her signature haircut, that triangular fringe. She's wearing a beige uniform of long, loose trousers and a flowy top, almost like hospital scrubs. And with his long arms draped loosely around her neck, connected to her leash, is the same sloth baku I remember from underneath Moncha HQ.

'Hello, can I help you?' says Monica Chan, not an ounce of recognition on her face.

Kai, Tobias and I all stare at her, and I've never been more grateful to have them by my side. If I was alone, I'd be terrified. But they don't look terrified – they look ... awestruck. I think they would drop down to their knees and bow to her, if they weren't so shocked at the fact we've *actually* found her.

Then I realize: it's the first time they've met her, this

woman who has been at the centre of our lives. Jinx curls around my ankles, staring at Monica too.

I know they're all waiting for me to speak. I'm the one who's met her before, after all. 'Monica, do you know who I am?'

'No, I don't think so. Have we met before? Should I know you? I'm really sorry; my memory is terrible these days. But I assume you've come here to join our wonderful community? You're just in time.'

I swallow, my mouth suddenly feeling very dry. 'Just in time for what?'

CHAPTER THIRTY-ONE

'WHY, IT'S ALMOST TIME FOR OUR annual celebration!' she says, a grin splitting her face in two.

I sneak a sideways glance at Tobias and Kai. Kai's mouth is wide open. Tobias is cooler, but I swear I see a bead of sweat drip down his temple.

'Monica ...' I say, and her head turns to me so slowly, she almost doesn't seem human. It nearly makes me forget the second half of my question. For a second, I wonder if Eric Smith's plans have taken a step further, and Monica is now totally automaton. What would that mean for her? For the company?

But then she looks at me and I know that she's real. She's just locked up in a different way. Her free will has been taken away. She's been updated.

What if it can't be reversed? says a tiny voice in my head. *What will that mean for her? And Mom? Will they be updated for ever, losing more and more of themselves ...*

I can feel the panic rising in my chest, but I try and push it down. I can't worry about that now. One thing at a time.

235

'Do you recognize Jinx?' I ask. I gesture to the cat baku at my feet, and he leaps up into my arms.

Her gaze follows Jinx, but all she says is, 'Who's Jinx?'

I can sense Jinx's disappointment that Monica doesn't recognize him. I wonder what it must be like to feel abandoned by your creator like that.

But no. She *didn't* abandon him. She tried to save him. That's why I have Jinx in the first place. She knew the danger he was in – and that she was in – and she chose to try to get him outside, where he might have the chance to survive, rather than be destroyed at the hands of Eric Smith.

Now, we need to do the same for her.

Kai echoes my thoughts. 'C'mon. We've found her now. We have to get her out of here.'

Tobias speaks up, because I seem to have lost my words. 'Ms Chan, I'm afraid that we can't stay for any celebration. But if you don't mind, can you come with us? We really need your help and we think that you're the only one who can help us.'

'Oh, I don't know . . .' says Monica. Her sloth's black-as-night eyes watch us with suspicion. 'I think I'd better stay put. It's not quite time for us to be outside yet. The others will wonder why I arrived so early.'

'I don't like the sound of this "annual celebration",' says Kai in a low voice.

'Me neither,' I say. 'Have you checked in with Ashley? Maybe we should send her a message to let her know we've found Monica.' I waggle my eyebrows in Oka's direction. If something bad is going to go down, someone needs to know on the outside.

'Good idea,' says Kai. He leans down to Oka's side, and records a message for Ashley. Then, for good measure (and something I've never seen from Kai) he takes out a pen from his pocket and writes down a note on actual paper. 'We can't be too careful,' he says. 'What if all the data gets erased?'

'Genius!' I exclaim.

He grins at me, then sends Oka on his way.

I exchange a look with Tobias, and together he and Kai step towards Monica. She stares at us placidly, that same serene smile on her face. That *creepy*, serene smile.

They gently take her by the arms and lead her out.

'No, I can't leave yet,' she says as she approaches the threshold of the door.

Did you see that? I ask Jinx.

>>I did. His voice is solemn.

The sloth had tugged on Monica's leash as the two boys were moving. He's the reason that Monica's come to a stop – why she fears crossing the threshold of the door. The sloth is preventing her from leaving.

We have to find a way to disable her baku.

>>I'll handle it. In a flash, Jinx leaps up and on to Monica's free shoulder, taking a swipe at her baku.

What happens next is less expected. The sloth swipes back, attacking Jinx with extendable hooked claws.

I yelp, but Jinx darts out of the way just in time. His electronic fur stands on end, and he hisses with anger.

'Aero, help Jinx,' says Tobias.

Like the team that I know they are, the two bakus work together, perfectly synchronized. Outside of the battle arena, Aero isn't free to attack the sloth directly, so instead Tobias instructs him to flap his wings violently in his direction, creating enough of a distraction to the sloth to cause him to lose focus on Jinx.

Jinx doesn't have the same restrictions as Aero. He uses the momentum shift caused by the distraction to push the sloth completely off balance. Although the sloth has long limbs, he's not able to right himself quickly enough to stop his leash detaching from Monica's ear.

Monica doesn't move, allowing the action to unfold all around her, until the sloth falls – when she automatically reaches out to catch him.

The boys step forward then, grabbing Monica beneath her arms.

Jinx settles on Monica's shoulder in the sloth's place, and although it sends a stab of jealousy to my heart, he looks as if he's about to leash up to her.

But then he pulls back.

>>Stop that sloth!

I run around the boys, darting towards the sloth, preventing his attempt to lunge forward towards Monica. I don't want to grab him directly in case he turns those claws on me, so instead I grab hold of the carpet he is standing on. I drag it back so that he slides into the other room, and I slam the door over the loud baku howls of alarm. How very un-sloth-like.

Also, not very 'content'.

Maybe Eric Smith's code isn't perfect after all.

With the sloth safely out of commission, we quick-time it to the front door.

All in, it's taken us about an hour.

So far, so good. We should make it back in time to stop the convention after all.

We head down the path leading through the village, Aero flying ahead of us. I'm next, then Monica, then the boys. Jinx is still balancing on Monica's shoulder, and now that she's not connected to her baku, Monica seems happier to follow us. My mind races to figure out the next step of the plan. We had been so focused on finding Monica, we hadn't really given enough thought to the logistics of what we should do once we had her.

All I know is that we can't let Eric Smith capture her again. I turn around to face Tobias. 'Tobias, once we're out of the dome, can you get a car ready for me? Zora and I will take Monica back to the authorities in the city and ask her how to reverse the update. Once we're safely far away from here, you and the rest of the team can stop the convention.'

We're almost at the end of the path, just passing the convenience store. We're almost at the path that will lead up towards the door in the dome. We're so close . . .

There's an explosion . . . of confetti all around me.

Dozens of people – all with sloth bakus leashed around their necks – emerge from the houses. 'Welcome to our annual celebration!' one of them says.

'We hope you can join us,' says another, his hair swept into a perfect sideways parting.

Tobias and Kai are struck still with shock at the sight of all the people who are surrounding us. But none of them look surprised or alarmed to see us, considering that we're intruders from the outside world. They look perfectly serene, dressed in the same beige outfit that Monica is wearing.

It's like a cult.

A Moncha cult.

'I'm sorry, but we can't,' says Tobias, keeping his cool as always. 'We have to go. We'll, uh, be sure to come back another time.'

'Oh, I understand. Hopefully we'll see you again soon.' And to our amazement, the man steps aside. So do all of the people, giving us a clear pathway out of the village. We hustle through them, trying not to make eye contact.

And then I make eye contact.

'Uh, Lacey?' Tobias stops and turns around when he notices that I'm no longer with them. In fact, I'm stood stock-still in the middle of the crowd. 'Come on, we've got to go.'

'What's her problem?' hisses Kai.

I swallow, completely unable to move. It's like I've been paralysed – my body feels like it's been dipped in ice. My hands are numb. My feet are numb. My brain is numb.

Finally, I manage to find the energy to lick my lips. It brings enough moisture to my dry mouth to spit out some words. 'I . . . I think this is my dad.'

CHAPTER THIRTY-TWO

I'M VAGUELY AWARE THAT TOBIAS AND KAI are shouting – at me, at each other – I can't quite tell. It's like I've descended into a trance. I walk slowly towards the man in the crowd that I barely recognize. Is this my brain playing tricks on me? Some kind of wishful thinking?

He's a total stranger, a vague approximation of the person from the photographs I've seen. I try to match him up with that man. The man in the white lab coat. The man with the beautiful German Shepherd baku.

I squint my eyes. Is this really him? Or am I just seeing what I want to see?

But I don't *see* the resemblance. I feel it. It's a punch in the gut. It's a pull – a fish hook that's got me by the cheek and is luring me in with every step. That tug is deep in my belly, in my soul. The man's eyes are artificially serene, and – most importantly – show no hint of recognition back. But I have to find out if my gut instinct is right.

Another part of me senses Tobias walking towards me, cautiously approaching, as if I'm some sort of wild animal.

I might go mad if he tries to stop me – lash out with my claws and hiss with my teeth and slash at him until he turns around and leaves me. I think he understands that, and that's why he keeps his distance for now.

'Jinx, do something!' I hear Tobias say.

>>Lacey — we have to get Monica out of here. Then we can help your mom and your dad.

I know what Jinx is saying makes sense, but for once, I can't listen to him. This is something that I have to find out for myself. If I don't ask now . . . if I let myself be torn away . . . I'll always wonder.

'Excuse me, sir?' I say, finding my voice at last.

He looks at me, and smiles. When he does, that fish hook tugs even tighter; I almost jump forward with the force of it. But the smile is accompanied by totally blank eyes. 'Yes?'

'What's your name?' It comes out as barely a whisper, but it's enough for him to hear.

He sticks his hand out to me, totally unaware of the turmoil that is roiling through my body at that very moment. 'My name is Albert Chu.' He gestures to the sloth around his neck. 'This is my baku, Lacey.'

Now I react. Tears spring up into my eyes. 'Your baku's name is Lacey?' I whisper.

'Yes – isn't it a nice name?'

'That's my name. Dad? Dad. It's me.'

Do I detect something? A flicker of confusion or recognition or maybe even a flash of anger out of the person who's trapped underneath? A million questions are running through my mind. Has he been here this whole time? Is he under the influence of the update? But how can that be possible? How long has this been going on?

And did he volunteer for this program, knowing that he would forget about Mom and me?

Can we reverse it?

'Oh, you must have confused me with someone else. How nice that you share a name with my baku! That's a great coincidence.'

My mind is racing so fast, I jump when Tobias touches my arm.

'Lacey – I know you think this is your dad . . .'

'It *is* my dad.'

'Right, yes, I believe you, and that is absolutely wild, but we have to go.'

'You're telling me I should just leave my dad here? To . . . whatever Eric next has planned?'

'We need to get Monica out and far away from here first. That way we can stop the update from being rolled out, figure out how to reverse this thing and *then* we can get your dad back. Don't you see? We have to do things one step at a time, but we won't forget about him. Jinx will record it all. Come on.'

'But . . .'

'Look, Lacey. He's been here for . . . god knows how long. He can last one more day. I promise you, we won't let a minute longer go by than we have to before we return and get him. The minute we get back and bring Monica to my parents then everything will be right again.'

I hesitate, chewing my lower lip. I know Tobias's logic is sound. But I can't tear myself away. Not now that I've found him.

I didn't even know I was looking for him, until he showed up right in front of my eyes.

I can sense the others – not Tobias and Kai, but the rest of the creepy Moncha cult – all staring at me, those strange grins on their faces. My curiosity gets the better of me and I sneak a little sideways glance in the direction of the other inhabitants. They really do seem geared up for a celebration. One is carrying a cake, some have streamers in their hands. It looks more like a children's birthday party than an annual celebration.

A thought strikes me. What if this happens every day, here? Everyone loves a celebration, a piece of cake, a reason for the community to get together . . . it would fall perfectly into the 'make people happy' category. A birthday every day! An excuse to celebrate! I bet some people would hear that and it would put a smile on their face.

'Lacey, please.' There's more than a hint of desperation in Tobias's voice now. I have no real concept of how much time has passed, but I know that it's ticking by.

I run up to my dad, heedless of his reaction towards me. 'I will be back for you, Dad.'

Then I turn back to Tobias, catching the look of relief on his face. I'm about to smile back, to say 'okay, let's go,' when my brain registers the words that he said just a moment ago.

'What did you mean by, "when we bring Monica to my parents"?' I ask, frowning.

Tobias opens his mouth, then closes it again, clearly caught off guard. 'Nothing, I meant when we take her to the authorities, or to BRIGHTSPRK, that's all. Slip of the tongue, I promise.'

'I wouldn't make promises I couldn't keep if I were you, Tobias.'

A man exits from the closest cottage, and my heart immediately drops. He's not wearing beige like the others, and at his feet is a black jaguar.

It's Nathan.

CHAPTER THIRTY-THREE

I STUMBLE BACKWARDS UNTIL I BUMP INTO Tobias, and I grip his hand tightly. His palm is as clammy as mine is, and I think he's trembling too.

'You think I didn't realize you all were up to something?' Nathan asks, stalking closer with his jaguar baku at his side. 'I knew there had to be a reason Tobias invited some pathetic level 1s and 2s to our Christmas party. I overheard a very interesting conversation between Mom and Tobias, then when you left this morning, I followed you all . . . and what do I find but you trying to kidnap the CEO of Moncha Corp?'

'Nathan, please,' I say. 'You don't know what Eric Smith is trying to do. He's developed this update and if we don't get Monica out of here . . .'

'Let me stop you right there,' he says. 'You think I don't know about the update? I'm Eric Smith's personal intern. Of *course* I know. I know even more about this than our parents. Dad might work on the team, but he thinks we're tweaking baku code. So naïve. When Tobias came to them about this, they had no idea what he was talking about.' He turns to

Tobias. 'You should have come to me instead. I could have arranged for you to have a position in the inner circle too. But now, you've given our parents just another reason to be disappointed with you.'

Tobias scowls, a sheen of sweat on his brow. 'Nathan, leave us alone. We're getting out of here. There's three of us and one of you . . .'

In response, Aero lets out a piercing cry, spreading his wings. Oka snarls, gnashing his jaws.

And Jinx hisses, his back arched.

Nathan's eyes light up at the sight of Jinx. 'Really, Tobias, I expected better of you. You think I came here on my own? Mr Smith is going to be so pleased.'

'I am indeed.' Eric steps out of the same cottage, following in Nathan's footsteps. Wrapped around his neck is his red panda baku, his dark eyes flashing. Behind him is a security team, all with dangerous panther bakus at their feet.

Immediately I fear for Jinx, so I crouch down and scoop him up in my arms. He doesn't resist.

>>Don't let him take me, Lacey.

My heart pounds in my chest. He sounds . . . scared. *I won't*, I think, with all the ferocity I can muster. *He won't get anywhere near you.*

With more confidence than I feel, I jut out my chin. 'You can't get away with your plan for the update now. Not when so many of us know the truth about what it does.'

'I have a solution for that,' he replies, this time sounding as serene as the Lake Baku inhabitants. He gestures to his security team, and three of them step forward. In their arms are four sloth bakus, ready to be powered up and leashed – to us.

Panic rises in my chest, and both Tobias and Kai gasp in shock as they realize Eric is willing to update them too. 'It's not just us! People on the outside know too . . .' I cry. I don't know if that's really true, but we've been sending messages to Ashley, and she would have sent them on to Zora and River back at Tobias's cottage.

'Oh? And how is that going to happen.' He steps aside.

'Oka!' Kai cries out from behind me.

My hand flies up to cover my mouth. Oka is there, but he's a crumpled heap on the ground at Eric's feet. And behind the unconscious baku is Ashley. One of the security team members is dragging her out from inside the cottage. There are tears in her eyes. 'I'm sorry. They caught me almost straight away after you left. He's . . . he's got Jupiter.' And sure enough, I see Jupiter pinned beneath the feet of the security baku nearest to Ashley.

'It's not your fault,' I say to Ashley, into the silence left by Tobias and Kai. I'm surprised by the lack of protest I'm hearing from both of them, but especially by Tobias. He's supposed to be our leader, and he's letting us down at the crucial moment. I turn back to Eric. 'This isn't right!' I shout. I feel every bit the teenager, caught up in a fight that's far too big for me.

'Things would have gone so much smoother if you had simply let your little beetle baku update you, as I instructed it too. But Tobias and Kai and Ashley – it doesn't have to be this way for you. You can have your bakus back. As long as you give up this quest to stop the update from rolling out this evening. Otherwise – I'll have no choice but to pair you up with one of these sloth bakus … and your originals will be destroyed.'

To their credit, Ashley and Kai both hesitate. But when Ashley yelps out a cry of alarm as the security panther sinks his clawed paw deeper into Jupiter's body, I give her a nod. They both rush forward, collecting their broken bakus. Ashley mouths 'I'm sorry,' to me, but I don't blame her. I know the connection they both have to their bakus.

I would never want them to be separated.

'How about you, Tobias?' Eric asks, looking up at Tobias's beautiful golden eagle baku.

'Lacey, I …'

'Take Aero,' I say, my voice soft.

'But …'

'Come on, bro. I think Mom and Dad want to have a word with you.' Nathan folds his arms across his chest.

Tobias looks at me, but I studiously look away. If I look at him, I risk breaking. I risk crying my eyes out, when I still need to be strong.

Tobias steps forward, but Nathan puts his hand possessively on his shoulder, dragging him further into the fold. I catch his eye and shake my head a tiny bit. There's no point him protesting here, not with Aero at risk. He gives me the tiniest nod back, and Nathan manoeuvres him away.

I exhale sharply.

It's just you and me now, Jinx.

He doesn't respond, but instead I feel him vibrate in my arms, burrowing his face against my stomach. I feel my pulse slow, my breathing become more regular. Jinx is calming me down, and in response, I feel my mind sharpening.

'Pardem, why don't you leash up where you belong?' Eric says, once my old teammates and the security team accompanying them are out of view. Monica's old sloth baku shoots me an evil look as he languidly crawls towards his owner. Eric looks back at me.

>>I hate him, hisses Jinx.

Jinx, you should run away now. You're faster than them. I know it.

>>I'm not leaving you to face him alone.

I pull him close and bury my face in his fur.

'That's sweet,' Eric says. 'Your friends have made the right decision, you know. You should trust me that this is for the best.'

I glare up at him. 'You put me in a coma.'

For the first time, a flicker of annoyance crosses Eric's face. 'If my team had reached you before that silly boyfriend of yours, we would have had you back on your feet in no time. We had an antidote – I just needed to stop you so I could question you. You don't understand, Lacey. I'm not some evil guy out to harm you. In fact, I admire you. I think you're smart and a brilliant engineer, with a fantastic and agile mind – you'd be an asset to the Moncha Corporation.

We need people like you working for us. In fact, I want to offer you a job at the end of this, once you've graduated from school – whether that's Profectus or St Agnes. But I need the robot that's in your arms.'

'But *why?* Why do you need him so bad?'

'That, my dear, is far above your pay grade.'

I see him about to gesture to his security team – maybe to relieve me of Jinx. I grip him tightly and ask Eric another question to distract him.

'Why have you come here?' I blurt out. 'You could have sent one of your minions, like you did to my apartment. Shouldn't you be … I don't know, preparing your big announcement?' My mind is racing to try and think of a way out, but there isn't one. All I can think to do right at this moment is to try to keep him talking, even if what I'm saying is meaningless blather.

I almost laugh out loud. I feel like I'm in a movie, acting exactly like it's been scripted. And maybe we are all just robots, programmed to behave in predictable ways. If that's the truth, then Eric Smith won't be able to stop himself from talking up his grand plan, even though he could take Jinx right now and destroy him before my very eyes.

I almost breathe an audible sigh of relief when Eric's eyes turn slightly misty. He looks almost proud of himself when he says, 'Ah, my announcement will take care of itself. I know you don't like it, but it's a good plan, you know. Most people accept the status quo, remain in their dead-end jobs, their miserable routine, their 9-5 that makes even the

251

interesting seem mundane. Moaning on a Sunday afternoon, waking up with dread on a Monday morning, enduring hump day, getting drunk on a Friday – same old, same old. Except they don't really *want* to change it. So, why not allow people to keep that routine and yet be happy? All we do is make a little tweak to their ambition. They get to live their normal lives, without uprooting themselves in pursuit of some unreachable, impossible dream, and – most importantly – they can be happy.'

I swallow, my mouth so dry with fear that I can barely speak. 'How do you know they're happy?'

'The bakus are the biggest data mine in the world and Moncha has the best scientists to analyse it. By any metric available to us, the volunteers under the update are happy. And you know what? There was only one thing that we needed to tweak. Ambition. That was all. Once that was gone, everything else fell into place.'

I shake my head. I can't control my emotions any longer, and a trembling that began in my feet travels all the way up to my body. Our bakus record all of our conversations and all our movements, they're with us every hour of the day. I never realized just how sinister that could be, until seeing what could happen when that data became the property of someone like Eric.

'That's sick. If people knew . . . they wouldn't go for it.'

'Of course they would. In fact, they *will*. Don't you realize? We haven't just implemented this all at once. This is something I've been working on for years. Almost a decade.

Your mom has just had the very latest upgrade. But her department have been our guinea pigs for years – the next stage of volunteers after those at Lake Baku, of course.'

The truth slaps me across the face. Both of my parents have been pawns in Eric Smith's game. My dad may have been one of the very first. And now to learn that the gradual changes I've felt in Mom, that I just put down to ... I don't know ... what it means to be an adult? Her ... settling for her lot in life? They were not that at all.

I think about the cookbooks I found in the garbage bag, the ones I have stashed away in the corner of the locker – along with the photographs and letters from my father – so old-fashioned in our era of modern technology. The acceptance letter to a top cooking school, the dream of travelling to Paris, to Florence, to Istanbul, to try the food and indulge in her passion. Mom and I haven't gone on holiday for years – but it's nothing to do with a lack of money or desire – the way I thought it was.

It's been because of Eric Smith all along.

My throat constricts at the thought of what our lives could have been like, had Mom not been subject to the update. What could she have become? Would we have been happier if she had been able to pursue her dreams?

What if she pursued her dreams, and failed? Would that have made her miserable? But the point is, she will never know. She was never given that choice.

And then there's my dad? One of the original subjects of the update, living out his days at Lake Baku in blissful (is that the right word?) complacency, a walking zombie with no mind of his own.

I take steps backwards from Eric, not wanting to get swept up into his twisted logic.

'Once people know about this, you will be forced to stop,' I say, shaking with anger. This man has taken so much from me and from my family. While I still have my own mind, I won't ever stop fighting him.

He presses his fingers against his temples, and I sense now that he is getting tired of me. I have to find a way out of here. Or else Eric Smith will force the update on me and these might be the last words I ever care about hearing. *Jinx, any ideas?*

>>I'm thinking . . .

'Oh, Lacey,' Eric continues. 'This has been Moncha Corp's core goal since Monica and I founded this company. *How can we make people happier?* I've simply . . . accelerated things.'

'If this was really a "shared" company goal, you wouldn't have had to lock Monica away.'

Now it's Eric's turn to look disgusted. 'You think her laser-like focus on creating that . . . that *thing* . . .' he looks over at Jinx, his face screwed up as if he wants to spit on him, 'had anything to do with following our company ideals? Trying to create life – she's not Dr Frankenstein. You think that I am evil, but Monica had the biggest ego of us all – she had the grandest designs; she was the one who thought she could play God! You idolize her but you didn't see what she had become. If she cared so much about her precious company, how would I have been able to take over so easily? At any point she could have raised her head and seen the truth, but she kept her nose firmly buried in that thing's machinery. If she wanted to stop me, she would have.'

I shake my head. But even as he speaks, I feel like I can recognize what he is saying. When I get working on a project, it's as if everything else melts away and nothing else matters. The world could be descending into chaos, meteors could be raining down, aliens could have landed, zombies could have risen up out of the ground, but if I was down in my locker and in the middle of tinkering, I don't think I would have cared. What if Monica had been like that too? Had she just passively let all this happen, allowed Eric to go ahead and build the community around Lake Baku, let him steadily release updates to some of her most dedicated staff, while she play-acted at being CEO, all the while developing her obsession?

And yet the result of that obsession is Jinx. Could I be too angry about that? Maybe in order to create something so amazing, something so innovative and out of this world, something so ... real ... it required one hundred per cent devotion.

Even to the total detriment of everything else.

Tears well up in my eyes. 'I want to go home,' I say. 'You ... you've ruined everything for me. First you took away my dad. That's him, isn't it? That's him out there with another one of those sloth bakus ...'

'I know you think I'm evil. And ... yes, we had some

hiccups along the way. Some – accidents.' He actually has the audacity to look sad, his palms open towards me as if he's asking for forgiveness. 'That is your father out there. One of the good ones. The best ones. He volunteered for this program early on. He knew what he was risking – for technology to advance, we had to have test subjects. We needed to try the bakus out under every condition. And that meant getting things wrong sometimes. You must understand that, as a creator. How many times did you get things "wrong", before you were able to get it right with Jinx?' He almost looks like he wants to cry.

I clench my fists. 'My dad wouldn't have volunteered if he'd really known the risks. There's no way. How long was he supposed to be in Lake Baku? How long was that test really supposed to last?'

Now Eric looks distraught. I wonder if he did care for my father, but then – he can't have done. He let Mom and I believe that Dad had disappeared . . . that he'd just left us. At any point, he could have come to us and told us the truth: that Dad was here, living life under this dome. 'We've come such a long way in the decade since Albert . . . your father . . . volunteered. And it was thanks to his sacrifice that we were able to improve the technology.' He must catch the look on my face – a look of disgust, of disbelief – because his tone becomes more urgent.

I want to scream at him: DON'T YOU KNOW YOU WILL NEVER CONVINCE ME?!

I want to rail at him, to hit him with my fists and scream

my lungs out, I want to tear at him with my teeth, I want to become a feral beast, just to show him exactly what he's done to me – to us – and how I will never, ever forgive him.

But I don't do any of that. I'm strangely calm, my expression neutral – I don't even let tears roll out on to my cheeks, even though they're desperate to. It's driving Eric wild – I can see that. He wants some sort of absolution from me, and I'm not about to give it to him. The only sign – if he could see it – is the way that I'm gripping Jinx tightly to my chest, and the way that I can feel his paws pressing against me, showing his presence. But I know he's doing more than that. He's soothing me, keeping me calm.

>>Stay strong, Lacey.

You too, Jinx. I won't let anything happen to you. He might be trying to convince me that what he's done is noble, but I won't be sucked in.

'You know something, I knew Albert well. He was a good man. And he was so happy when you came into this world. His vision for bakus was so far beyond what even Monica and I could have imagined. He wanted bakus to be body-independent – sorry, a technical term there – but essentially he thought that bakus could be passed down from generation to generation, become receptacles for our memories and a constant link between families. Why do you think we make it possible for people to upgrade rather than replace? Keeping a baku for life is what makes people happy.

'Isn't having Jinx with you making you happy?'

'But Jinx isn't controlling me; he's soothing me!' I

shout back, fiercely. 'He's not altered any of my hopes and ambitions, or made me forget my feelings. He's helping me *manage* my feelings. It's not the same thing.'

Eric shrugs. 'Semantics. Now, hand Jinx over to me.'

CHAPTER THIRTY-FOUR

THERE'S A ROAR OF AN ENGINE AND another door to the dome flings open. Standing, silhouetted against the bright white winter light, is Zora – and a man it takes me a second to recognize.

'Lacey, don't you dare give that man anything!'

My heart lifts at the sound of Zora's voice. It's as if all my prayers are answered at once.

Once they step into the dome, I gasp. Next to Zora is Mr Baird. I'm immediately comforted to see his calm, confident face, his unwavering air of authority even in the face of Eric Smith, one of the most powerful men on the planet. Seeing him, a huge weight is lifted off my chest.

I hadn't even realized how much it had been worrying me that we hadn't been able to find him before – that maybe it really was going to be us against Moncha Corp. But a representative from another huge corporation, a proper adult in a position of power, someone the authorities would listen to? Surely it will be impossible for Eric to push the update now.

I look back at Eric, whose face is bright red. 'Get that baku!' he cries out to his security team.

Now, Jinx – run!

We both bolt at the same time. I sprint to Zora and Mr Baird, as fast as my feet can carry me. Jinx speeds away towards the trees, the security panthers chasing after him. But he's faster than them; I know he is. And he can't be tracked now he's disconnected from the cloud. *Lose them, Jinx, you have to lose them.*

The fact that he doesn't waste any energy on a reply, I take to be a good sign.

Zora grips my arm instinctively, her fingers digging into the flesh of my bicep. But rather than chase after Jinx and me, Eric simply laughs. The sound sends a shiver down my spine.

'Derek Baird, is it? Of BRIGHTSPRK?' Eric Smith looks down at his red panda, whispering some sort of command. 'Yes, I remember – the corporate spy who worked with us for so long. What a shame BRIGHTSPRK might not have long left for this world. You've seen the writing on the wall, haven't you, Derek?'

I look up at Mr Baird – whose face is looking a peculiar shade of grey. But maybe that's from seeing inside the dome. At least – I really hope it is.

Or maybe he looks so strange because Mr Baird doesn't have his owl baku any longer. Instead, he has one of the BRIGHTSPRK halos, discs of light that plug into the neck the same way as bakus, perform the same functions, but are so … cold, is the only way I can describe it. They're the opposite of the baku – they can be so discreet as to be almost totally invisible, designed to be an accessory, as bold or invisible as you prefer, to be a fashion statement or no statement at all. The devices aren't meant to be companions.

Eric's red panda baku turns his head towards his master, whispering something. 'I need to be getting back for the convention,' Eric says, spinning on his heels.

'There's not going to *be* a convention now that BRIGHTSPRK know about this. We'll tell everyone before you can get on stage. Once people know what you have planned . . .' My words spill out of my mouth thick and fast, unleashed with the confidence of having my best friend and Mr Baird beside me.

Mr Baird puts his hand on my shoulder – steadying me, but also stopping me. I flick my eyes up in his direction and his mouth is set in a firm line. He gives me a gentle shake of the head. 'Let's get out of here,' he says. 'I've got a car outside.'

'All you're doing is delaying the inevitable, Lacey,' Eric says again. 'I will push the update today. And then I will find and destroy that baku of yours.'

'Never,' I reply, defiantly.

'Come on, Lacey,' says Zora.

I tear my eyes away from Eric Smith and search the crowd of Moncha-zombies for my dad, taking a final look at him. I have one final spark of hope that he will recognize me, but it's quickly dashed. 'I'll come back for you,' I whisper, before allowing Zora to half-drag me out of the door of the dome where there's a private car waiting for us. I feel the shock of the cold air around me as we leave the fake sunshine and warmth for the real world.

'That was unbelievable,' says Mr Baird, once we're installed in the car. 'I'd heard rumours about a test facility but to see it in person . . .'

'You mean the place where my dad has been imprisoned for the past ten years, and which was used to develop an update that has changed my mom?'

Mr Baird shakes his head. 'I'm sorry, Lacey, of course that's what I mean. It's horrendous. How he thought he could get away with this . . . But don't worry – we're not going to just leave your dad. I've let my superiors know where this place is; the police will be there soon.'

'So Eric won't be able to push the update?' I lean back in the car seat, relieved to have a piece of good news.

'He won't. Everything is in motion to stop him in his tracks. It's not just the authorities we will notify. We'll push this out to the media too. Moncha Corp and Eric Smith are through,' says Mr Baird. He instructs the car to take us back to the BRIGHTSPRK offices in Toronto. It won't take long in the superfast car.

I wrap my arms around my body, my head spinning with everything that we've learned. I feel like my heart is torn in so many different directions.

Finding Dad alive – but zombified.

Finding Monica – but not being able to set her free.

Watching Jinx run away from those security bakus – and praying he escapes capture.

Being able to stop the update from going out wide – but not being any closer to knowing how to reverse it.

I need my mom back. The *un*updated version.

'Lacey, what you and your friends did today – it was incredibly brave. My mind is still trying to process it all.'

I'm trying to process a lot, too. 'Thanks, Mr Baird. But wait – how did you know where to find us? I tried to get in touch with you a few days ago.'

'I was deep in hiding, I'm afraid. It was a condition of my BRIGHTSPRK contract. But your friend here managed to get word out to me.' He nods at Zora.

'How did you manage it when we couldn't?' I ask my friend.

'Well, Jinx might be an ace hacker but I'm also a super coder,' she replies with a wink. 'I set up a tracker to search the internet for all details associated with the person who once owned the owl baku that your teacher had. Then it pinged up with this number, I called it, and got an answering service. I left a message and a few minutes later ... he called me back. I told him to get here as soon as he could.'

'You're amazing but ... how did you know we needed help?'

'When River and I didn't receive any messages from Ashley for over an hour, I knew something bad must have happened. I left Tobias's family cottage in secret to meet Mr Baird on the main road, and it was a good thing I did – I was cut off from River too.'

Linus squeaks. >>Lizard hasn't responded to any of our messages.

'They probably threatened to destroy Lizard if he didn't cooperate – I don't blame River,' I say.

'I have to say, I was pretty surprised to get the call from Zora,' says Mr Baird. 'But once she told me what was going on, I dropped everything to get up here as fast as possible. It's unbelievable. The update cannot be allowed to roll out further.'

Then Zora reaches out and grips my hand. 'Lacey ... did you really see your dad?'

I nod, biting my lower lip.

'Oh my god. That's huge. Are you okay?'

'I don't know,' I say, honestly. 'I mean ... he's alive. But who knows whether he will ever be back to normal. He had such an early version of Eric's update. It might have permanently damaged his brain, as far as we know.'

'We'll find out,' Zora says, fiercely.

'And BRIGHTSPRK will help,' affirms Mr Baird. 'We will find a way to reverse everyone who has been updated so far.'

'I hope you can,' I whisper. I want to believe that BRIGHTSPRK would have the answer, but I know it's not going to be easy.

'Can you show us what else you saw inside the dome, Lacey? It's important that we know everything.'

I nod, and pull Slick out of my pocket. He's almost drained of power, so I plug him into the car's built-in charger. He opens up his projector and we cycle back through the footage. It's clear that we have enough to prove to anyone what was going on. I'm so grateful to have him, for once.

Zora doesn't even bat an eyelid when Eric's soliloquy comes on, and the extent of his plan comes to light. 'I don't think I'm surprised at anything, any more,' she says, when the footage ends.

'But what I still don't understand is why he wants Jinx so badly,' I say. 'Jinx was out in the wild for a month, and no damage was done to Moncha. Can't he just be left to live in peace?'

'There must be a reason,' says Mr Baird.

'When Jinx comes back, I'll ask him,' I say, with more confidence than I have.

'When?' Mr Baird asks, one eyebrow raised. 'Do you think he escaped from Lake Baku?'

'I have to believe it.' I lean back in the car and turn my head so that I'm facing the window.

Even though Jinx is too far away by now to be able to hear me, I talk to him. *I just don't know if we're doing the right thing. Leaving Dad there, not having Monica with us . . . I feel like we've come away with nothing.*

As if I could hear Jinx's reply, there's a little doubting *and . . .*

And I can't believe Tobias told his mom. After all our planning, all the measures we took . . . I trusted him.

He betrayed me.

I wonder what he's doing right now. Tobias would have had to go back to the cottage and his parents. Would they consider what happened to be a triumph for him, or a failure? Maybe all Tobias needed to do was prove his own loyalty.

He's done that. To his parents, to Moncha Corp – and not to me.

But who am I to him, anyway? His high school fling? The girl who has a big crush on him, who he indulged for a while?

It doesn't matter who I am to him. What matters is that the next phase of the update doesn't roll out, that we figure out how to reverse it so I get Mom back. And maybe Dad too . . .

With those thoughts swirling in my head, the adrenaline rushing through my veins finally drops. The leather seats seem to mould around me, and I feel my muscles relax for the first time in a long time. My eyelids droop, and the scenes of the Canadian countryside rushing by lull me to sleep.

CHAPTER THIRTY-FIVE

WHEN I WAKE UP, WE'RE BACK AT the BRIGHTSPRK headquarters, a tall office building uptown. For a moment, in my post-waking-up haze, as we pull up outside the tower block, I think Mr Baird might have driven me straight home, and my heart lifts. I'm not used to being so far away from home for so long – and with everything that's been going on, I'm yearning for my own bed and a hug from Mom.

But I can't go back and face Mom, not yet. Not until I have a way to reverse the update. And not until I can give her a solid answer about Dad.

Zora reaches out and squeezes my hand. 'I wonder what my sisters are up to at the moment.'

I give her a small smile. Inside, though, I'm cursing myself. I've been so wrapped up in myself – and the discovery of my dad – that I haven't been thinking about Zora. Her family all have low level bakus, and would be in line for the next phase of the update.

'I bet they're missing you a lot and can't wait for you to be home.'

'Yeah, so they have someone to bug all the time,' she replies, dryly, but I can tell there's a twinge of sadness there. I know she's missing them – although it would take a lot of arm-twisting before she would ever admit it.

Mr Baird places his hand on his halo and his face turns pale.

'What is it?'

'We have to hurry,' he says. He rushes out of the car, not even waiting for us to follow. Zora and I exchange a look, then scramble out of the car after him.

Mr Baird looks over his shoulder as he jogs up the stairs. 'Eric Smith has pushed *up* the convention again. To now. It's all over the news.'

'What?' I cry out. 'But you said we were able to stop him from going ahead at all?'

'Lake Washington is so remote, it takes time for the authorities to check out our information and to get up there . . .'

We're swiped through the building security quickly, and taken through to a huge open-plan cafeteria space, with long rows of benches and tables, all very metallic and clean. A few eyes turn towards us as we enter, but most people are laser-like focused on a screen at the far end of the room.

Mr Baird ushers us towards one of the tables, facing the projection – which covers almost the entire back wall. It's more than an ordinary projector screen, of course.

BRIGHTSPRK have such a different ethos to Moncha Corp: everything is slick and modern, not focused on comfort but on design. Moncha was one woman's vision, whereas this company has cycled through many different owners and leaders. Still, I wonder now which one is going in the right direction. With only one person at the top, once that one person is corrupt, nothing is fail-safe. At least BRIGHTSPRK seem as intent on keeping their house as clean as they are their products.

Projected from the halos, the image on screen is crystal clear. It's almost like we're live at the convention after all.

Even the buzz from the crowd inside the Washington cottage is perfectly audible. The baku-cameras (most common are doves) are trained on the crowd, flying around to show off all the important people who are there. My heart twists as I spot Tobias standing to one side, with his parents. His dad has his hand on one shoulder and Nathan is at his side, beaming.

I hope that's the outcome Tobias wanted. Even though I wish he'd stood by me . . . can I blame him for wanting to be accepted by his family?

'Even after knowing what they've done to your mom and dad . . .' mutters Zora beside me. Clearly *she* hasn't forgiven him.

I lean into her, appreciating her support.

Then, the atmosphere in both rooms changes. Something is happening on stage.

Normally, this is when Monica would come out and put

people at ease. I think that's what lots of people are still expecting, even though Monica hasn't been seen in months.

But it's not Monica *or* Eric who appears on the stage. It takes me a moment before I register who it is.

'Is that . . . Mayor Coleman?' says Mr Baird.

'Who?' I ask, with a frown.

'The mayor of Toronto,' he replies.

Zora and I exchange a look. 'What's the mayor doing at the launch of a Moncha product?' I ask.

'Not just *at* the launch. Introducing it,' Zora says.

We turn our attention back to the announcement. Sure enough, Mayor Coleman is kicking off the speech. At first, I barely take in what she's saying, my brain is whirring as to what it could all mean.

But then it becomes crystal clear in an instant. 'The City of Toronto has been proud to be a part of the Moncha journey, supporting Monica from her very first steps as a tech entrepreneur into the multinational corporation we see in front of us. We were delighted when Eric approached us with an exciting new venture, which will see the city partner with Moncha Corp to provide bakus for all of our residents, to serve as a model for all cities of the future. And, in an act of tremendous generosity, Moncha have donated level 1 bakus to anyone who hasn't purchased one so far – Merry Christmas, everyone!' A video flashes up behind her: of postal workers in Moncha-branded uniforms delivering brand new shiny insect bakus throughout the city. There are line-ups around the block for free 'leash' installation clinics.

And then a montage plays of how harmonious life is when people and bakus work together: city workers cleaning up the streets with their loyal retriever bakus, maintenance workers fixing street lights with magpies and – worst of all, for us – the Toronto police with brand new, shiny, sharp-toothed panther bakus.

While we've been away, Monchaville has expanded.

And as the mayor speaks, a baku appears from beside her, a beautiful level 3 Great Dane. There's a huge burst of applause from the audience, which the mayor bows to receive, placing one hand on her Great Dane's back. Then Eric walks on to the stage, reaches out and takes the mayor's hand. He looks so smug – as if all his chickens have come to roost at the same time. He's the man who's laid the golden egg: he's managed to get rid of his partner, and secure the biggest deal in Moncha history, all in one fell swoop.

With a single update.

If every person in the city has now been given at least a level 1 baku … that means millions of people will now be updated.

There's only one conclusion: we can't trust the authorities now. They're in Eric's pocket. I'm glad that we decided to come here, to the headquarters of one of Moncha's biggest rivals. It's one thing to convince politicians to be on your side. But another to convince a rival firm. Surely they would do anything to see Moncha Corp taken down.

I try to turn my attention back to what Eric is saying now. 'Thank you, Mayor Coleman. We're delighted to partner with the City of Toronto to make it one of the best and *happiest* places to live on the planet. And now, for the next stage of our big announcement. We've been working around the clock on the latest update – which is about to revolutionize your lives. This update will bring your bakus even more in sync with your needs, taking even more decisions off your hands to help *you* lead your happiest life ever. This is the biggest improvement to happen to bakus, well, since the very first baku was released! We want everyone to access this update at the same time, so if everyone would plug into your leashes . . .'

'No!' I cry out. But at the same time, all at once, I notice a buzzing from around the room. Mr Baird's halo is glowing, and he's staring down at a projection on his hand. More of the BRIGHTSPRK employees are doing the same.

Soon, it's everyone in the room. Everyone at BRIGHTSPRK is receiving a message. I turn to Zora, who grips my hand. 'What's going on?' she whispers to me.

'No idea,' I reply.

The look on Mr Baird's face is not good, though.

'What is it?' I ask him.

'We've just had a company-wide message come through.' Mr Baird isn't really looking at me though. He's looking around at all his co-workers, the buzz in the air almost impossibly loud. 'Moncha has taken over BRIGHTSPRK. We're all receiving an update to our halos.'

All of a sudden, his eyes open wide, as he realizes the implication of what he's just said. He raises his hand to rip the halo off his head – but too late. It flashes and changes colour, and Mr Baird goes stock-still.

It happens all around us, to everyone at BRIGHTSPRK.

'We should get out of here!' Zora says.

There's a fierce buzzing in my zipped-up pocket too. Slick is begging to be updated.

Zora's hand flies to her shoulder as well – Linus is bounding up her arm, aiming for the leash. >>I've just received notification of the latest update! squeaks Linus. >>We should leash up now and then I can process it.

'No!' shout Zora and I in unison. Zora is just quick enough to grab Linus before he connects, and she stashes him in my other zipped-up pocket. 'But he's a level 2!' Zora cries out.

'But Eric Smith knew you were at the Lake too. Or maybe ... maybe the update is going out even wider.' I feel sick as the words leave my mouth.

'Oh god, Lacey, I have to get home.'

I nod, then look up at Mr Baird, still clinging on to a scrap of hope that this is all a big mistake – and that Eric Smith hasn't been able to snatch a victory from the jaws of certain defeat. 'Mr Baird? Are you all right?'

But when he looks at me, his eyes are totally blank. 'Miss Chu? What are you doing here?'

CHAPTER THIRTY-SIX

'LACEY, LET'S GO, NOW!' SAYS ZORA, dragging my arm.

We spin on our heels and run, causing havoc as we topple over benches and chairs in our wake. No one pursues us, but we run as if we're being chased by the fiercest of security bakus.

Once we're outside and clear of the BRIGHTSPRK building, we slow our pace – but only barely. 'I have to get home!' says Zora, striding down the sidewalk. 'I have to warn my family.'

'Of course! But we have to warn *every*one,' I say, hurrying to catch up with her. 'Will Linus still let you send out a message without connecting to your leash?'

She slows down. 'It's worth a try.'

I unzip my pocket, carefully keeping my hand around Linus's small dormouse frame the whole time, making sure he doesn't leap towards Zora's leash. I pass him over to her, and Zora holds him with equal caution.

'Let's do it. We need to get on the St Agnes message board and warn everyone at school.'

Zora nods. 'It'll sound better if it comes from me – no offence. You're still seen as a Profectus student.'

'None taken.'

There are no cabs on the street at all and we don't want to take the subway and risk losing signal. Zora uses Linus to hail a ride-sharing driverless car instead.

'Mom isn't messaging me back,' says Zora, her voice trembling with worry.

'He won't get away with this,' I say, my fingers curled up so tightly in my fist, I might draw blood.

No wonder Eric allowed us to leave with Mr Baird. He was never worried that BRIGHTSPRK would be the ones to stop us. We should have gone straight to the authorities. Maybe bigger than the police. To . . . the federal government, or somewhere that isn't yet under Moncha's control, where there's still hope that they have their own minds.

My stomach churns. I have a feeling that's not the end of it either. If he's thought of how to stop his rival corporations, and how to control the city's power, he may already have thought how to stop the government too.

The driverless car pulls up, and we hop in – grateful for both the warmth and the way we're able to speed through the empty streets of the city. I'd forgotten it was Christmas Eve. Most people would be at home, with their families. *Updating* . . .

When the car pulls up to our condo building, Zora rushes to the elevator, with me following swiftly behind.

'Miss Chu, Miss Layeni, Merry Christmas,' says

Darwin, our building's porter, cheerfully oblivious to our panicked state.

I divert my run to his desk – he has a level 2 baku, a ferret. 'Darwin, tell me you haven't updated Treasure yet.'

'Why, of course I did! Just a few moments ago. It's the best decision I've made this year.' He grins widely at Zora and me. It's like he doesn't even register our bright red faces and wild, windswept hair, let alone the panic and worry in our eyes.

I groan loudly, and Zora is mashing the elevator call button, now even more desperate to see her family. Finally, there's a ding as the elevator arrives, and we rush inside.

'Let me know how they are,' I say, when it reaches Zora's floor.

She grabs my hand and blocks the elevator door from closing with her foot. 'I know this is hard. I know it seems like the complete end of the road, and that Eric has anticipated our every move. But we can't be the only people in the world who feel like the update is wrong. We'll find supporters. We'll tackle this together. I just have to check on my family first.'

'Of course,' I say. 'Go!'

I slump against the handrail as the doors slide shut again.

Going to see Mom now, knowing that she is already under Moncha control, wanting to tell her about finding out where Dad is after all these years and yet knowing that she won't understand what that means ... it will feel like my heart is breaking over and over again.

PART FIVE

THE ARMY

CHAPTER THIRTY-SEVEN

I NEEDN'T HAVE WORRIED SO MUCH. DESPITE my dread, when I let myself into the apartment, there's no one there. Mom must be working.

This is possibly the worst Christmas Eve in living history. I plop down on one of the stools in our kitchen, leaning my head against the counter, too tired to even think about making myself anything to eat.

Then, I hear a quiet tapping. I leap to my feet and rush to the window. I throw it open as fast as I can. Jinx squeezes in through the frame. 'You made it! You're okay!'

>>Of course I'm okay. Did you think they could catch me?

A swell of emotion overwhelms me at the sight of him, and tears pour down my cheeks. Jinx is okay. At least *one* thing we did today has gone right.

'Have you heard what Eric Smith did?'

>>He's pushed out the update to all level 1s and 2s.

'We couldn't stop him, Jinx.'

>>You did your best, Lacey.

Jinx curls his tail, projecting what seems like a hundred different screens in front of me, each showing a different news outlet reporting on the update. The news is overwhelmingly positive, Eric's smiling face front and centre. Jinx pushes the positive ones to the back and shows me a few dissenters, who are questioning Monica's absence and are sceptical about the changes to the terms and conditions.

>>Look, there's still something we can do. We can get in touch with these journalists, tell them the truth, try to stop it. We should run away from here tomorrow, set a base somewhere, from a different city. Maybe if the city won't listen, then the country's government will? You can't give up, Lacey.

I wipe the projections away. 'Anything we do will be for nothing if we can't reverse the update. And we don't have Monica to ask.'

Slick pipes up from my pocket. >>You have a message from Zora.

I scramble to take him out of my pocket, and he projects the message to me: MY PARENTS UPDATED, is all that it says.

The weight of today comes crashing down on me. I've never felt so helpless in my entire life. There's no one to ask for help. The people who were supposed to care – our parents, teachers, the rival firms, the government ... they're already under Eric's influence.

Even Tobias went behind my back, wanting his family's

280

approval. Kai, Ashley, River – this isn't really their fight. They couldn't risk losing their bakus, and in a way I understand that. Their bakus are their companions. They're too high level to be subject to the update.

Only Zora is with me.

And I worry it might not be enough.

I push Jinx away, turning my face from his. It's only a matter of time now before he is destroyed too. I can't save him.

I can't save myself.

I can't save Monica.

I can't save my mom. My dad. Zora's family.

And I certainly can't save the world.

Slick quivers on the countertop. Maybe I should just leash him. Allow the update to go through. Then everything would be fine. I wouldn't feel this pain, this anxiety and uncertainty. One tiny push of a button and it would all go away for ever. I could be content. I would forget this whole messed-up situation.

But I know I will never do that. I feel it growing, a seed burrowed deep into the bottom of my skull. If it means never having a baku again – then so be it. But I won't let myself become a mindless drone of the Moncha Corporation. The *new* Moncha Corporation.

For once, I don't want to be Monica Chan. I don't want to follow in the footsteps of my father.

I just want to be me. On my own path.

But walking that path is going to have to wait until tomorrow.

Today, I just want to burrow deep down into my duvet and forget that the whole world exists.

Especially to forget that tomorrow is Christmas Day.

I wake up in the early hours of the morning to a jangling at the front door. I leave my room to see Mom walking in. She's wearing a little Santa hat, and Petal is playing Christmas tunes over her speaker. She's humming gently to herself.

She looks like she's about to head straight to her bedroom, but I cough as she passes me by.

Mom's eyes widen in surprise but then she smiles. 'Merry Christmas, baby girl!' Mom says. 'You're here!'

I rush over and wrap my arms around her so tight, she expels her breath in a small 'oof'. I bury my face into her fuzzy Christmas jumper. 'I found Dad,' I whisper into the fabric.

There's a jolt as she pushes me away – and the gesture fills me with hope. As if I've shocked her out of the update, reached some part of her that's buried deep. But Petal comes and settles on her shoulder, alarmed at the sharp spike of her heart rate.

Just as quickly, that spark is gone. Her next words are said in a deadpan tone, so different from her happy, chirpy Christmas 'good morning' a few minutes ago. 'That's not possible, Lacey. Your father is gone.'

I search her eyes for any hint of recognition, but there's no point. 'Mom, I know it's Christmas but I left your present down in the basement. Do you mind if I go and get it?'

'Not at all, honey.' Her bright, chirpy tone is back. 'And then Petal has given me a great recipe that I can try, sent to me this morning by the Moncha chefs! You're going to love it.'

I smile weakly. 'Sounds good.'

She walks past me, shutting herself in her room. Jinx slinks out of my bedroom, curling himself around my feet.

>>To the basement?

I nod. I think about checking in on Zora, but then she hasn't checked on me either – maybe she wants to be left alone, after the update to her family.

The locker is happily un-Christmassy. I pull the sleeves of my hoodie down over my hands, trying to keep myself warm in the chilly basement. I shouldn't be down here. I should be upstairs, in my warm condo, helping my mom make Christmas cookies and watching our favourite movies on television.

I walk through the basement to see if Paul is there. I want to talk to him, to fill him in on everything that went down at Lake Baku. But his locker is empty, the cage dark. I slump my shoulders, disappointed that he didn't stick around to hear from me. But then again, Christmas is the one time that he spends with his family from out of province. Can I blame him if he wants to be with family right now?

Jinx tries to slip into the locker behind me. I look down at him, blocking his path through.

They're coming for you, you know. He won't stop. There's no reason for you to stay with me. You proved you could blend in with the real stray cats and avoid getting caught. Even though saying it breaks my heart, I keep going, attempting to harden my thoughts so he can't read my real feelings. *You should just go.*

He looks up at me and blinks, not saying anything.

GO!

Footsteps sound in the darkness and my breath hitches – no one should be around here at this time. It's early Christmas morning. They've come for him, even sooner than I could have predicted.

'Slick,' I whisper, patting my pocket. 'Turn on the light.'

The light in my locker flickers on with a reluctant hiss – even it doesn't want to be disturbed this early. When my eyes adjust to the light, I see a tall, skinny figure with a pale face, clutching something close to his chest.

Carter.

Jinx! I scream inside my head. Jinx darts in between my legs, and I slam the locker door shut, fumbling with the lock.

When it's firmly closed, I swallow, putting one hand out to grip the edge of the locker doorframe to steady me. 'What are you doing here?'

He shrugs. He looks different to normal ... smaller, or something. He's hunched over, his jacket pulled tight across his body. I don't trust him.

'It wasn't hard. When you didn't show up at the convention, I knew you were back in the city. And I know this is where you used to fix Team Tobias's bakus ... Figured it was as good a place to start as any.'

'What do you want? Aren't you supposed to be with your dad? Shouldn't you be revelling in the fact that the update went out?'

'Look, Lacey . . .'

'You and your father have taken *everything* from me!' I shake the cage door, filled with rage. 'You can't have Jinx too. Leave us alone.' I feel bolder than I have in days. Stronger too.

'Your dad wasn't the only one trapped at Lake Baku,' he shouts through the mesh grating as I spin around, turning my back.

I ignore him as tears spring up into my eyes. I don't want to speak to him about my dad. Rage burns in my mouth like acid, but I don't give him the pleasure of turning around. My fingernails dig into the palms of my hands. How dare he. After what his dad did. How dare, how dare, how dare . . .

'My mom was there too.'

His words stop me in my tracks. At first, I don't turn around. I listen. I wait for the sound of his heavy breaths to change into vicious laughter. I expect him to say 'JOKING – loser' and then throw something at my head. That would be my typical interaction with Carter.

But nothing in his tone of voice sounds like a joke.

Jinx? Do you believe him? Jinx doesn't answer. He's hidden himself in the shadows and this is one situation where my baku can't help me. Do I trust Carter or not?

I swallow and spin around on my heels, slowly. To my surprise, Carter's eyes are glassy with the sheen of tears. His jaw is set, like he isn't sure if he should trust me either.

'What did you say?' I need to hear him say it again. I need to watch him as he talks, to search his face for any signs of imminent betrayal, or joking.

'My mom was at Lake Baku too.'

'For how long?'

He shrugs. 'Years. I didn't know. When I was eleven, she just up and left ... I never got a straight answer from Dad about where she'd gone.'

A frown flicks its way across my face. All this time, Carter had been going through the same thing as me. All those times he'd niggled at me about my dad's absence, as if it was my fault.

He knew exactly what buttons to press – because his own were being pushed at the same time.

'But ... that doesn't make sense. I thought the whole reason you got your boar baku was because of your mom.'

He nods. 'It was. Hunter has been with me for a lot longer than anyone knows. Mom picked him out for me when I was just a kid.'

'But you're not allowed a baku until—'

Carter rolls his eyes. 'Right. But remember who you're talking to for a second, will you, Lacey?'

His tone instantly annoys me, but then I realize: he's right. Of course his family could bend the rules. They *made* the rules. 'Anyway, when I was at St Agnes, Dad made me swap for a dog baku, so that I didn't appear too different from anyone else. But once I got into Profectus, I demanded to have Hunter back. After all, he's the only thing I had left of my mom.'

'How you convinced your mother to buy you that thing . . .'

Eric had said that to Carter on my first day at Profectus, after his speech to the entire school in the arena. I remember being shocked that he'd been so rude to his son; I'd almost felt sorry for Carter in that moment.

'Your mom bought it for you . . . and then she disappeared?'

'Yes. I only found out where she'd really gone just after you did,' he continues. 'They're not at Lake Baku any more, though. Dad had to move all the "volunteers" from Lake Baku to the downtown HQ last night until he can figure out somewhere else to keep them.' He looks down at the ground, and grips the bundle tighter to his chest. My eyes flicker down towards it, wondering what he could be concealing. 'After she left, all I ever wanted to do was prove myself to my dad. To be good enough. To be worthy of his attention – and more than that. His confidence. I wanted him to tell me what was going on at Moncha, to let me in on his plans. But he never did, until today. And now look at me. About to betray him. I guess he was right. I wasn't ready to be a part of his team, after all.'

'Wait . . . what?'

'I know, right. Finally something we can agree on. No one should have their future taken away from them, Lacey. The update – it's not right. So . . . I want to help you bring down my dad.'

'Are you serious?'

'I am. And I know how I can prove it to you.'

'How?'

287

'Will you let me in so I can show you?'

It could still be a trap, of course. He could be a much better actor than I give him credit for, just pretending that his mom is wrapped up in this whole thing. But then I think about whether I want to take that risk. Jinx can protect himself; I know that. This is someone asking for help. And I want to be the type of person who will give it to them.

'Okay,' I say. I step forward and undo the chain to my engineering cave.

He steps in swiftly, barging past me, and for a moment my heart hitches in my chest. What if he's about to destroy everything?

But instead he puts the bundle down on my work surface and unwraps the dark grey blanket, revealing a rumpled form of a broken boar baku.

My hand flies to my mouth and I have a sharp intake of breath. It's Hunter, but almost irrevocably destroyed. That's why he looked so different – he didn't have his baku at his feet. I didn't notice in all the intensity of my rage. Now, my focus is on the baku, and I rush forward, trying to assess the damage. It's bad. He looks as if he's been rolled over by a truck.

'What happened?' I ask. If there's one thing that I've never had to wonder about with Carter, it's his devotion to his baku. He wouldn't have let this happen out of choice.

'This is what my dad does when I decide to disagree with him.'

'Eric did this?'

Carter nods.

I whistle through my teeth.

'Do you think you can fix him?' The hope in Carter's voice almost breaks my heart.

'We can definitely try.' My brain is immediately putting a plan into action. I pick up a pair of oversize tweezers from my toolbox and start by separating out some of the broken pieces that need to be thrown away, from what I think can be salvaged. I know that I have some of the shiny red metal wiring that matches in one of my containers, but if we want to get him absolutely back to perfect then we may have to scavenge for some new parts.

'So, you'll help?' Carter asks.

'Of course,' I reply. 'Look, you and I have had our differences but that's no reason to take it out on a baku. I was just thinking, I have a lot of the parts and Jinx here can pull up the schematics and help me. For some of the stuff that I don't have, we might have to go scavenging if you're up for it . . . or maybe you can afford to buy it new?' I shrug. I realize that Carter is still the son of one of the richest people in the city. He might not have to go scavenging. He might be able to access the spare parts we need legitimately.

Carter wrinkles his nose. 'I . . . I'm not sure I can pay you. My dad's not exactly in a generous mood towards me at the moment. But I can offer you something else.'

I raise an eyebrow. 'What's that?'

'I think I know how to reverse the update.'

'WHAT?!' I drop the tweezers on to the desk with a loud

clatter. My eyes are as wide as saucers. 'You know how to reverse it?'

'I think I do. I think you've had the key all along.'

'The key?'

'Why do you think my dad has been so desperate to capture that baku of yours? There's only one thing that can stop him in his tracks – and it's hidden inside your baku's code.'

Jinx is the key.

He emerges from the shadows – one paw, then the other, slowly catching the light. He stares up at me, his shiny black eyes unblinking.

>>Tell me what I have to do.

CHAPTER THIRTY-EIGHT

'SLICK, SEND A MESSAGE TO ZORA TELLING her to meet us at my apartment ASAP. Make sure to write that it's an emergency.'

\>>Done, says the beetle baku.

It doesn't take long for her to respond. Zora is there when we step out of the elevator on to my floor, her face puffy from crying, but she does a double-take when she sees Carter exit with me. 'What's he doing here?'

'It's okay. He's come in peace. He's helping us.'

Zora shakes her head. 'Are you serious?'

'Listen, Zora. Carter's mom was a Lake Baku prisoner too. She was one of the updated.'

She blinks several times, her gaze shifting between Carter and me, trying to figure out whether there's some sort of trick. But she knows me better than that. There's no way that I would voluntarily side with Carter, not unless it was absolutely necessary.

'Zora, he thinks he knows how to reverse the update.'

He nods. 'I do.'

'Can you trust him? What does he want in exchange for that information?' asks Zora, crossing her arms over her chest. My heart swells with love for her. She is the very best of friends – always looking out for me.

'I'm helping him fix his baku, which his dad destroyed. But come on – there's no time to waste. We have to see if his theory works.'

I fumble with my keys, barely able to get the door open, I'm so nervous. Carter and Zora are both right on my heels. Once I manage it, Jinx streaks past me, the fastest of all of us.

Mom is in the kitchen, Petal fluttering around her head. We get to the kitchen just as Jinx is bounding up her leg. 'What are you doing?' she cries out. 'Get off me.'

But before she can protest too much, Jinx leashes up to her. The first time he's leashed to a person since I let him go at the cat park.

Zora, Carter and I hold our collective breaths. Mom's eyes go blank, her arms falling limp. Petal is frantically buzzing up against Jinx, trying to get at the leash. I capture the butterfly baku in the cup of my hands, and pass her across to Zora.

'Mom?' I say, after a couple of seconds go by. *Jinx, is it working?*

>>I . . . I'm not sure.

I grip one of Mom's hands, holding it in both of mine. Then, a second later, I feel her fingers squeeze mine back. Light returns to her eyes, and Jinx releases from the leash. 'Lacey?' she says, turning to me. 'Oh, my darling girl, are you okay? Why are you crying?' She pulls me into a big hug.

292

I can't help it. I'm sobbing now. My mom is back. Zora claps her hands together and fist pumps the air, while Carter slumps against the counter, relieved. 'You're back, Mom, you're back!' I say, when I'm finally able to talk again.

'I feel so strange,' she replies. 'Like I've had the strangest dream.'

'But you're okay, now,' I whisper. 'You're awake.'

The revelation slowly dawns on me. 'Zora, we have to go to your family now.' I kiss Mom on the cheek. 'I have so much to talk to you about, and so much to explain. But Mom . . . promise me something.'

'What, honey?'

'Don't leash up to Petal until I tell you too. Promise?'

'Lacey, wait – you can't just . . .'

'I have to go, Mom! I'll be back as soon as I can!' I cry out, before racing to the stairwell to join Zora and Carter.

We take the stairs two at a time, jumping down and using the banisters as a pivot. Zora's braids are flying out behind her, and Carter and I can barely keep up.

Jinx is at her feet, though. He knows now that he can help.

It takes a good few minutes for Jinx to reverse the update on Zora's parents, and by the time he's done, they're as fired up as we are – outraged by the stories that we have to tell.

'We have to do something!' says Zora's dad, Michael, his voice booming in their small apartment.

'Mrs Layeni,' I say to Zora's mom. 'Can you go to my mom and bring her here and make sure she's okay? I don't want her to be alone after what she's gone through.'

'Of course! But honey, where are you going?'

I exchange a look with Zora, and then we both look at Carter, who is hanging back against the wall, his head low. 'Jinx can't go to everyone in the city individually and reverse the update, so we have to figure out a way to spread it more widely.'

'I'm on it!' says Zora, and I can see from her expression that she's already thinking through possible options.

'And while she's doing that, I have a favour to complete . . .' I gesture with my head to Carter, who perks up.

Alesha, Zora's oldest sister, is raging. 'You said you put a post up on the St Agnes message board, little Z?'

Zora nods.

'We'll amplify it. Thank the lord we didn't all update. I was just about to when Zora came running in. We'll try to get to anyone else who hasn't updated yet to make sure they don't. I can't believe what Eric Smith has done . . .'

'Anything we can do to help – just call on us.'

I smile gratefully at Zora's family, but I'm itching to get back to the basement. There's a different kind of urgency now that we have a way to reverse it.

Maybe Monica did know what she was doing, after all. If it was only a matter of time before someone tried to manipulate her technology, then she needed to make sure there was an antidote.

Jinx. My beautiful, difficult, independent, snarky, incredible baku was the key all along.

CHAPTER THIRTY-NINE

J INX PLUGS INTO THE COMPUTER IN THE basement, and Zora stares at his code as it appears on the screen in front of her. The last time we looked at his code, he'd been under the influence of a black mark, which disables bakus. Now, he's giving us free access to a code, and Zora is gobbling it up with her hungry eyes.

After she's looked at it all twice over, she plugs Linus in as well, so that she can see the update code side-by-side with Jinx's.

'Seriously? This is amazing ...' Her eyes scan the code. 'I think I know how I can separate out a reversal of the update ... but it's going to take some time. You need to figure out how we then get it to the rest of the city.'

'I've thought about this. We have to reverse Monica first – then she can issue the command to go out to all the bakus that have been affected,' says Carter. 'But we are going to need a distraction if we're going to get into Moncha HQ. Something big and public, that will draw attention away.'

It still feels strange to me to be working with Carter,

who's been my rival for so many years. But now we're working towards the same goal . . . we actually make a pretty good team. 'Do you think anyone else will listen to us?' I ask. 'The news outlets that Jinx showed me were almost overwhelmingly positive.'

Carter laughs, and the sound puts me on edge. He seems to understand that, as he turns serious almost immediately. 'Have you checked the Profectus forums recently?'

'No . . .' Then it hits me. 'Oh, of course! Profectus students won't have been affected because they all have level 3s and above!'

'Right. You've got some of the most popular kids in school – Kai, Ashley, even that strange dude River – all fired up about how unfair this is. Of *course* people are listening.'

My eyes open wide. 'They're still trying to protest the update?'

Carter nods.

I take a deep breath, and leash Slick up to the mains. After a few seconds, he buzzes to life. >>Hello, Lacey. I'm afraid I'm running an old operating system. Soon I will lose functionality if you don't allow me to update my systems.

It's another automated message. I ignore it, and clear my throat. 'Slick, open the Profectus Student app and flashes side-by-side,' I instruct.

There's a brief moment where I'm not sure if the baku's going to obey my command (it would be just my luck to have *two* disobedient bakus in my life) but then Slick obliges.

Within a few seconds, both the apps are projected side-by-side and I try to take in the deluge of messages that flood through both apps.

> What can we do?

> This is bananas – I'm scared to even turn my baku on.

> Seriously man, I'm accessing these apps on a PC like some kind of millennial.

It's clear that I've missed a load of messages, and I attempt to scroll backwards to find out what was said in the beginning. I scan for handles that I recognize – like Tobias's or Ashley's. But the messages have been completely scrubbed.

Carter leans forward. 'That's odd ... there were loads of messages complaining about the update yesterday.'

'Look!' I point to one of the latest messages.

> They're erasing these boards as fast as we can post! What are we going to do?

> Did you see that they've made it mandatory for all level 1s and 2s to update before the New Year?

> Crap – I just saw that too.

I stare at Carter. 'They actually *do* care.'

'It's the same on the St Agnes forum,' says Zora. 'And my sisters are firing up all the upper grades right now. If we figure out a plan then I can totally post a message there – get Linus to send out a call to action before the New Year.'

'So not all St Agnes kids updated last night?'

Zora shakes her head. 'I guess a lot of teens are smarter – and more savvy – than Eric thought. He released it too quickly, too widespread. We might want to fit in and be part of a crowd, but some of us definitely don't want to be *told* what to do.' She looks up at the screen and tuts. 'Okay, while you two are thinking of a plan, I need to properly concentrate to get to grips with this code,' she says. 'And since I don't have Linus, I'm going to have to block you out the old-fashioned way.' She swings around, searching my shelves. 'I know I stashed a pair of heads around here somewhere. Aha!' She reaches behind one of my boxes and pulls out a pair of garish pink headphones, each ear-covering almost the size of her face. 'They're noise cancelling as well. No disturbances.'

'Aye, aye, captain,' I say to her.

Then, just like that, it's just Carter and me once more. We eye each other across the table, both of us feeling awkward.

'Any ideas?' I ask him. To distract myself while Zora is working, I pull the wrecked remains of Hunter towards me, going in for a closer inspection.

Carter sighs with relief when I start working on it – and I realize how worried he must've been that I wouldn't uphold my end of the bargain. This is someone not used to trusting anyone.

For a second, I feel sorry for Carter. Growing up with a dad who constantly puts him down, his mother gone, always having to put up a front, never knowing if anyone was his friend because of *him* or because of who his father is.

I pull down two pairs of safety goggles from the shelf behind me, and hand one of them to Carter. He takes it with surprise. 'You want my help?'

'Of course. Two hands are better than one.'

'What, are you going to run a full health-and-safety briefing next?' he says, but he grimaces, as if ashamed of his own defensive words.

'If you don't want to lose an eye, you gotta take precautions. Haven't you learned anything at Profectus?' I nudge him in the side to show I'm joking.

Cautiously, he smiles at me. He's surprisingly helpful, too. He leaves me to work, and instead spends a suspicious amount of time studying my toolkit. But then, when I need the right tool, he's already got it out and ready for me. Maybe he's not as useless as I once assumed.

'I always liked this kind of stuff, but Dad was much more the "just buy a new one" type.'

'Yeah, he strikes me that way. I hadn't even realized that your mom wasn't around. You were sometimes so cruel about my dad . . .'

Carter shrugs. 'Defence mechanism? But also, obviously Dad didn't want it to become common knowledge that

Mom had gone. Or maybe he wanted her out of the picture – somewhere nice and easy to control. Turns out, if you're a psychopath in business, you're that way at home too.'

'I'm really sorry you had to deal with that.'

Again, he shrugs. 'Better for me to find out now, I suppose.'

'Aren't you worried that this might mean you lose both your parents?'

Carter stops what he's doing (messing around by stripping some wires, ready for me to solder) and stares at me. 'I hadn't even thought of it like that.'

I cringe. 'Oh. Sorry.'

'You don't think that the update can be reversed that far back?'

I think back to the dead eyes, the placidly cheerful actions of updated people inside the Lake Baku dome. They've been living like that for years – over a decade. Is it possible to come back from that? What would it be like if you hadn't had to use your mind – your real mind – in years?

If it isn't possible . . . it will be agony. To have found Dad again, but then not be able to get him back properly . . .

But I can't look into Carter's face and tell him that I don't know if his mom will ever be back to normal. Mostly because that would mean me having to confront that same fact about my dad. I'd rather not think about it just now, and try to concentrate on saving the world instead.

'So, tell me the story of what happened exactly?'

Carter sighs. 'So, I saw Monica, my mom, your dad and

the others being loaded into vans last night and one of the guards let me know the destination. There's not a lot of people who will keep a secret from the son of the acting CEO of one of the world's biggest companies.'

'Guess there have to be some perks,' I say, wryly.

'Exactly. I confronted my dad before he was due on at the convention and that's when . . . this happened, with Hunter. So I stole one of the cars while he was on stage to take me down here to find you. Wasn't too difficult. Honestly, I don't think Dad even cares where I am most of the time.'

We both jump as one of Hunter's legs jerks to life, his cloven hoof scraping along the metal surface of my desk. 'Ah ha! Looks like the connections aren't too broken then!' I exclaim. 'That's good – it means the motherboard hasn't totally been destroyed. It's just mechanical repairs he needs – we'll be up and running, no problem.' Carter looks delighted, his eyes lighting up. I use it as my opening.

'But how are we going to get into Moncha HQ?' I ask. 'It's not as if I can just walk in there . . .' I'm sure that I'm on the top of the security team's watch lists.

'So somehow we're going to have to divert the security team's attention,' says Carter.

'I guess so.'

>>We could create some havoc! It's the first time Jinx has spoken up in a while. >>Storm the gates?

'Or something that would create even more attention,' I say, raising my eyebrows. 'A proper protest. One that the media will be interested in covering.'

301

'Well, I'm sure Dad's one step away from *owning* most of the media, so it would have to be something BIG.'

'Something they won't be able to ignore, or hide.'

Carter looks at me, his eyes searching my face. 'You have an idea?'

'I think I might.' Focusing on work – on engineering – opens up another part of my mind to solve problems. My solution is a bit out there, and I'll need a lot of help with it. *Including from you, Jinx. You're going to have a big part in this plan.*

>>Whatever I can do, Lacey. I'm here with you.

Good.

I look up at Carter. 'If we're going to make it work, we're going to need more than just Profectus and St Agnes teens on board. We're going to have to get *every* teen who hasn't updated in on it. A totally coordinated attack.'

'We'd better get the word out then.'

CHAPTER FORTY

THE IDEA IS A CITY-WIDE PROTEST. THE *non*-updated teens of the city, as many as we can round up, are gathering at a few major hotspots so that we can protest the update. The date is set for New Year's Eve, and we need to get as many people as possible to join us.

But even before we can properly get organized, Eric Smith throws a spanner in our plans. He must have noticed that thousands of teenagers weren't updating – the numbers not computing, not adding up – so they decided to ramp up the consequences. Update by New Year or else the un-updated bakus would be put out of commission. We lost a few supporters that day, scared of losing their companions.

So instead, they lost their minds.

The days in between Christmas and NYE are both excruciatingly long and way too short – Zora works around-the-clock on the code, Carter goes back to his dad, acting like nothing is happening, apologizing for his outburst – hoping to lull his dad into a false sense of security – and

I enlist the help of Jake to rally the troops – thanks to his skill at running an underground Baku Battle gambling ring, he's the master of keeping things under the radar while still spreading the word, and he's devised a series of code words and false leads in case Moncha is watching.

They're not the only ones who know how to be sneaky.

There's even word that some people are using handwritten *letters* to pass the word around.

Talk about old school. I'm surprised there are still enough of us left who know how to use a pen and paper.

On the morning of December 31st, Zora and I are the first people to show up outside one of the locations – City Hall – the strange buildings that curve like wings around the public square. It's freezing cold, but we're not planning to stay here long. I dig my hands deep into the pockets of my winter coat. Jinx curls around my legs, a black mark against the white snow. Now that we're confronting Moncha, he doesn't want to hide any more.

'Do you think anyone will show up?' I ask Zora, shuffling nervously.

'I hope so. Wow, look at that.' Zora gestures behind my shoulder.

There's a new addition to the popular neon T-O-R-O-N-T-O sign, a tourist attraction next to the public ice-skating rink. It's a back-lit statue of a raccoon baku to signify the new partnership between the city and Moncha Corp.

Even despite everything happening today, I chuckle. It's a fitting choice.

I still love bakus. It was a question everyone asked us on the forums: *Are you trying to ban all bakus?*

There's only one answer to that: of course not.

'Holy bakus, Lacey. Look.' Now Zora is pointing at the street just behind the ice rink. We can see a couple of pink and orange jackets, bright against the otherwise grey backdrop of concrete high rises and dirt-covered snow banks. 'They're from St Agnes, I'm sure of it,' she continues.

Okay, Jinx . . . our part of the plan is in action. Now you have your job to do.

>>I'll be back before you know it.

I look down at the watch I took from Mom's bags. Such a strange thing to have on my wrist, so analogue and mechanical. I quite like it. I might keep it.

I need the watch, because I no longer have a baku. I place Slick down on the ground at my feet, his switch powered 'down', so he's one of the first bakus involved in the protest.

More and more people start arriving in the square. I swallow down my surprise and the tears that threaten to spring up in my eyes – I thought that maybe our class group would come along, the ones who knew Zora and me personally, but there are kids from all grades here – and from different schools too. No one knows how to get the word out like teenagers.

And today, we have rallied.

Because of the cold, there's not a lot of chitchat. But our plan isn't to stay for long. One by one, in the courtyard of City Hall, the students unleash their bakus, power them down so they can no longer move and leave them in the snow. Animals great and small – from beetles and birds and tiny mammals like Linus, all of that expensive technology, immobile and frozen like statues – litter the ground so that it is impossible to walk into the building without taking notice.

Because we love our bakus. We love the technology.

But we are not going to be ruled by it.

Moncha Corp got one thing right – we want to build the future. Not have it taken from us.

There's a screech of tyres, as a van branded with a local news network logo pulls up outside City Hall. Zora puts her hand on my shoulder. 'I'll organize things here, make sure that the media gets the message. You better hurry along to Moncha HQ. Put my brilliant code into action.'

'You bet. You've done an incredible job,' I say, giving her a quick hug, muffled by our respective down jackets. She's right; I don't have a lot of time. I have to join Carter at Moncha HQ. But I feel buoyed by what I'm seeing at City Hall. If St Agnes teens have shown up, maybe Profectus and other schools will too.

This is something that affects all of us.

A ride-share car takes me down to the east side of the city, where Moncha HQ is located. This is going to be a much trickier part of the plan, where I'm going to need every inch of my skill to make it happen. I don't have Slick with me to check what's happening and to see if I have any messages. I have my old phone, the one with the broken screen, but not many people have the number. I just have to trust in the people who are leading this with me. Zora over at City Hall. Carter at Moncha HQ. Jake on his app. And Kai, River and Ashley, who've taken the lead on rallying Profectus teens. I have confidence in all their abilities.

But I've heard nothing from Tobias. I kept expecting a message, half-hoping it was him whenever Slick buzzed.

You're not together, remember? He did that when he chose his family over you.

I steel myself, gritting my teeth. I don't have time to moon about over a boy. I have a job to do. The relationship drama can come after.

There's an electronic beep inside the car. 'I'm afraid I'm not authorized to take you any further,' says the robotic driver.

'What? Why not?'

'I'm afraid I'm not authorized to take you any further.'

We're still a good few blocks away from the headquarters, so I have no choice but to head the rest of the distance on foot. I mutter curses under my breath – this must be yet another way that Moncha are trying to discourage the protest – by making it difficult to even get close to their headquarters. The plan is spiralling out of my control, each side of the battle attempting to outwit the other. All I need is a little longer. A little more effort.

I'm running late now. I pick up into a jog, my breath streaming out in front of me like I'm a fire-breathing dragon. A dragon with enormous boots on to ward away cold toes and a jacket so big I look like the Michelin Man.

But then my breath is almost stolen away from me as I

finally round the corner to Moncha HQ. There are baku statues everywhere here – and not just level 1s and 2s. Because these are mostly Profectus teens, there are higher level bakus too – dogs and cats, monkeys and birds – scattered all over the red brick courtyard. It's a jaw-dropping sight.

The media have made it to the scene. It's strange to see them scrambling with old-fashioned cameras, as the baku birds they would traditionally use are refusing to display any footage. Between this and the cars, Eric Smith is really digging in. The measures smack of desperation. He must know his time is running out.

Especially because his son is out there, leading the revolution.

I can see Carter across the square, giving a statement to the media. I head over to listen to him. He sounds louder and more confident than I've ever heard him, channelling his normal arrogance to *my* cause for a change. He emphasizes how the protest isn't because we don't want our bakus – we love our technology – but because we *cannot* update – not until there are assurances in place that bakus will never be used to adjust our personalities.

Crucially, I notice that he is also attracting the attention of the Moncha security – exactly as we had planned. I can see the slick black panther bakus gathering behind him in front of the main door to the building.

'Oh, there you are!'

I spin around to see Kai, River and Ashley waving and running up to me. Their faces are bright red with exertion, eyes shining with excitement. 'Happy with the turnout?' Ashley asks.

'Happy? I can't believe it . . .'

'I know. But you've got a lot of people behind you, Lacey. We're all worried about this update,' says Kai.

River sticks his hand out to me. There's a pass inside. 'Carter told me to give you this. Good luck. You'd better hurry. I don't think we'll be able to keep the protest up for much longer. Rumour has it they're bringing the police in to shut this all down and clear the bakus.'

I take a deep breath, taking the pass from River's hand. He grips my fingers as we touch. 'Don't worry, you got this,' he says.

'And if I don't?' I ask, swallowing hard.

'It's not all on you. We're behind you. They can't ignore us, Lacey.'

'I know. You've done your part. Now I've got to do mine and reverse this update once and for all.' We shake hands properly this time, as if we are generals on a battlefield. Ashley gives me an enveloping hug. Then, they turn around and walk back towards the sea of frozen bakus. I take another moment to admire it. This is what a lot of tiny drops of concern can raise: an ocean of protest.

There's a nudge against my boot. I look down to see Jinx at my feet.

>>Everything is ready.

You have your army?

>>I have them in place.

Good. Let's do this.

>>I have found an unobserved entrance you can use.

My heart skips a beat. You mean, we can use?

>>I must go a different way.

So I have to go in alone?

>>You won't be alone for long. I promise.

What if Eric finds me first? What if we get lost or separated or it's too late . . .?

>>We won't.

I crouch down, staring into Jinx's shining dark eyes, the eyes of the little creature who has stolen my heart. Once again, perhaps for the last time, I have to trust him. I close my gloved hand tighter around Carter's pass, programmed from his baku.

The side door is much more low-key than the front, a staff entrance that might go unnoticed to the untrained eye. If Jinx hadn't pointed it out to me, I don't think I would've found it on my own.

I take a deep breath and walk up to the door. I touch the pass against the brick wall, feeling a little silly. I steel myself for the pass not to work, for the technology to somehow realize that I don't have a baku with me – only a plain motherboard coded to resemble a baku's entry code to a scanner. But it's not that sophisticated. It recognizes Carter's entry code from the pass River handed to me, and the brick wall melts away to reveal the interior of the building: the long hallway paved in dark hardwood and the brightly coloured walls.

At least Eric never pulled the plug on his son's access to the company headquarters.

Now I follow the map that Carter hand-drew for me. It's hard to navigate in the building, as there's little-to-no signage anywhere – only miles of painted walls, hung with large pieces of valuable artwork. Why would anyone need signage when their bakus could guide them, and who went anywhere inside the headquarters without a baku?

Luckily, Carter has taken this into account. At any other time, I would have been surprised by his scrupulousness, but then – I wouldn't have given him the time of day before now. Funny how events can turn even your best judgements on a dime. Even as little as a month ago, I would have said there was no universe in which Carter and I would be friends.

Now, we're working together. Maybe still not quite friends, but collaborators.

A shared goal will do that.

'Turn right at the rainbow artwork,' reads his note. 'Following the blue wall – not the red.'

That's not hard to find. I quickly come across a cascading rainbow of lights, streaming down in an endless waterfall. It would be almost hypnotic if I didn't have a job to do.

I duck into a doorway as some Moncha employees cross the path I'm meant to take, but they're walking fast, concentrating on information being fed to them by their bakus. 'Do you know what's going on outside?' one of them says to the other.

'No idea. But I think they're sending a panther baku team out there now to disrupt the protest.'

'There's one at City Hall too. And in High Park. Our resources are going to be really stretched.'

'Stupid teenagers, what are they even protesting about? The update is a *good* thing.'

Then they move away from earshot. My stomach churns. Eric has all his employees blinded to the true nature of the update. And soon the security teams are going to be mobilized in force.

That means I have to make my move even faster.

Once they're out of sight, I dart down the hallway. It widens out into a mezzanine-type space, with a set of sofas to one side, and small hammocks for bakus to rest in. I have an eerie jolt of recognition as I realize that the map is leading down towards the arena. I stare down at the paper again, re-reading the directions and checking myself against the landmarks Carter has identified. I'm going the right way. Eric is holding Monica and the other Lake Baku 'volunteers' in the team rooms of the Baku Battles arena.

And why not? It's the perfect hiding place. Quiet. Secure. Private. Large enough to fit all of them in.

I take a deep breath before I open the door. *Jinx . . . I hope you're coming.*

CHAPTER FORTY-ONE

THE TEAM ROOM IS STILL SET UP AS I remember it, with the names of the Baku Battle team captains on the doors: Gemma, Dorian, Pearce, Elektra ... and Tobias. Each in their own, specially chosen font. My paper sign is gone.

It's a stark reminder that those battles were only a month ago, and yet so much has changed since then.

I shake my head. I can't be dragged back into nostalgia. I need to get to the arena.

But the door opens before I even touch the handle. 'Who let you in here?' barks a familiar voice. My heart sinks and I close my eyes. I was hoping to have found Monica by now.

I open my eyes, slowly, willing with every movement for this to be a dream. But it's not.

Eric is standing there, with Monica in tow, surrounded by a security team with their sophisticated panther bakus. The sloth, Pardem, is still draped around her neck – she's still under the influence of the update.

'It's over,' I say, although my mouth is almost completely dry. 'I've come to reverse the update.'

'No one can reverse the update,' Eric says. 'Now move out of my way. Monica is going to make a statement to the press herself. It's time to show the world that *all* of Moncha supports this update. Then everyone will fall in line.'

'But it's not true,' I say, attempting to stall him, darting out in front of his path to prevent him from leaving the team room. His red panda baku bares his teeth at me, but I stand my ground. 'Monica, please listen. You can't allow Eric to do this. This is your company – your life's work.'

But she just stares at me blankly, the ghost of a smile on her face. 'The future of Moncha Corp is safe in Eric's hands,' she says, with all the charisma and conviction of a drowned rat.

Eric doesn't waste any time. 'Get her out of the building. She's trespassing.' He signals to his team, who grab me roughly beneath the arms. They half-drag me back through the door.

'I can walk!' I say, trying to shrug off their grip. But they keep their hands on my shoulders, perp-walking me out. I feel like a criminal. *Jinx, where are you?*

Hope drifts further and further away as we reach the huge, wide-open lobby, its once comforting plant-and-light-filled interior now a place of dread.

But Eric stops a few feet away from the front doors, and the security team stop too. I crane my neck to see what's happening.

And that's when I see him: Jinx, standing in the middle

314

of the Moncha HQ atrium. The cat baku looks so small amongst the huge surroundings, but his presence is big enough to stop us all in our tracks.

I just hope he's brought his army.

'Oh good,' Eric growls. 'You brought that thing straight to me. Now I don't have to go looking for it to destroy it.' He snaps his fingers. 'Security, get that baku,' says Eric to the guards behind me.

>>Are you ready?

Ready.

'Jinx, do it!' I cry out loud.

He sprints towards us and I stumble backwards. My arms flail in the air, swinging like a windmill, throwing my captors off-balance. Then the atrium is a flurry of commotion as we're surrounded by a sea of cats – a mixture of real and baku – all of them under Jinx's command. They pour out of the walls, having hidden in the nooks and crannies meant for bakus. Jinx melts in amongst them, disappearing as they swarm across the lobby floor, crawling over the sofas and jumping over railings, surrounding the feet of Eric, Monica and the security team.

The security bakus are instantly confused. They can't attack the real creatures because of their inbuilt safety systems, but they also can't seem to tell the real Jinx from the doppelgangers. They are able to find the other cat bakus, and they disable them with a swipe of their paws. But there's still too many.

Even I am taken aback. When Jinx told me that he

would be able to confuse Eric by bringing other cats into the building, I was expecting three or four other cat bakus – nothing like this. I certainly didn't realize that while I was away, Jinx was able to befriend real cats – the ones that haunted the parks of the city, the descendants of pets that people used to keep before bakus became the norm. He's created a cat army.

Eric is aghast. He tries to shield Monica from the wave of cats, but they're covering her now, crawling up her arms and legs. She stays stock-still, unperturbed by this strange encounter.

But Eric can see one particular cat aiming for the leash at Monica's ear. He lunges towards Jinx, but I jump into action too. I barrel my way through the cats and into him.

He's more solid than I realize, and I don't manage to topple him over – only knock him slightly off course. But it's enough time. Jinx plugs into Monica's leash, the sloth struggling to the ground under the weight of other cats pinning him down.

There's a beat as both of us watch what's about to happen to Monica. I close my eyes, whispering a prayer to whatever tech gods might be out there, listening. But Eric reacts faster than me. He snarls like an animal, pushing me off him and reaching towards Monica.

I stumble on to the floor, sliding on the slick polished surface. One of the security guards strides forward and grabs me underneath my arms, clutching them behind my back. Eric grabs Jinx and throws him to the floor, and I cry out, watching my friend being treated that way. He lands on his feet – but only just.

'We have to get out of here, now,' says Eric. 'You, take Monica,' he says, pointing at one of the guards. 'And grab Pardem. We have to make sure that everything is to plan before proceeding.' Then he turns to the guard holding me. 'Escort Miss Chu out of the building and make sure she has no ability to get back inside. If she's ever seen here again, confiscate her baku and disconnect her leash. She'll be banned from ever being able to own a Moncha product again. And get these mangy creatures out of here.'

Just like that, I'm frog-marched out of the building as Monica is taken the other way. All the cats – including Jinx – dissipate into the various hallways. I hope that means that Jinx has escaped, and is unharmed. I have no idea if Jinx managed to uninstall the update in the short period of time that he was leashed up to Monica.

Or has all of this been in vain?

CHAPTER FORTY-TWO

THE SECURITY TEAM UNCEREMONIOUSLY pushes me out of one of the side entrances to Moncha HQ, tossing me so I tumble into a snow bank that's built up along the edge of the sidewalk. I zip up my jacket, and pull my gloves back over my fingers. But I find myself frozen for a different reason. I have no idea what to do now. I don't know if our plan has worked, or if we're in as much trouble as before.

If it hasn't worked . . . how will we be able to reverse the update? Will Jinx have to find every single person in the city, one-by-one? And what if Eric rolls the update to the rest of the country, to the world? What then?

Then, there will be no stopping him.

I have to find out if it worked. I dash around the corner to the main courtyard. I have to stop to take a breath. It's amazing to see all the bakus sitting outside, still as statues. Amazing how such a simple demonstration can be so powerful. I hope it's catching the media's attention. Or will Eric find a way to play this out as something *positive* for

Moncha? I don't know how, but if anyone can manipulate the situation, he can.

A crowd has gathered at the front entrance of Moncha HQ, in front of the imposing double-doors. There's a ring of media, cameras and microphones pointed at the doors, and then a wider circle of people around it. I feel sick to my stomach. It looks like Eric is still planning on making some sort of statement to the public. If he's willing to do that ... it doesn't look good to me.

'Lacey!' I hear my name being shouted from across the street.

I look up to see Zora barrelling across towards me. She crashes into me, her arms thrown around my body, squeezing me in a hug. When she pulls away, she asks, 'Did it work?'

I bite my lower lip. 'I don't know.'

'You don't know? But ... the word is that Monica is about to give a speech.'

'Jinx connected but I don't know if he had enough time to reverse the update completely.'

Zora bites her bottom lip, chewing it furiously. There's a commotion at the front of Moncha HQ, and all of a sudden, lights come on around the door. Zora grabs my hand. 'Come on. We have to watch. We have to find out.'

I allow her to pull me through the crowd, pushing our way past the journalists and crowd of onlookers who have gathered around. I don't know what to expect. I don't know who is going to appear at the door.

The gates open – and out steps Monica Chan. And on her shoulder . . . is Jinx.

I swallow, tears welling up in my eyes. Tears of relief.

Jinx touches his tail to Monica's throat, amplifying her voice so that she can be heard by everyone. Bird bakus descend from the sky, suddenly permitted to film again – Monica must have reversed the ban, wanting everyone to hear what she has to say. The reporters jostle and clamour for space, everyone wanting the best angle to film from.

As for me? I feel as if the entire world grinds to a halt. I don't feel anything any more: I don't feel the cold of the air, or the wind on my face, or the heat of adrenaline in my cheeks. I'm holding my breath, wondering what Monica is going to say. Wondering if what we did worked.

Wondering if our teamwork is enough.

I exchange a look with Zora, and then across the way, I see Carter, his eyes wide with happy surprise. Kai and Ashley grin at me, and I see River's head poking up behind. Jake catches my eye and winks. I scan the crowd, looking desperately for one more face.

But he's not there.

I feel a wave of disappointment, but then I turn back to Monica. *Please be all right, please be all right*, I whisper.

I hear Jinx's voice in my head. >>Do you doubt me?

Never, I think, fiercely.

Silence descends on the courtyard as she steps forward.

'In light of recent events, including an unauthorized update pushed through to certain level 1 and 2 bakus in

Toronto, Moncha Corp have agreed to submit to a full and open government investigation.

'As CEO of Moncha, I take full responsibility for the update and the resulting problems it has caused, and want to apologize unreservedly for the actions of certain members of my company. A reversal – developed by a group of dedicated and brilliant young coders and companioneers – is being issued as we speak, for all people and bakus affected.

'Although I have always tried to operate under a culture of openness, it is clear that there were members of my corporation that felt differently. While glaring security leaks have obviously been revealed, please rest assured that we are working hard to make sure nothing like this ever occurs again. We are cooperating with other creators of personal assistant tech to create global regulations for our industry. But, if the recommendation is that we shut down production of the bakus, then we are prepared to take that step.

'In the spirit of cooperation, Moncha will now work with the City of Toronto and BRIGHTSPRK on ways to make baku technology even safer.

'We are confident that together, we will come up with a solution and keep bakus safe for everyone to own. After all, I know that I couldn't possibly live without my baku.

'Could you?'

A world without bakus? It seems unthinkable now. They are so integrated within our society. People want to use the technology, now that we know it exists. We can't go backwards.

We can only learn how to use it responsibly.

There's a flurry of questions as Monica finishes speaking, but to me – it's as if the universe has condensed into this tiny moment.

'You did it!' I squeeze Zora's arm. 'Your code worked! Everyone is going to be back to normal.'

'We did it. *We* did it, Lace,' Zora replies, her bright white teeth shining with the biggest grin I've seen in a long time.

Yet my jaw drops before I can reply. Because Monica is looking directly at us. She's waving away all the questions, telling reporters that she'll have another press conference in a week, announcing all the changes in regulation that they will go through. Then she walks straight towards Zora and me.

She extends her hand to us.

'I have a lot to thank you both for,' she says.

I stare at her, scanning her face for traces of the update. But her eyes are bright and clear, and she seems to be standing taller than the last time I saw her at Lake Baku.

'May I be the first to extend you an invitation back to Moncha HQ? I want you to have a front row seat to all the changes that are being made.'

CHAPTER FORTY-THREE

TWO DAYS LATER, WE STEP INSIDE Moncha HQ, this time in the footsteps of its founder. A sort of reverential silence descends on us both as we enter the building. Even though this is now the fourth time that I've met Monica – this is the first time I feel like I'm meeting the *real* person. And I'm more scared than ever that reality won't live up to expectation. Jinx is by my side, his tail lifted high in the air.

>>Relax. The real Monica is the best. You're going to love her.

'Wow,' says Zora, her neck craning back. 'Linus, make sure you're taking loads of pictures.'

>>I'm on it.

I grin. I forget that she's never been inside the headquarters before, the impressive cathedral of glass and light and greenery. It's not an opportunity that many people get. 'This place ... it's like baku-Disney World,' she whispers.

Monica hears her, and laughs. 'Not a bad idea, Miss Layeni.'

We jump, not realizing that Monica was standing so close by. 'Oh, you can call me Zora, Ms Chan,' Zora stutters.

Monica nods, 'And you can call me Monica. We're all friends here.' We come to a stop in the centre of the foyer, at the edge of a bubbling fountain. She smiles, the full intensity of her gaze upon us. 'Well, Lacey and Zora, I can't thank you enough. What you did to reverse the update ... it worked. In fact, there are many people here who would like to thank you.'

All of a sudden, people appear from every doorway, and even at the balconies looking down on to the foyer. They launch into a voracious round of applause that echoes off the red brick and surrounds Zora and me with happiness and praise. Even the bakus give us a little siren song, chirruping or stomping the ground or barking and roaring to join the chorus.

'It wasn't just us,' I say, the blush rising in my cheeks.

Monica smiles at me. 'I know. And I've invited some of the others along too ...'

She gestures behind me, and I spin around. The first person I see is Carter. He has Hunter next to him, restored to perfect condition. We nod to each other, still guarded in our interactions. I don't think I'll ever like him, but I do trust him a lot more. I know his devotion to his baku, and that reassures me.

Next to Carter, I see Kai, River and Ashley, and their respective bakus. They look slightly sheepish to see me, even Kai, but I run at them, wrapping my arms around all three and pulling them into a big group hug. 'I'm so glad to see you! Thank you for everything you did to help organize the protests.'

'Way to go, Lacey,' says Ashley. 'You did it. You and Zora pulled through when we gave up.'

'And hopefully we'll be seeing you back at school, yeah? I want to be on your team next year,' says River.

I smile. 'You better believe it.'

I look over River's shoulder, but the person I'm really looking for isn't there. I'm not surprised any longer. Every day that goes by, I expect to hear from him, and every day ... I'm disappointed.

Then, I see him. Or rather, I see Aero. He swoops over our heads, still one of the most magnificent bakus I've ever seen. I follow him, watching him dive and soar, before landing on the shoulder of his owner.

The rest of my friends step aside, to give us some space.

'Hey, I'm sorry—' says Tobias.

'Hey, I'm sorry—' I say.

We both speak at the exact same time.

'Jinx,' Tobias says, with a small smile. I smile back at him. 'Let me go first,' he continues. 'I am so sorry, Lacey. I know I betrayed your trust. I was a coward, and I have no excuse.'

'I can hardly blame you for wanting to confide in your parents,' I reply.

His face screws up into a scowl. 'I never wanted it to go further than that but Nathan overheard – and he ran straight to Eric. I'm so sorry. I should never have betrayed you.'

'I wish you'd reached out to me sooner.'

'I know. I wish I had too. But my parents banned me from contacting you . . .'

'It's okay, it's over now,' I say. It's true. The stakes have been so high – with minds and dreams on the line – I don't want to hold a grudge when everything ended up going to plan. 'Friends?' I ask.

A spark of disappointment flickers across Tobias's face, but he nods. 'Of course,' he says, his voice soft. 'Friends.'

Monica claps her hands together, and we turn around to face her. 'All right, now that we're all here . . . let's head up to my office. I've got a lot of explaining to do, and I want your group to be the first to hear about any of it. Before we have any sort of public press conference or anything.'

The crowd gives us another cheer as Monica leads us over to the elevator. It warms my heart to see all the employees so glad to have their fearless leader back.

We take the elevator to the very highest floor, which opens up directly into her office. It's decorated in typical Monica style – a bit mid-century modern, with eclectic touches – lots of resting places for bakus, and plenty of lush green foliage. She gestures for us to take a seat on big, comfy golden leather couches. But I can't sit down. Because I'm too excited. There are lots of people in the office that I recognize: one is Mr Baird, back with his owl baku.

The next face I see is even more surprising. 'Oh my god, Paul? Is that you?' Paul and his lemur baku George are standing right by Monica's desk. I run up to him and give him a big hug. He guffaws in surprise but hugs me back. 'Well done, my favourite tinkerer,' he says, gruffly. 'Well done.'

Before I take a seat with the others, Monica pulls me to one side. 'Lacey – I trust your mom is okay?'

'Yes, she's much better, thank you. Grateful for the offer of compensation.' Everyone who was forced to receive the update is being given a pay-out. 'But I mean ... she has a lot of questions. And most of them are about Dad.' It's the question that I've wanted to ask the most, ever since the reversal went out to the wider public.

Did it work on the volunteers at Lake Baku? The ones who had been under the influence of the update for so much longer? I've been in constant contact with Carter, who'd been given the same information – that the volunteers were being looked after, but that there was no concrete news on their progress so far.

It's been the most agonizing wait.

Monica nods, her mouth drawn into a thin line. 'Of course.' She gestures over my shoulder to Carter, and he rushes over. 'I wanted to be the first to tell you both. Everyone who was imprisoned at Lake Baku, including your mom, Carter, and your dad, Lacey, are being treated with the utmost care, as we speak. Many of the volunteers suffered greatly at the hands of my former business partner. I swear, if I had known what was going on up there—' Her eyes flash with anger. 'Of course, it's no excuse. I never should have taken my eye off Eric's work; I should have been more questioning, more demanding.

'But that's in the past now, and it will never happen again. All the volunteers have made good progress and we're confident we'll get them back to their normal selves. I promise, you and your mom will be able to see Albert again before too long. He is desperate to see you both. Carter, your mom too. It's going to take a lot of patience – and rehabilitation – but you'll have the full resources of Moncha at your disposal.'

My heart soars to hear that he is okay, and that the update isn't permanent. I know it's going to be hard on my mom, that there will be a lot of residual anger and frustration and tears over the lost time we could have had with him.

But the important thing is that he's coming home.

'Thank you,' is all I manage to utter.

She gestures for me to take a seat, so I squeeze in between Ashley and Zora on the couch. I lift my eyes up to Tobias, and then quickly look away again. *Friends*, I say firmly in my mind.

>>Yeah, right, says Jinx, and I have to stifle a smile.

'My dear friends,' Monica begins. I want to listen to her, but movement down around her ankles distracts me. It's a loping gait that I recognize, and then the baku comes fully into view: the sloth, Pardem. I recoil in disgust. I want that baku as far away from me as possible. Even Jinx tenses in my arms, the way I've noticed bakus tense – he seems to vibrate at an even faster speed, his electronic hum seeming even louder.

'It's okay, Lacey,' Monica says, clocking my reaction. To

my dismay, Monica scoops the sloth baku up into her arms, and connects him to her leash.

'No!' I cry out.

Monica shakes her head. 'It's all right; there's no update in his system any longer. I've grown attached to this baku and decided to keep him. Despite what he represents. Because it wasn't his fault. It was his programming.'

It takes a few seconds for me to recover my breath, but she's right. The sloth bakus were never the problem. The update was.

Doesn't mean I find the sight of them any less triggering, though.

'I'm sure you're all wondering how things at Moncha are going to progress from now on. Most of you heard my press conference a couple of days ago. Of course, I have resumed my position as CEO of the Moncha Corp. Team Happiness has been disbanded and, after thorough interviews and investigations, it's clear that most employees were kept in the dark about the team's true objective. He kept the circle extremely small. The fault lay alone at the feet of Eric Smith.' At this, her gaze falls solely on Carter. 'I know it's been a difficult week for you, Carter, and I thank you for all your help. Eric has given himself up voluntarily to the authorities, and he is being processed as we speak. The likelihood is that he will spend the rest of his life in prison.'

'As long as I get my mom back, then that's what he deserves,' Carter says, sticking out his chin defiantly. I have to admire him. I can't imagine what it would be like to know that my dad was behind a plot like this – and that I might never see him again, except behind the bars of a prison cell. Deserving or not, it's got to be tough if that's your parent.

Monica continues: 'As you've probably noticed, your old teacher, Derek Baird is here. He is a senior VP at BRIGHTSPRK. Plans are full steam ahead to work with him and his team at BRIGHTSPRK, the City and other big technology companies to come up with proper legislation to regulate the advanced technology that we're all developing at lightning speed. But one step we've taken is the formation of an impartial board, who will oversee all the developments here at Moncha Corp – total transparency. And Paul here, one of my former board members, is going to oversee that.'

I grin, seeing the pride on Paul's face. I'm glad he's back in a position he deserves.

Monica continues. 'It's clear that I wasn't careful enough in planning for the time of my demise – whether that's accidental or done through malice. We need better protections in place, so that we can protect the future of bakus – and the future of all of us – going forward.'

'So ... you're not going to have total control any more?' I ask Monica.

She shakes her head.

'Won't you find that hard?'

She smiles. 'The bakus were always going to outlast me, Lacey. That was always the plan. One day, one way or another. I've always known that. I selfishly thought that I could do everything all on my own – and still be the creator and innovator that I've always been. But I took my eye off the ball, and someone immediately took advantage of me. We need people who aren't going to do that. This is the right thing to do. The right way forward.

'And Moncha Corp is never going to let you down again.'

CHAPTER FORTY-FOUR

MONICA ASKS ME TO HANG BACK, once her speech has finished. The others leave, except for Mr Baird, Paul and Tobias. Zora lingers too, but I get Slick to send Linus a ping for her to wait for me downstairs. Zora holds my gaze for a couple of seconds, then nods. She slips into the elevator with the others, and then I turn my focus back to Monica.

Her lips bunch up to one side, and her sloth, Pardem, hangs heavily on her shoulders. 'There's just one more thing, Lacey.'

'Yeah?'

'It's about Jinx ...'

At the tone in her voice, Jinx jumps up into my arms, and I hold him there. I stroke his head. At his request, I don't use him as my baku any more. I have Slick for that – and now that there's no danger of the beetle injecting me with poison or updating me, I feel much more comfortable in his presence.

She exhales deeply, and glances at Mr Baird and Paul, who

both nod. Tobias comes and stands by my side. I'm glad to have the weight of him, his solidness, near me. I feed off his strength, and try to stand a little taller. 'Here's the thing, Lacey,' she says. 'You and I both know what Jinx is – what he represents. If it becomes widely known that this sort of technology is available, it would also be incredibly dangerous. As dangerous as the Team Happiness update was, but in reverse. It would be hypocritical of me to allow it to be out there. No one can know how close we have come to creating something *real*.'

At her words, I pull Jinx closer. How *close* she came to creating something real? There was nothing close about it. He *is* real. He's real to me. His emotions, his feelings, his spirit – those are all real. So what if he's made of metal and wire, of code and electricity? He's alive. And he's my friend.

Monica sees my actions – sees my arms wrap around him tighter – and she bites on her bottom lip.

'Lacey, we're all in agreement here,' says Mr Baird.

Paul nods as well. 'We all love Jinx. But if the wrong people were to get their hands on him, you know what could happen.'

'No one will,' I say, blood rushing into my face. I bite down hard on my back teeth, setting my jaw to try and stop tears from flowing. I don't want them to know that I feel weak in this moment. I want to look strong. But then I realize that I can look strong, even if my tears flow. It's holding emotions in that causes weakness – fissures that grow into cracks that entire minds can fall into the depths of. A tear rolls down my cheek, and then another.

'The public can't find out what we've created here. Even Eric Smith didn't realize Jinx's full power.' Monica's voice is soft, but I feel the betrayal in it. I know what they're about to ask me, and I can't stand the thought. 'Lacey, I'm very sorry,' Monica says. 'But we have to destroy Jinx.'

'No!' I cry out.

'I don't want to either. But the board agrees – it has to be done before we can move forward.'

'No, it doesn't!' I exclaim. 'You haven't even written the full agreement yet – or named the full board. How can it already be a condition? What if I can prove that he won't do any harm? He's not even acting like a baku any more!'

Monica smiles wanly at me. 'But you know that's because we can't let *anyone* know about him. Can you imagine the chaos? If you keep Jinx, even as just your companion, you'll be spending your entire life looking over your shoulder, wondering who is going to try and take him. You won't be free.'

Her voice softens. 'All the notes about how I created him have been destroyed. They never made it up on the cloud. He is the last remaining piece of evidence of what I did. I broke the rules. Now we have to make sure nobody else can replicate what I did. It's for the best.'

Jinx purrs in my arms, his fur sending out comforting vibrations that calm my nervous system. >>It's okay, Lacey. I expected this. The world isn't ready for me yet.

The tears continue to flow down my cheeks, in a steadier stream now. 'But I can't lose you. Not after everything we've been through. Who is going to help me graduate Profectus, for one thing?'

Jinx winks at me. >>Ugh, I suppose Slick will just have to do. Didn't you have plans to companioneer him into a level 3, once upon a time? And then, more quietly, he says, >>This won't be the end, Lacey.

But what if it is . . . there will never be any baku like you again.

>>That's for sure.

His tone is still cheeky and mischievous, but there's a hint of sadness in there too. I know that he will do anything that Monica asks.

I'm going to miss you.

>>I know. But you've trusted me this far, right? Just one more time.

I nod. I can't bring myself to say the words, I simply loosen my grip, letting my arms fall to my waist. Jinx jumps down, and saunters across to Monica.

She kneels down to pick him up. 'You were my finest creation,' she whispers into his fur. Then, she passes him over to Mr Baird, who immediately fixes him with a black mark designed to immobilize him.

Sobs wrack my shoulders. I knew keeping Jinx would be too good to be true. I should have enjoyed more time with him. I should have cherished even more of the moments. I should have recorded his cheeky voice so I could play it whenever I need a boost.

I squeeze my eyes shut, and feel the weight of Monica's hand on my back, comforting me.

I open my eyes and watch as Mr Baird walks Jinx into the elevator.

I swear, just for a second, I spot one of his tiny, black pointed ears give a twitch.

And I'm left with a spark of hope.

EPILoGuE

THREE YEARS LATER

LINING UP TO CROSS THE STAGE ON MY graduation day at Profectus, my heart swells with pride. My fully upgraded level 3 scarab beetle baku, Slick, buzzes around my head, his wings now extended (using a superlight material) so he's twice as big as before. With retractable legs, a reinforced carapace and super-strength horns, we headed off several challengers in the Baku Battles. We won this year, of course. Team Lacey kicked butt and took names.

'Miss Lacey Chu!' My name is called. I automatically turn to face the crowd before I step up on to the glossy hardwood flooring. I see my mom's face there, beaming. She waves at me and I lift my hand to show that I've seen her.

And still the thing I can't get used to most of all. My

dad is there next to her, his face glowing, his grin wide and teeth gleaming. Around his shoulders is the sloth baku, Lacey, that had been his long-time companion at Lake Baku and that he still can't bear to be separated from. Around Mom's head floats Petal. Even though she could have any baku that she wanted now that we live on Companioneers Crescent, she didn't want to change either. That didn't mean that she didn't allow me to make a *few* tweaks of my own, though – and now Petal never gets tangled up in a scarf.

There's an after party to celebrate the graduates. Monica Chan is here, to celebrate with us all.

She pulls me aside, and I still find myself a bit tingly at the prospect of being so close to my mentor. In the years since what was known as the Happiness Conundrum, she has somehow managed to guide the company from strength to strength. 'So Lacey, I understand that you're *not* going to be taking your prizewinners' internship?'

A blush rises in my cheeks and it creeps all the way past my hairline. I can't believe still that I hit 'reject' on the guarantee of a job at Moncha Corp – and not just any job, but one that would put me in direct contact with my idol every single day.

But I've realized something along this journey.

It's not that my lifelong dream has been to work for Moncha.

My goal has been to *be* Monica Chan.

And the only way that I'm going to be able to do that is

to go out there on my own and get some life experience – to see exactly where my future is going to lead.

'No,' I say, in a voice barely louder than a whisper.

She smiles. 'That's a shame. Are you sure I can't change your mind? You could come and try and be part of the future. Now that you've graduated ... Your place is here.'

'Thanks, Monica ... but I want to try and find my own way for a while. Maybe I'll come up with an invention as great as the bakus.' I feel cheeky as I say it, but I have to be truthful. Now I want to work until my idol has become my rival.

She laughs, but there's nothing unkind in it. 'I understand that impulse better than you know. And somehow, I don't think you'll be alone.' She looks over my shoulder, where Tobias is standing, shoulder to shoulder with my mom and dad.

'No, I don't think I will be,' I reply, with a smile of my own.

'But you know, if you ever change your mind ... your baku knows how to reach me.' Pardem reaches out and touches Slick's outstretched limb. 'Now he has my direct line, so we can make sure that we can communicate.'

'Thanks, Monica.'

She reaches out and touches my chin. 'You're going to do amazing things, Lacey Chu. Don't give up.'

And then she's gone. Moved on to the next person.

Slick raises one of his legs. >>Ready?

'Ready,' I say. I'm free now. Graduated from Profectus. No job offer on the horizon. I can tinker away to my

339

heart's desire. I can travel. I can search for inspiration.

I turn to Mom and Dad. 'I need some air. Is that okay?'

'Sure, honey. We'll be right here.'

'Everything all right?' Tobias frowns, looking concerned. He's been working at Moncha now for the past two years, making a name for himself in the design division. He knows all about my choice, because we're still great friends.

And still *just* friends.

'I'm fine, I promise. I just need to go outside.'

'You've done good, Lacey Chu. And you're going to do great things.' He reaches down and kisses me on the cheek. I blush. I still can't help how cute I think he is. Then I step away, moving quickly along the path that Slick is projecting in front of me, to the exit that will bring me fresh air – and a little solitude.

I push open the doors on to a balcony, and take a deep breath in. From this vantage point, I can see right over Lake Ontario, a huge sparkling expanse of water that stretches as far as my eye can see. I lean out over the railing, taking in the view, and feeling the warmth of the sun shining on my face.

There's a thump next to me, the sound of metal scraping against metal, and I smile.

If anyone were to look out on to that balcony at that precise moment, they would have seen a different baku at my feet – not a scarab beetle (who is now guarding the door), but a little black cat so slinky and perfectly formed that they might have mistaken it for a shadow.

'Thanks for waiting for me, Jinx,' I say, with a grin.

>>Any time. So, now what are we going to do?

'I guess it's time to figure out how I'm going to change the world.'

>>Together.

'Together.'

Jinx.

ACKNOWLEDGEMENTS

Books are always a team effort, and I'm so lucky to have the very best around me! Thanks as always to the brilliant folk at Simon & Schuster Children's UK: my sparkling editor Lucy Rogers, marketing and publicity gurus Eve Wersocki-Morris and Olivia Horrox, and the best cover designers an author could wish for, Jenny Richards and Jesse Green. Also I'm very lucky to get to work with the Sourcebooks team across the pond, with particular thanks to my editor Annie Berger.

My champion and agent is the illustrious Juliet Mushens. Her two adorable cats Luna and Neville cause more mischief than any baku! And thank you to Molly Ker-Hawn, for helping to bring Lacey and Jinx to North America.

To my writing friends – Kim, Emma, Jessie, Amie, Laure, Juno, Zoe, Laura, and James, thank you for being the best advice-givers, listeners and cheerleaders on this wild journey! Also a special shout-out to Keith Stuart, who helped put *Jinxed* into the hands of some people who really are trying to design the future. So cool!

Special thanks to Chris, for helping me to climb giant

mountains both metaphorical and very real. And the *Jinxed* series couldn't have been written without the unwavering support of my parents, Angus and Maria, my sister, Sophie, and my friends Sarah, Adam, Tania, Maria Felix, and Natasha . . . I'm so very lucky to have you all in my life.

READ THE FIRST
Book IN THE
ELECTRIC SERIES!

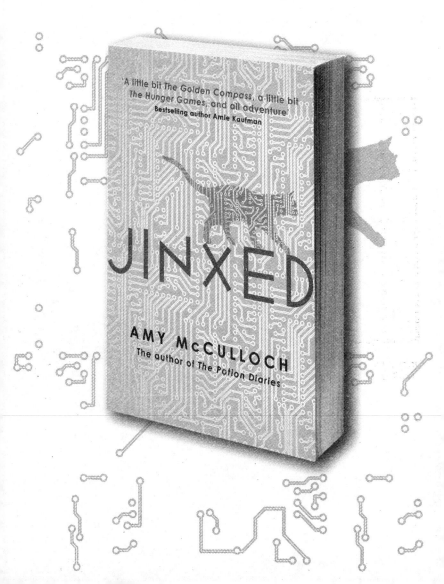

'A little bit *The Golden Compass*, a little bit
The Hunger Games, and all adventure'
Bestselling author Amie Kaufman

JINXED

AMY McCULLOCH
The author of *The Potion Diaries*